CROW

CROW

a novel

AMY SPURWAY

Edited by Bethany Gibson.
Cover and page design by Julie Scriver.
Cover illustration by Julie Scriver, based on a work by Potapov Alexander, Shutterstock.
Printed in Canada.
10 9 8 7 6 5 4 3 2 1

Library and Archives Canada Cataloguing in Publication

Spurway, Amy, 1976-, author
Crow / Amy Spurway.

Issued in print and electronic formats.
ISBN 978-1-77310-023-4 (softcover).--ISBN 978-1-77310-024-1 (Kindle).--
ISBN 978-1-77310-025-8 (EPUB)

I. Title.

PS8637.P88C76 2019   C813'.6   C2018-904590-6
                                        C2018-904591-4

Goose Lane Editions acknowledges the generous financial support of the Government
of Canada, the Canada Council for the Arts, and the Province of New Brunswick.

Goose Lane Editions
500 Beaverbrook Court, Suite 330
Fredericton, New Brunswick
CANADA E3B 5X4
www.gooselane.com

FSC
www.fsc.org

RECYCLED
Paper made from
recycled material
FSC® C103567

To the people who are my roots and wings.

A.S.

1 THE DIRT

I come from a long line of lunatics and criminals. Crazies on one side of the family tree, crooks on the other, although the odd crazy has a touch of crook, and vice versa. I am the weary, bitter fruit—or perhaps the last nut—of this rotten old hybrid, with its twisted roots sunk deep in dysfunctional soil. Some even call it cursed, this family tree of mine. But if you ask me, that's all a pile of superstitious bullshit. Like I said, we're just a bunch of lunatics and criminals.

"Get your bony arse out of bed before I kick it out." Mama clomps into my room at the crack of dawn, thumping a laundry basket full of wet clothes down at the foot of my bed and flinging the window wide open, like some kind of sunrise-loving lunatic. Threatening to kick my arse, like a criminal alarm clock with big, flat feet.

My mother, Effie Fortune, is the sanest, straightest one of the bunch. After all these years, I realize that threatening to kick my bony arse out of bed is her way of saying I love you. Mama's the reason I came back to Cape Breton. Not that I had much choice.

I want to tell her that I had that same nightmare again. The one with the flock of birds that laugh at me and the tree that uproots itself to chase me across a swath of black and barren land. The monster branches grab me when I stumble, and squeeze the life out of me, while the birds all fly around cackling. The first time I had that bad dream was one week ago, when I still lived in Toronto. I woke up gasping and retching, and then I vomited all over my bed. Both of my arms dead as doorknobs, my head pounding, and my eyes unable to focus, it took me almost an hour to pull myself together enough to clean up the mess. In the end, I biffed the creamy satin bedding in the dumpster out behind my condo because I couldn't stomach trying to wash it. Puke-covered designer sheets chucked in a dumpster. Of all the genuinely sad and jarring circumstances of late, that one foolish detail was somehow the final straw. I called Mama that night to say I was coming home.

So here I am.

When I try to speak now, all that comes out is a low groan, which Mama takes as the kind of willfully inarticulate protest she would've got from me when I last lived here as a lazy, melodramatic eighteen-year-old.

"You've been laying in that bed since you got here. Damn near a day and a half. It's no good for you. And that laundry won't hang itself." She shoves the basket closer to my bed with her size-nine clodhopper.

Again, I open my mouth to say something, but Mama's already hustling out the door and down the hall before any words make it out. But that's all right. I didn't come here to argue with my mother, even though a vestige of my saucy teenage self is alive and well, and on familiar turf. I came here so Mama could take care of me. So I could gather the strands of my life together and weave them into some kind of coherent story about who I was and where I came from, before it's too late. Before I forget. Before I'm just a memory here.

See, I'm dying.

But where are my manners? We haven't even been properly introduced! Just let me pull on my fancy pants, flatten my hair, and slide into my smooth, persuasive Multi-Level Marketing expert voice.

Good day. I'm Stacey Fortune, former manager of marketing communications for the Canadian division of Viva Rica! The Essence of Inspiration!

What's that, you ask?

Viva Rica is a carefully crafted and ludicrously expensive blend of eighteen essential superfood extracts that supports and stimulates the flow of health and wealth to a handful of folks at the top of the company pyramid, by pushing highly sophisticated twenty-first-century brainwashing sales and recruitment bullshit through a dedicated network of wishful-thinking super juice junkies. We'd be proud to have you and your twenty closest friends join our rapidly growing global distribution family! The greatest journey starts with one small sip!

That's the kind of marketing prowess that could have earned me the prestigious Viva Rica Juicy Details Award, which recognizes excellence in convincing desperate people that pawning off crates of fifty-dollars-a-bottle blueberry juice on their friends and family is their ticket to entrepreneurial bliss. Unfortunately, I lacked the kind of bubbly ambition that would have helped me float all the way to the top of the Viva Rica pyramid. Probably because I didn't drink enough super juice. It gave me gut rot.

How about an introduction that's a little more down to Earth? One where my pants are clean but not fancy, my hair is only a tad ratty, and my voice has just the faintest hint of a charming yet ambiguous East Coast accent.

Hihowareyataday, I'm Stacey Fortune. Up until two weeks ago, I was the picture of a strong, successful, independent urbanite woman. I had a mediocre career, an overpriced condo in downtown Toronto, and a hilarious story about how I empowered myself to blow gobs of money on stupid shit in the name of retail therapy after I gave my cheating fiancé the boot. Then I got diagnosed with three highly unpredictable — and certainly inoperable — brain tumours, which sporadically turn my limbs to Jell-O, my eyes to kaleidoscopes, and my head into a world of hurt. Now, I'm holed up in my mother's small and scruffy trailer on small and scruffy Cape Breton Island, holding out little hope that the doctors in this Have-Not Hellhole can do much to stop me from morphing into a paralyzed bag of piss, drool, and babble before I unceremoniously croak.

Hair, pants, and tone be damned, let's just cut to the chase.

Hi. I'm Stacey. But you can call me Crow. How 'bout bein' nice to me. I'll be dead soon.

A few pages in, and I just blew the ending of this story. That's all right. It's painfully predictable anyway. I really should have just written *Girl gets tumours, girl loses mind, girl dies, the end* on a sheet of loose-leaf, slapped it in a damn Duo-Tang folder and been done with it. But that is not the style of a masochistic narcissistic drama queen such as myself. Get comfy and get the tissues, dear. This here is a proper Cape Breton tale of shame and woe. Grabs at the heart strings and tugs.

All the old dolls will click their tongues and say, "Yes, poor Crow Fortune. Deathly ill with the tumours smack dab in the middle of her brains. What a sin. So young. What, thirty-something was she? Makes ya wonder, don't it. About them Fortunes and the...you know."

Because nobody will come right out and say it. It's always whispered every time something terrible happens to one of us. *The...you know.* The thing that makes us lunatics, or criminals, or both. The thing that cuts us down in the prime of our lives. The curse of the Poor Unfortunate Fortunes. They say it goes back generations. I say it's a convenient cover for people who are prone to poor life choices, bad luck, and bouts of lunacy. Either way there's a story here about me, about my people, about this place, and I need to be the one to tell it. If only to myself. Get this life of mine down on paper while I still can. That's item number one on my bucket list. Or, my Fuck It List. Because fuck it, I'm dying, so I'll say and do whatever I want now. But first, I better get those towels out on the clothesline before Mama has a conniption fit.

[···]

My feet are barely planted on the worn vinyl of my bedroom floor when my phone buzzes. A text message from my best friend, Allie, reads simply: *Mom's gone.*

Allie's mother, Reenie, is dead.

Reenie Walker had been dying in fits and starts ever since she was diagnosed with ALS when Allie was in tenth grade. One year later, the woman who built her family's log cabin home with her own two hands couldn't hold a teacup. Allie sold her beloved Shaggin' Wagon to buy her mother a wheelchair van just before graduation. And while I was gallivanting around Toronto, pissing away my blueberry juice money on napkin rings to match the seasonal centrepieces on my dining-room table, Allie was a decade deep into being her mother's full-time caregiver in a tiny Halifax apartment decorated with tubes, monitors, and forgotten dreams. Reenie lived far longer than anyone expected. I can't tell if that was a blessing or a curse.

Oh honey. I'm so sorry. R U ok? I text back.

Which is stupid. Of course she's okay. Allie Walker is always okay. She's been preparing for her mother's passing for years. Talking about it openly. Looking forward to the kind of freedom that would inevitably come once this hard, sad chapter of her life closed. Of course there will be grief. Guilt, too. It so happened that Reenie died on the only night in ten years Allie was away from her bedside. It was a quick jaunt to Boston, for her first real job interview since her mother got sick. A big medical research company was looking to hire a patient and family coordinator for a project in Nova Scotia. Allie applied on a whim and was shocked when they called her back. Even more shocked that the position came with flexibility, benefits, training, and a paycheque well beyond the pittance of her mother's disability pension. So, Allie missed out on the last act of unflinching love that she'd been dutifully rehearsing in her head for years. The moment where she would hold her mother's hand, kiss her on the forehead, and whisper, "I love you, Mom. You can let go now." Instead, it was a home care nurse who didn't know that everyone called her Reenie, and not Irene. But Allie is and will be okay. The woman's a rock.

I'd be lying if I said I'm not relieved as Allie details her return and her plans to be back in Cape Breton for the foreseeable future. If there's one person besides Mama I'd want by my side to hold *my* hand, kiss *my* forehead, and tell *me* it's okay to let go, it is Allie. Allie understands the slow-motion betrayals of a sick body. Allie can stomach suffering. Allie will help me die.

My phone slips from my increasingly clumsy hand and into the pile of dank, dusty stuffed animals I shoved to the floor when I arrived thirty-six hours ago. I can't be bothered to dig for it now because the morning cacophony of physical and sensory chaos has begun. The faded collage of magazine ads and rock god posters plastered on my bedroom wall becomes an amorphous blur. A jackhammer headache ramps up in jig time, and my stomach clenches into a wretched knot of nausea. I try to stand up in the beats between my head's pounding and my gut's lurching. With a spinning head and ringing ears, the first two tries don't pan out so well, but the third time's the charm. I'm on my unsteady pegs. Upright. Feeling like I might barf. Sorry Mama. That laundry is going to have to hang itself.

I teeter down the hall and into the kitchen, focusing on the repeating pattern of wheat sheaves and horseshoes on the linoleum floor to steady my balance. Through half-squinted eyes, I watch in the wobbling shadows as Mama's thick, sturdy legs stride toward the phone mounted on the wall by the kitchen table, and it takes me a minute to realize that the phone has been ringing. Which goes to show how screwy my brain's processing is and how loud my tinnitus gets, because Mama's got the phone ringer volume set on stun. I see Mama's lips move, but struggle to sync up her mouth with the words because of the lime-green squiggles and blushes of dusky red moving in sweeping circles around her head. More delightful distractions courtesy of the foreign invader in my sensory cortex. Another reminder that this body, this brain, these perceptions of mine are not to be trusted.

Speaking of things not to be trusted, it is Aunt Peggy on the phone. There is only one reason Peggy ever calls Mama. Probably the only reason Peggy ever calls anyone. She must have dirt. Peggy isn't smart enough to be a real criminal, and she's too lazy to be a proper lunatic. To compensate for those failures, she puts all she's got into being a pogey-scammer, as well as a nasty, gossipy big mouth.

Mama fields Peg's urgent dirt calls at all hours of the day and night. There was the three a.m., "Effie! They just arrested Boots Johnson on the DUI. Drunk as a skunk, down past the gas station in The Mines. He never was any good. I could tell by the smell of him!" And the crack of dawn, "Effie! Milly Pike's house got broken into. Made off with all her OxyContin." Then twenty minutes later, "Effie! Update! They found that little MacKeigan one, not Squirrel's daughter, the other one. The one who don't wear bras and always has her arse crack hanging out the back of her drawers. Face down in the field down behind that skater park with B&E gloves and an empty pill bottle. *Tsk tsk tsk.*"

As if Mama gives a damn.

Once my eyes adjust to the kitchen's brightness, the swirls around Mama's head slowly recede into an ordinary grey blur. There are tears swelling in her eyes. Despite my ringing ears and screaming headache, I can hear Peggy breathlessly spreading the details of Reenie Walker's death, which she heard from Shirl Short, who heard from Cindy Grimes, who is sleeping with Allie Walker's father. No doubt that old pack of hyenas will be itching to rip into the meaty saga of my upcoming demise, and Peggy will have the perfect excuse to throw herself a pity party in my name. *Pfft. Over my dead body, Peggy Fortune.* That's another thing for my Fuck It List: to tell that one off, once and for all.

I want to start now. I open my mouth to yell, "Shut your trap, you gossipy old quiff!" at the nattering presence on the other end of the phone. But no words come out. Instead, I throw up all over the kitchen floor.

"Listen, Peg. Gotta go." Mama smacks the phone and her soulless sister into silence. She sidesteps the puddle of vomit, puts her huge, gruff hands on either side of my throbbing head, and pulls me closer toward her for what I expect will be an awkward but tender peck on the cheek. Instead, she grips my skull a little too tight and sighs, "I'll go get the Javex. That puke pile won't clean itself."

That's why I came home. Because puke piles won't clean themselves, and because I need my mother to help hold my head together while what's left of my life falls apart.

While Mama is Javexing the bejesus out of the floor — as a hotel chambermaid of thirty-five years, she is professionally trained to Javex the bejesus out of anything — the phone rings again.

I stare at it, paralyzed by the terror of no call display. *Should I pick it up? It's Mama's house, she should answer. What if it's Peggy? Don't wanna talk to her. What if people don't know I'm home, or why? Worse yet, what if they do?*

"Answer the goddamn phone, fool!" Mama yells.

I'm met with a velvety voice, punctuated by a crisp Indian accent. It's my new neurologist at the hospital here. Dr. Parvati Divyaratna.

"Good morning, Stacey," she says. "I am calling with good news."

Dr. Divyaratna tells me that my medical file arrived from Toronto. The last MRI got some good, clear images of the tumours. Not only are they very photogenic, but their locations are also "clinically interesting." And, an appointment opened up for ten thirty this morning because one of her other patients "came to the end of a long journey" last night.

"Who's that?" Mama asks as I hang up.

"Dr. Divyaratna," I say, proud of how easily her name rolls off my tongue.

"Oh, the Choco-Doc."

"Jesus, Ma, don't call her that."

"G'wan it's just a nickname. She's dark and she's sweet. Beats the hell out of what they used to call her."

Which was the "Darkie Doctor," since she was a young, brown-skinned physician tending to a slew of culturally cloistered old white people. Now she's the Island's only neurologist. Everyone's terrified she'll up and leave like so many have, so she's downright revered. People bring her homemade bread and fresh-from-the-boat lobster. She never pays to have her car fixed or her driveway plowed. But they don't call her the Choco-Doc to her face, now do they? A name like that's only said in whispers, the same way folks refer to a local farming family as the Chickenshits. Everybody calls them that, but nobody ever says it right to them.

You'd think my mother would know better. They still call her Scruffy Effie behind her back, and she pretends she doesn't know. My nickname is not a whispered-behind-my-back kind of thing. I'm forever Crow because I stole a piece of gaudy costume jewellery from the Bargain Store when I was five and a half years old, and Peggy caught me. She thought it was a riot, and couldn't wait to tell the world: "That one, snatching the shiny things. Just like a little crow!" The story fell away as I got older, but the name stuck. So I embraced it. Even though it's a reminder that I'm part criminal.

Right now, I feel more like a complete lunatic, standing

in the kitchen blubbering like a baby because my doctor thinks that having photogenic tumours that are "clinically interesting" and getting a dead guy's appointment slot somehow constitutes "good news."

Mama wraps her mighty arms around me, cradling the back of my head in her hand. My snot and tears stream all over her broad shoulder as she tries in vain to smooth my hair with her chapped and calloused palm, managing only to snag and pull it. I hug her back harder than I've ever hugged anyone before. It's like hugging a rock. I hope she won't crumble and crack under the weight of grief when I'm gone. Maybe my twenty-year absence was good practice for what's to come.

"Listen, missy," she says, giving my head another squeeze before prying herself out of my death grip, "you need to go down to The Wharf. Blow the stink off of you." Then she dumps her floor-washing water down the kitchen sink, puts the kettle on to boil, and stomps off down the hall.

The housebound hermit stink that needs blowing off now first crept in while I was still in Toronto. In the days after my diagnosis, I called in sick to work. I was scared shit-less to leave my condo in case I had another neurological malfunction in a sea of indifferent strangers. But when the pile of greasy food delivery containers and the stench of my own armpits reached a certain point, a different dread set in. What if something ruptured, or my brain short-circuited while I was all by myself, my door locked and my phone out of reach? What if it happened while I was all scuzzy and sad like this? Or while I was on the toilet? What if I just died alone there, and the cops only found my body because the dude next door complained about the smell?

So I tried going back to work. Because that's what people do who have bills to pay, fears to run from, and a life to feign. They brush their hair, put on some clothes, swallow some pills, and pretend everything's fine. Pretend the drugs that are supposed to make the symptoms go away *aren't* actually making things worse. Pretend their brain *isn't* a time bomb. I should have known better than to tell anyone at the office what was going on. Maybe I did know better, but I did it anyway.

"Awww, Stacey." Ami, the product PR guru—who passed for a friend some days—frowned a little when I told her, while her glued-on eyelash fringes fluttered at hyper-speed. "You *have* to try the Viva Rica Detox Flush."

I wanted to tell her that she just *had* to shove a bottle of blueberry juice up her ass. Instead I smiled. Nodded. Fluttered the mascara-clumped stumps that pass for my eye-lashes back at her. The next morning, I called in sick. The day after, sicker. Until finally, after ten days of swinging between numbness and dread, there came some clarity. Punctuated by the dumpster top thudding shut on my balled-up silky, pukey bedsheets. I called Mama. Started planning my exit.

Here and now, there's no point in getting dressed or making any attempt to look as though I've done anything other than roll out of bed. That is the beauty of being in the woods. No one to impress, least of all the nosy neighbours who'll be peering out windows and driving in slow motion to take a good long gander at who's doing what, where. I slide on a pair of old flip-flops and head down the road to the second-most sacred place on the planet.

The massive U-shaped concrete structure that sprawls out into the deep water is technically "the wharf" where a ferry once docked and crossed the narrow channel in this part of the Bras d'Or Lakes, until they built the big bridge in the sixties. But "The Wharf" is so much more than just the old ferry dock. It is the surrounding beach and woods. A place of myth and memories. A holy site of secret rebellion, and the backdrop for stories you sure as hell won't hear at church teas and knitting circles. Stories that my generation relives in loud, raucous roars around bonfires and at kitchen parties. Maybe even at funerals. The good ones, anyway. The Wharf is where I built my first sandcastle and had my first swimming lesson. It's where I had my first kiss, my first cigarette, my first swig of Golden Glow apple-flavoured wine-like product. It's where Allie and Char and I hosted the infamous annual May 2-4 drunken debauchery camping excursion known as Fucktapalooza. It's also where I'd go to be by myself and to talk to my father. Not that he ever talked back.

That's another little scrap of the story I need to stitch into what's left of my life. Exactly what manner of tragedy befell the eighteen-year-old kid they all called Smart Alec Spenser, who went and knocked up his family's poor young housekeeper, Scruffy Effie Fortune. Smart Alec was last seen walking this very road twenty-seven days before I was born, headed down to The Wharf to his brand new, freshly christened fishing boat, *The Anastasia*. Two days later, *The Anastasia* was found run aground on the far shore of the Bras d'Or. There was no sign of Smart Alec. Except for a broken beer bottle and a bloody T-shirt on board. You can imagine all the whispers that little mystery spawned, what with the Spensers being a pack of ruthless business kingpins on the brink of being scandalized by a bastard baby, and the Fortunes being a bunch of dirt-poor, cursed lunatics. The last person to see Smart Alec alive was my mother. She swears to God her final words to him on that cool October evening were, "You're a foolish son of a bitch. But I love you."

[···]

"Christ Almighty, child, I didn't mean for you to walk! Get in." Mama huffs out the window of Bessie, her beat-up maroon 1995 Toyota Corolla as she rolls up alongside me. I'd been traipsing down the dirt roadside for a mere seven minutes. Five more, and I'd be there. It seems silly to get in the car. But I do it anyway. I plunk my arse down in the front passenger seat and promptly start to argue with her.

"Ma, it's not far."

"I don't give a flying fiddler's fart if it's within pissing distance. You're in your friggin' pyjamas, no bra on, your hair's a rat's nest, and you're..."

Silence.

"Ma, I'm fine."

She cocks her eyebrow to an angle that says, Liar. Then she slams on the brakes.

"Fine? Fine. Get out then. Just don't come cryin' to me when Peggy goes telling everyone and their dog that you were down at The Wharf this morning dressed like a streel."

"Please. I've got better things to cry about."

"Suit yourself. I've got to go lend Flossie Baker a hand. She hurt her hip again. I'll pick you up at nine thirty-five on the nose for that doctor's appointment. Here. Hot tea in that there cup thing of yours."

"Thanks, Ma. Loves ya," I half snort as I grab the travel mug from the console and get out of the car.

"Damn right you do!" I hear out the window as she wheels around and drives off.

I saunter down The Wharf road, a little afraid that I've jinxed myself with that foolish bravado, that I *will* wind up having a seizure, or going blind, or losing control of my legs, my bowels, or my mind down here by myself. But there are worse places for those things to happen. In a dank corner of the Bloor Street subway station, in the middle of the morning rush while doing a walk of shame home from a one-night stand, for example. Want to know what happens when a messy-haired, smeary-eyed streel of a woman crumples to the ground in a mess of vomit and piss and rolling eyes, then and there? Throngs of people just keep walking. A transit cop will tell her to move along. When she tries to explain that something is wrong—that she usually has tidier hair, less slutty clothes, and the ability to control her bodily functions—the words come as a slurry string of garbles, so he'll call 911 and describe her as an unidentified incoherent female. Through a crack in the visual chaos of swirling colours and light, she'll see the cop shake his head and hear him on repeat, until the paramedics arrive: "Ma'am, tell me your name and what you're on." The nurses will smile their best pity smiles when they see she's got no one to pick her up at the hospital at discharge, and a cab driver from Sudan will be the first one to hear the news that she's got brain tumours.

I was more alone in that city of two and a half million people than I am here. At least if I keel over down at The Wharf, somebody will know who I am. Maybe even care. That's the beauty of these particular woods, and of being a bit of a big deal around here. Even when it seems like there's

no one around, somebody's watching. Waiting for something—anything—to happen. Especially to the likes of me.

As the summer sun ascends, my senses come to rest on
what I'd been too busy to notice was missing from my life all
these years I've been away. The mesmerizing dance of light
on waves. The lullaby rhythm of waves on the shore. The salty
stank of rotting seaweed and jellyfish corpses, inexplicably
mingled with the smell of…marijuana?

Willy Gimp's truck is parked on the beach, just down past
the wharf itself.

Willy Gimp's real name is William Matthews Jr., but the
only people who call him that are people he hates—doctors,
lawyers, cops, and judges. He was born with a twisted-up
right side. An arm that defies cortical orders to co-operate.
A hand whose default is tightly curled and fisted. A foot that
turns in and drags a bit when he walks. A slight tension on
the right corner of his bottom lip, giving him a perpetual
smirk. Hemiplegic cerebral palsy, in medical terms. A "gimp,"
according to his old man.

When he was five years old, Willy Gimp wanted to play
hockey, but his father laughed. "That body will do you no
favours. Best learn to use your head, Willy Gimp." And so
he did—out of spite and pride—use his head instead. Willy
was smart as a whip. He was also bad at sports and worse
with girls, so he had ample time to hit the books. More than
anything else, he used those brains to get in and out of
trouble.

Willy lived just off the highway between Loch Bhreagh
and the turnoff Down North, a stretch called Centre Loch
Bhreagh Bay Look-Off, according to the road signs. He
was a year ahead of me in school, but in grade twelve, he

transferred from the preppy-ish, small-school comfort of Loch Bhreagh Rural Consolidated to the industrial remedial program at the mean concrete edifice on the hill between The Mines and the Northside, in Town. Sullivan High School was its real name. But everybody called it The Jungle.

Why did sharp-as-a-tack Willy Gimp go from being honour roll at LBRC to being a grease monkey in The Jungle? Two reasons. He decided he wanted to be a mechanic, and The Jungle was a bigger market for the phenomenal pot he grew in the backwoods of his grandfather's property in Big Harbour. Gimp had been growing it since he was sixteen, and smoking it since he was twelve. Said it eased the spasms in his arm and leg and made the stupid people of the world just a little more tolerable, funny, even.

But Gimp was a businessman at heart. In grade ten, he had both the wit and the balls to turn his little grow-op into a "hypothetical" Junior Entrepreneur Club project, complete with a detailed business plan, thorough analysis of the competition, and a kick-ass marketing strategy. He didn't win any prizes for it, but he managed to drum up a fair amount of non-hypothetical business. Within a year, he had a sizable stash of cash and contacts, and it was time to grow the business. So he ventured into The Jungle, already well known and much sought after. By the end of grade twelve, Willy Gimp had enough money to put himself through school to become a licensed mechanic. He bought his own garage and a three-room shack on the highway into Town, where he fixed cars, pumped gas, and moved massive quantities of pop, chips, and weed.

Ten years ago he got busted, charged with trafficking, and went to jail, where he was, of course, a model prisoner. He meditated and lifted weights. He studied environmental ecology, philosophy, and got a business degree. He made friends with everybody—the inmates, the guards, the janitors, the spiders in the corner of his cell. Willy Gimp emerged from the clink stronger and smarter and better connected. He got home, fixed up his little house and his garage, and went back to rebuilding his business.

And now, here he is sitting in a shitty old truck, having a little wake-n-bake at The Wharf.

I sneak down along the beach, making sure to stay out of range of the truck's mirrors, which Willy Gimp is no doubt monitoring with due paranoia. Then I duck down low and creep right up alongside the passenger door. I pause for a moment, listening to the first few bars of The Doors' "Hello, I Love You" swagger out the driver's side window on a waft of pungent smoke, then rise sharply to rap my knuckles hard on the window and bark, "Out of the truck, Mr. Matthews" in my best cop voice.

Without flinching, without trying to hide the joint, without even taking his eyes off the copy of the newspaper that lies splayed across the steering wheel, Willy Gimp grunts loudly, "It's legal. I got a medical licence. Ya can fuck off now, thanks." He glances up, sees me, and everything turns on a dime. His bloodshot eyes brighten and widen. A laugh shakes through his shoulders, cracking his face into a crooked smile.

I ignore the quick flicker of orange fireworks that my eyes invent around his ears, and smile back.

"Ohferthalovagod, Crow! What's goin' on? Christ, get in the friggin' truck and come have a puff with me, woman!" His spastic arm deftly swings the door open, and I climb in.

"Real cops don't ever come to the passenger side window, eh. Or pop up like a friggin' jack-in-the-box. I figured it was Shirl Short comin' to hassle me. Lucky I didn't chuck a piss jug at ya."

Before I can ask Gimp if he really does still keep piss jugs in his truck like he used to, he passes me the joint. I hesitate. The voice of the cop on the Bloor Street subway platform ebbs into my mind. *Tell me your name and what you're on.* Maybe I shouldn't smoke weed. Then again, I'm home now and on borrowed time. So maybe I should.

Fuck it. Me and Gimp are gonna sit here in his truck smoking a doobie, listening to The Doors, waiting for Shirl Short to come hassle us, just like we did when we were teenagers. Except now, Willy Gimp is hot.

He'd always been kind of cute, I guess. Big green expressive eyes rimmed with long dark lashes. Soft, black, laissez-faire hair that curled when it got too long. Smooth skin. Straight teeth. But he was tall and scrawny. He wore socks with sandals. His skid metal T-shirts had cigarette packs rolled up in the sleeves. He wore jogging pants and had a mullet long after those things were unacceptable and long before they became fashionably ironic. He walked funny. He moved his arm funny. He was a bizarre combination of genius and clown. Nobody was ever entirely sure what to make of Willy Gimp. He certainly wasn't dating material, by any means. But that didn't stop me from sleeping with him for most of high school. Not that I ever admitted it.

It started off innocently enough. A pity lay, really. We hooked up at a bush party one night when I was in grade ten, and he drunkenly confessed that he was a virgin. So, compassionate little hussy that I was, I dragged him up to the road and into the back of Allie's car—the legendary Shaggin' Wagon—to give him a memorable first fuck. And that was supposed to be the end of that. But a few weeks later, when I realized Trevor Jessome was using me to get back at Allie, I ran to Willy, looking to use somebody myself. When Weasel Tobin broke my heart along with the pointer finger on my left hand, I ran to Willy for some tenderness. When Duke Clarke humiliated me with the Clap for Crow stunt at my graduation ceremony, I ran to Willy before I ran away. In fact, I kissed him goodbye at this very place the night before I left, planning never to return.

But here I am. And here he is now, middle age just beginning to touch and shape him. His hair is delicately salt and peppered. His face is ever so slightly etched and imprinted with the joys and pains of the last twenty years. His chest and arms—even the gimpy one—are still thin, but muscled and defined beneath his snug white T-shirt. Beautiful artwork is inked into his skin, a vibrant and detailed oceanic sleeve tattooed down to his left wrist. Not bad for a forty-year-old pothead mechanic. Perhaps another pity lay might be in order. Assuming he'll take pity on me.

There isn't much need for us to catch up on the ordinary details of each other's lives. Facebook made those kinds of reunion conversations more or less obsolete, and good old-fashioned gossip fills in the gaps. I know that he still has the garage. He knows that I made a life selling super juice. I know that his father died two years ago and his mother shacked up with his uncle. He knows that I flew Mama up to Toronto every Christmas, and that she'd bitch about being there the entire time. I know that he was engaged to Chrissy Parsons, but that fell apart a year ago when she pumped every dime he'd been saving for their wedding into a slot machine, and then got onto the hard drugs. He knows that I was engaged to the world's biggest douchebag, until that douchebag got caught putting his penis in places his penis should not have been. Namely, in his boss's mouth.

"Lookin' some good there, by the way," he grins. "Come back just to show off or what?"

This. This kind of thing right here is what I've been dreading. How do I tell people that my secret to dropping the extra twenty pounds I lugged around most of my life wasn't hot yoga or detoxing? And then how do I fake optimism, and pretend I haven't leapfrogged over the normal seven stages of grief, and invented my own single stage: Surly and Reckless Resignation to Being Doomed. And where is that goddamn gossip network when I need it? I've been home for nearly thirty-six hours. That's more than enough time for Peggy to have told everyone and their dog why I'm back so I wouldn't have to answer any questions, and everyone could just greet me with pity and pleasantries. But no, I've gotta do *this* batch of dirty work myself, I guess. Thank Jesus it's only Willy Gimp. And thank Jesus I'm good and stoned now.

"I'm back living with Ma because—" I pause, inhaling sharply before crushing the roach out in the ashtray. "I got diagnosed with brain tumours. Inoperable ones." And then I ramble. "Wow, that's good weed. I haven't smoked weed in a really long time. Like, ten years. In Toronto I hung around with all these hipsters so it was all blow and Jägerbombs. But this is way better. Not skunky either. Hey, got 'Roadhouse Blues' on here? Haven't heard that tune in for-fuckin'-ever. God, did I always talk this much when I was stoned? Got any Visine? Or Doritos? The munchies, man. And the pasties."

I remember the tea in my travel mug, take a gulp, and nearly spit it back out all over the dash of Gimp's truck. My chattering mind and my pasty mouth expected my usual gently steeped loose leaf green tea with bits of toasted walnuts and praline sprinkles, candied pineapple, flower petals, and other bits of artisan tea goodness. Fruit tea, Mama calls it. Whether that's because she thinks it is actually made of fruit or because she figures only "fruits" drink it, I'm not certain. Instead, I get a scalding mouthful of Effie Fortune's Stovetop Sludge, which I could probably bottle and market as a potent detoxifying tincture, if I wasn't so busy getting ready to die.

"God, Crow. That's terrible. I don't even know what to say." Gimp leans across my lap to rummage through the console for his shot glass and scissors.

"Me neither." I take another sip of tea, this time managing to swallow it without making a scene. "Allie's on her way home, too. Her mother finally died."

"Well, Little Mary Sunshine, so much for polite stoner small talk. You're only slightly less depressing than neo-con newspapers and government-run education." He drops a fat green bud into the shot glass, and starts chopping it with a methodical tenderness, watching the scissor blades pinch and pierce the whole sticky mass into crumbs and slivers. Talking to it, practically. "Death, eh? Shitty reason to come home."

"Death's the only reason to come back to this shithole," I say, staring out the window. The sun has hoisted itself higher into the sky, putting the run on the remnants of early morning mist. There's not a breath of wind. The water is dead calm, an acquiescent mirror for the sky's vanity. All that showy light and colour and vastness.

"Shithole?" Willy's voice cracks with feigned offence. "Nah, b'ye, this here's a good place to live."

"I need a good place to die," I mumble, returning my attention to the enclosed comfort of the truck. "Remember my cat Whipper?"

"That the one the coyotes ate, or the one that played the piano?" he asks.

"No, he was orange." I give his bad arm a flirty shove at the precise moment he begins to shake the carefully chopped pot into the rolling paper he has cupped in the other hand. But Gimp doesn't drop so much as a crumb. And his eyes never leave the narrow sphere of the task at hand. He hasn't looked at me since I said the word *tumours.*

"Whipper had a tumour in his gut," I say. "The day after we found out, he ran away. A week later, I found him right there on the wharf, sprawled out on the edge overlooking the water. Dead as a doorknob. That cat did the same thing I'm doing. Haulin' ass home. Looking for a good place to curl up and die."

"Flawed analogy." He shakes his head but keeps his eyes fixed on the delicate mechanics of his one-handed joint rolling. "You're doing the opposite. Whipper left home. Went somewhere different. Somewhere lonely. Where the people who loved him wouldn't see him go all twitchy. You're the reverse Whipper."

"Dammit," I say. "I *am.* Well, better chop that story out of the blockbuster memoir I'm writing. Wanna party like it's 1995 with me in the meantime? I'll make you a chapter." I glance at him, toss my hair, grin, and start leaning in toward him.

"Ah, Christ!" Gimp jumps in his seat. "I gotta go! I hired that Edwards kid to work mornings at the garage, but don't trust him enough to give him keys. Betcha he's been standing outside with his thumb up his arse and his brain in neutral for the last fifteen minutes. Wouldn't just break in like anybody with half a brain would do. Kids today. Want a ride back to your ma's?"

"Oh. No. I'm fine. Thanks," I say, doing a shit job of concealing my sulkiness at being cock blocked like that.

He tucks the fresh joint behind his ear. "Nice seein' ya, Crow. Don't be a stranger, eh."

"Hey, maybe we can, you know...go for coffee." My shoulders lift in a fake-casual shrug, doing my non-verbal damnedest to remind him that "going for coffee" was our secret code for getting high and having sex in random parking lots, bushes, and occasionally beds.

"Yeah b'ye, that'd be r'oit awn," he says. No flirty wink, no devilish eyebrow arch, no goodbye pat on the arse as I get out of the truck. He peels away in a dusty grey haze, which my squirrelly vision tinges with swishes of murky blue.

Under the grandiose influence of unobstructed land, sea, and sky, with a goodly dose of pent-up sexual frustration and primo medicinal weed, I meander up onto the wharf and get the urge to do something crazy. Jump in the water with all my clothes on, maybe. No. Even crazier. A quick skinny dip. I shimmy out of my boxers and tank top. Do I do a flying leap off the wharf, dropping six feet straight into the deep, dark water, just like I did when I was a kid? Or do I go down to the shoreline and tiptoe in until there is enough cold and courage to force me to get ducked, the way the lame old grown-ups used to do when I was a kid? *Leap or be lame? Leap or be lame? C'mon Crow, what's it gonna be?*

While I'm psyching myself up, a long bank of blackish cloud comes out of nowhere and swoops in front of the sun, thwarting its warmth and light. The wind picks up. The water gets choppy. The rush of feeling cocky and crazy and cool was fleeting. Suddenly I am cold. And naked. Stoned, sick, and stupid.

I yank my clothes back on in a hurry. Then I walk back to Mama's, dragging my feet in the roadside dirt the entire way.

2 THE DUST

The Wharf is the second-most sacred place in the world to me. Back at Mama's I retreat to the first: my bedroom closet. I crawl in, just as I used to do when I was a drama queen of a kid. That closet was, and still is, a comfortable disaster that always made me feel held, contained. The late-August morning light that streams through my bedroom window is filtered and softened by the rainbow tie-dyed sheet that hangs over the place where a closet door should be. It's cozy and dim enough to curl up and fall asleep, but too dark to do what I've crawled in here to do. Especially since I'm old, stoned, and my vision is all screwy. I flip on the little night light that Mama installed when I was five to keep the monsters out, and begin to dig through the pile of long-neglected throwbacks. The only monsters here now are memories, and I need to touch every goddamn one of them at least one more time.

My fingers land on the shimmery cover of my junior high diary. A literary masterpiece if I do say so myself. Each entry a poignant coming-of-age vignette imbued with deep emotion. Which means I wrote down my moody teenage takes on whatever drama had unfolded that day, and dotted my *i*'s with hearts. I even worked in a little poetry here and there.

Who knew that love/ was a gift from above/ like a hand in a glove/ with no push or no shove? I did, at age thirteen, when I had a crush on a guy named Weasel.

Beneath the diary, there's a substantial pile of early nineties fashion relics. Skin-tight acid-washed jeans with zippers on the ankles. A pink crimping iron and scads of neon friendship bracelets. The electric purple suede jacket with ridiculously gigantic leather shoulders. I pick up the jacket, and my stomach turns.

The summer before grade nine, I saw it in the window of Rutherfords, the tony ladies' wear shop in Town. After fifty-nine kilometres' worth of garbage picking in roadside ditches on a government grant job, I finally had enough money to buy it. For twenty minutes, I preened and twirled and made sassy duck faces in front of the mirror in the store, pretending I'd just stepped out of a music video. When I asked Mama what she thought, she smiled a big broad smile, then started singing "Purple People Eater." Complete with a little dance. That was the first and nearly the last time I ever swore at my mother. I called her a bitch, threw the jacket on the floor with an angsty flourish, and stormed out.

Mama found me a few minutes later, sitting in the car, where I'd already resolved to blow all the money I'd saved on streel clothes, Doritos, cream soda, and smokes. Which I did. Mama's underbite pinched her top lip in a vice grip as she got in the car. She didn't say much. Just this: "Listen here, missy. I brought you into this world. You ever talk to me like that again, and I'll take you out of it."

A few months later, I opened my fifteenth birthday gift from Mama. The flying purple people eater suede and leather jacket. I never wore it. Not even once. I try the jacket on for size now. It borders on being too big but is still soft and supple and purple as fuck. Maybe Mama will have me buried in it. She might have to, since I sold all my good clothes on Kijiji before I left Toronto because I needed the cash. And because I'd look stupid wearing that kind of wardrobe around here. And because I probably won't be around much longer anyway.

Over in another closet corner, there's the pile of my high school era treasures. By grade ten, my muddy waters ran too deep for original poetry and bubble gum teen magazine fashion. My binders weren't identified by subject, but rather by the song lyrics scrawled on the covers. The Tragically Hip, for English. Sixties drug tunes, for chemistry. The most cryptic and depressing things Tori Amos ever wrote, for math. There's baggy jeans with ripped knees. Plaid shirts. A pair of busted-up red suede Converse One Stars, like the ones Kurt Cobain died in. Bought them with the tips I made waiting tables one summer. Mama gave me the gears for wasting money on something as foolish as a pair of brand name sneakers, when they sold ones "just like them" for ten bucks at the Bargain Store. I made a point of wearing them right to death. Maybe I'll be buried in *them*, too. They'll go great with the purple people eater jacket.

I emerge from the closet with an outfit to wear to my doctor's appointment and some reading material to kill the time. I'm wrapped in the nostalgia of worn denim and plaid, and a little black T-shirt with the word *skater* on it — an ancient artifact from the time before it was spelled with an 8. I flip through my grade twelve yearbook.

There we are, Loch Bhreagh Rural Consolidated School's Class of '95. Fifty young faces preserved in shades of grey.

Glossy, air brushed, and earnest with our First Loves, Final Destinies, and Favourite Quotes. Allie's long, pin-straight blonde hair spills over her shoulders onto her symmetrical, enviable rack. Her wide, steady eyes and her beauty of a smile. Allie's First Love was "Mom's chocolate chip cookies." Her destiny was to "buy a Shaggin' Wagon De-Luxe and change her name to Dr. Feelgood." Her quote, some trite shit about crying over spilled milk only making it salty for the cat, was stolen from a poster in the guidance counsellor's office. Allie spent a lot of time in there with me, handing me Kleenex as I sobbed to Mr. Patterson about another pet cat's tragic demise. He never caught on that such trauma only ever seemed to surface when Allie and I had double gym class after lunch.

A few pages later, there's my other best friend, kooky, cocky Char MacIsaac. She threatened the yearbook editor, Becky Chickenshit, with a puck in the tits if she printed her real name, which was Charlotte. Char's grad portrait looks more like a mug shot. Her snaggle-toothed smirk and angular, freckled face are framed by an electric mess of tight orange curls. Her slightly off-centre left eye is framed by a big black shiner that was too big and too dark to be air-brushed out without making the entire eye disappear. Which was fine by Char. She earned that shiner in a fight against Scary Sylvia out behind the rink after a dance. Char's First Love was "adrenaline rushes," her destiny was "to set the world record for full body orgasms while nude skydiving." And she quoted herself: "Shut up, before I puck you in the tits." Which Becky snuck past the yearbook staff advisor, because she was scared of getting pucked in the tits.

Every few months, I get a quasi-coherent Facebook message

from Char. Scattered stories about how she hitchhiked across Europe with a three-legged pit bull that she rescued from an underground dog fighting club. Detailed descriptions of her days spent teaching English at a posh private school in Thailand, and nights spent performing exotic, drug-enhanced sex rituals in the forest with men dressed as Buddhas. Tales of her tumultuous love affair with a twenty-year-old Congolese diamond smuggler. Somehow, that self-destructive danger junkie is still alive and kicking. Much to everyone's surprise.

I flip back to the page with me on it. My hair is poufed like a mouse-brown Christmas tree. My cheeks avoid looking chubby, more by good luck than good management. A tight pseudo-smile. My quote is from the chorus of "Me and Bobby McGee." The part about freedom. About having nothing left to lose. Attributed to Janis Joplin. Mama was miffed at me because I "knew damn well it was Kris Kristofferson." I also knew damn well that it was better to be cool than correct. First Love: "the sound of my own voice." Final Destiny: "to die a living legend."

"Oh, g'wan," Mama had said when I brought that yearbook home. "Legend in your own mind, that's what you are."

Little did we know I'd be back here, trying to live as a dying legend. I'm clutching at these silly, trivial remnants of my past, trying to patch over the frays, the rips, the tears in who I am, who I thought I was, and who I won't get the chance to be. Meanwhile, Allie stands on the brink of getting her life back, and Char is still off gallivanting around the globe like the reckless wreck she's always been. For a while I thought I had a shot at being a redemption story. The gritty Cape Breton girl who comes from multi-generational dysfunction but manages to pull herself up by the dirty old pit boot straps, go down the road, make a name for herself, and never look back.

First, I bolted to Halifax, where my nickname followed me, as did Char and Allie and half the people we knew. Because we all wanted to be anywhere but home. When I finished university there, the only logical step was to go bigger. Farther. To Toronto, where I could really morph myself into whatever I imagined I could be. Alone. Walking down Yonge Street that first time felt like floating, like I was this empty vessel being carried along by a cool current of anonymity. No one spoke to me, no one made eye contact, no one gave a rat's ass about my father's name or my mother's past or the fact that my skirt was too short and tight. I could be whoever I wanted. In Toronto, I was Stacey Fortune. Stacey Fortune was so urbane. Edgy but classy. Ate dim sum and drank Shiraz. Didn't cut and dye her own hair, or reek of pot smoke and cheap perfume. Stacey Fortune got into a course at a *Toronto* university and got a certificate. In marketing. She was going to make it on her own in the big city, come hell or high water. She hustled, she networked, and she landed a half-decent job. Eventually, she even landed a boyfriend named Dave, who played piano, downhill skied, and delivered pick-up lines in multiple sexy-sounding languages. Stacey Fortune was a success story. Crow Fortune was but an amusing anecdote that would linger in the gossipy minds of a backwoods island on the edge of nowhere special.

This time last year, I was prancing around Toronto with an antique diamond engagement ring on my finger, nibbling organic wedding cake samples, *oohing* and *aahing* at exotic flowers being beautifully humiliated into things called tussie-mussies and nosegays, and even entertaining the idea of growing another human being inside my aging uterus. It took me seven years of chameleoning myself into Dave Salyszyn's idea of wife material—worthy of his grandmother's jewellery and his unpronounceable last name. Then, when that particular version of Stacey Fortune's Dream Life went to hell in a philandering handbasket last New Year's Eve, I managed to ignore Mama's litany of "I told ya so's" and yank myself into yet another iteration of victory.

Stacey Fortune would go all *Sex and the City* Shopaholic Girl Power on this whole shitty deal. Because Kris Kristofferson was right, freedom *was* just another word for nothing left to lose. And once again I was free to be whatever *I* wanted, including—but not limited to—a nightclubbing cougar with no standards and several credit cards. Not Scruffy Effie's daughter, one of the poor cursed Fortunes from the Halfway Road. Not Crow, the high school scandal turned university Beer Pong champ, nor Stacey the smiling Viva Rica shill. Not even the future Mrs. Dave Salyszyn, uptown Rosedale yummy mummy to be. I was gearing up to be a friggin' phoenix, emerging in a flash of golden mid-life glory, rising from the ashes of an ego burned by other people's assholery. But I didn't get a chance to be a full-fledged phoenix because brain tumours have a way of fucking with such plans, and the phoenix life burns up a godawful pile of resources in a hurry. So here I am. Plain old Crow. Again.

Which means that my mother will still bust in through my bedroom door without knocking and scare the shit out of me. I used to roll my eyes and yam at her about it. She'd fold her arms across her chest, listen to me rant a bit, then snap, "What's this, the Greeting Gale Inn? *Knock knock,* housekeeping? Listen, this is my house missy, and I'll walk into a room as I see fit." Then, for the hundredth time, she'd regale me with tales about how the shack she grew up in didn't even have doors, and the bathroom was a three-walled outhouse in the front yard. "If you want privacy, go in to the bathroom and be glad the whole of the Halfway Road isn't watching ya piss."

Now, I don't protest, even as she thumps into the middle of my room and grunts, "You're not going to the doctor dressed like that? Like a friggin' lumberjack."

"It's retro fashion, Ma. And you're one to talk." I nod toward her ridiculous Greeting Gale Inn housekeeper's uniform. What kind of an arsehole makes his aging female motel staff wear pouf-sleeved, full-skirted dresses with white aprons while they make beds and scrub toilets all day? An arsehole by the name of Jason Gale. He was in my grad class, too. First Love was "money," Final Destiny was "to inherit his grandfather's motel," and his Favourite Quote was "Clothes make the man." So he makes my mother go to work dressed like a drab version of Alice in Wonderland. If she and the other women say a word about it, their shifts might get shorter and shittier. They might find themselves cleaning the rooms of every bedwetter, hair shedder, prom nighter, and honeymooner that comes through the front desk. And I know this. So I immediately feel like a heel for teasing Mama about the dress.

She picks up a teddy bear and whiffs it at my head, but misses by a mile. Then she pulls a small silver flask out of her Greeting Gale dress pocket and takes a swig.

Surprise, sur-fucking-prise. My mother drinks. She's not the falling down wreck-yer-life kinda drunk, although she can get a little mean on a Saturday night if she gets off the gin and on to the white wine. I'm not even sure she's what you'd call an alcoholic, especially around here. Not like her old man. Black Bernie Fortune was a notorious drunk, and Mama will be the first one to tell you that he's the reason she picked up a bottle in the first place. He threatened to beat her if he ever caught her drinking, and even in her youth, nothing flipped Effie Fortune's contrarian switch quicker than hypocritical authority. So when he said, "Stay away from the bottle," Effie went straight to the nearest bootlegger. As promised, the Old Man beat the piss out of her, and she took it with pride. She made a point of holding herself and her liquor in a way Black Bernie never could. Still, she can't sleep without a few drinks, she's unfit to be behind the wheel of a car more nights of the week than not, and she's burned a few bridges when she was in her cups. Figuratively speaking, of course.

Aunt Janice was the only one in our family who ever literally burned a bridge. But that's another story.

"What?" Mama says when I give her and the flask the side eye. "Gin's medicinal. No different from the dope you and Willy Gimp were smoking down at The Wharf."

And before I can stammer out a half-assed denial of what Mama somehow knew, she's headed down to the kitchen. There I find her, muttering an exasperated string of "Jesus, Jesus, Jesus" into the depths of her tea kettle. It has been sitting on the back burner, steeping and simmering for hours. That's the secret to Effie Fortune's Stove Top Sludge. The generous splash of milk and four spoons of sugar that leave a syrup at the bottom of the cup are just fancy flourishes. The essence of the brew lies in keeping the kettle hot all day long, and tossing in a new bag with the old every time more water is added. But you can only boil the bejesus out of old tea bags so many times before one of them ruptures. So there's Mama, cursing at the wayward clumps of tea leaves sullying her kettle.

"Opportunity for an upsell. A product add-on. Effie Fortune's Stove Top Sludge Tincture, now with Fortune-Telling Tea Leaves."

"Shush now, don't be talking," she says. "Old Black Agnes used to read the leaves. That's where all the troubles started."

Mama dumps the kettle contents into the sink and rinses it down the drain with a blast from the tap. But not before making a quick study of the remnants of the busted tea bag in the metal basin. I pretend I don't see her stare a second too long and purse her lips. And Mama acts like it never happened.

"Well, c'mon then, if that's what you're wearing."

[…]

The Middle Rear Road sits halfway between the picturesque village of Loch Bhreagh — a quaint little tourist trap on the other side of Ceilidh Mountain — and Town. *Town* is what us hicks from the sticks call the Northside and The Mines, and it is actually the amalgamation of a couple of OxyContin-ridden, call-centre-infested, coal-stripped craters that erupted in the armpit of the Island's industrial end. It's where both my parents were born and raised and most of their people still live. My doctor's appointment is a good shot deeper into the heart of Industrial Cape Breton, which is out in Town, Town. When you say it twice, everybody knows you're referring to our only half-assed crack at a city. A thirty thousand–person sputtering economic engine, with the beautiful BayFlower Mall, more cheap chain coffee shops than you can shake a stick at, and of course, the Regional Hospital. The Mines, the Northside, and the city itself all used to be boomtowns in their own right, back in the days of coal and steel. Nothing but busted now.

Mama curses under her breath every time Bessie's tires plunk through another pothole on the crumbling kilometres of the Middle Rear Road, but she still laughs about the time she filled those holes with clumps of forget-me-nots that she dug up from the ditch at the bottom of our driveway. This was her way of protesting the negligence of the powers-that-be on the Mainland, who forget that rural Cape Breton even exists when it comes time to spend taxpayers' dollars. When she was done, every hole had thick clusters of delicate, tenacious blue flowers filling the dangerous gaps in the collapsing pavement. A lovely way to make a point. Then old Mary Jessie MacRitchie ditched her truck swerving to avoid a pile of forget-me-nots, which she mistook for a dog. Mama doesn't laugh at that part of the story.

"Mary Jessie was damn near ninety," Mama snorts. "Shouldn't have been driving in the first place."

She cranks up whatever whiny old country singer she's got jammed in the cassette deck as we turn onto the highway that will eventually lead to some semblance of civilization, and I close my eyes in a vain attempt to curtail a fresh round of pounding head and screwy vision. I can't stomach the world as it rushes by the car window now, even if it is only swaths of stifled trees and clearings dotted with the derelict remnants of the Island's assorted failures. A shuttered gas station here. A rundown Pott's Coffee Shop there. The sad scrap of land that sits at the turnoff to the Halfway Road in The Mines, where Mama's family's shack once stood.

My uncle Gord sold the land when Black Bernie died. Everyone in the family was too broke to chip in on the burial, so Gord used most of the money from the property sale to pay for Black Bernie's velveteen-lined casket, a grand Catholic wake and funeral, and a gleaming headstone engraved with the words "Beloved Father." Mama was wild. Said they should have just pitched the old bastard's corpse in the ocean and let the eels and sharks dispose of him for free. Gord sold the land to my father's family, the Spensers, who planned to develop it as a gravel pit. The Spensers got the land for a song because nobody else in Town would dare buy it. Not after all that had happened there. Not with the earth still scarred from the night my great-grandmother Black Agnes went mad and burned her house and most of her family to the ground on the orders of a secret message she read in a tree's bark. Not with the whispers of how Black Agnes and all her descendants were cursed by the evil eye of some Lebanese gypsies from up Ferris Hill because she was stealing their tea leaf–reading business.

The Spenser gravel pit never panned out, so they sold it to their buddies in the municipality for twice what they paid for it, making out like the well-heeled bandits they were. The bandits they still are, no doubt. The only thing that stands on that land now is a cracked wooden billboard with peeling paint that used to read, *Welcome to The Mines. Rich in Coal and Hospitality.* Those things are long gone now, too.

Still, as we drive by the site of the Fortune's familial pain and undoing, Mama grumbles, "Never should've let Gordie sell that land. They ain't making any more."

"They should at least fix the sign," I say. "Maybe to say, *Welcome to The Mines. Rich in Drunks, Drugs, and Pogey Scams.*"

"Watch it, missy," Mama growls. "There, but for the grace of dumb luck, go you."

Dumb luck? Did my mother not get the memo about her whole damn family, us Poor Unfortunate Fortunes? Her grandmother Black Agnes got us all hexed in an occult turf war. Mama's father, Black Bernie, was the only one who survived the fire his mother set in her madness, and that's only because he was given away to the nearest neighbours when he was a baby. Neighbours who, by the way, all perished in a mysterious house fire of their own when Black Bernie was a teenager, just as he turned old enough to take a job in the mines and inherit the land his birth family left him. Mama's got eleven siblings, and those who are still alive are the epitome of ruin—largely due to some variation of the aforementioned drunks, drugs, and pogey scams. I'm thirty-eight years old, all of my cousins are already dead, and I've got inoperable brain tumours. Dumb luck, my arse.

[...]

My doctor's appointment goes something like this: *Blah blah blah*, three tumours. Tricky type. Trickier locations. Operation, impossible. One step at a time. *Blah blah blah*, biopsy for cancer. Hole in your skull. Hollow needles in your brain. But don't worry, we have robots. *Blah blah blah*, here's a booklet. And a drawing. Big words. Aren't you warm in that plaid shirt?

Except imagine all that delivered in a crisp, soothing, smart-sounding Indian accent. And in full, coherent sentences. I don't know what those coherent sentences actually were because I spaced out for most of the appointment. I smiled. I nodded. I said, "Okay," even though it wasn't. "Yes, I understand," even though I didn't. And "Thank you, Dr. Divyaratna" even though I wanted to tell her to shut up. Mama paid better attention, I hope.

On the drive home, Mama tries to talk to me. I try to answer, but I can't stop staring at the handy little diagram Dr. Divyaratna drew for me. The type of tumour is written in all caps at the top of the sheet, yelling "ASTROCYTOMA." There's a sketch of a brain that looks more like a sad, lopsided cloud. Crooked arrows label the frontal, parietal, and occipital lobes, where the three tumours live. The tumours themselves are represented by smudged-ink stars. By the time we hit the stretch of highway where the nearby Chickenshit family farm perfumes the air, I manage to peel my eyes away from the paper, but end up staring out the window through the same numb zombie eyes. I can't even bring myself to bitch about the stench for fear it will come out sounding like a sob.

I get Mama to drop me off at The Wharf, again, which is stupid because the August afternoon sun is now blazing. I am depressed and hungry. And dressed like a skater grunge lumberjack. Mama zips away, already late for her shift at the Greeting Gale. There is no one around. The water is more agitated than it was this morning, little whitecaps whipped up by the warm wind. The fractured light glinting and bouncing off the choppy surface is almost too much for my eyes. I close them, and smell roses, unsure if the scent is brought to me on the breeze from a nearby bush, or something dredged up by the astrocytoma tendrils that tickle my sensory cortex in mildly amusing ways. Frankly, I'd rather the smell of rotting seaweed and burning doobies. The smell of roses makes me nauseous. Dave the Douchebag ruined roses for me by having a dozen sent to my office every Monday morning for the twelve months we were engaged because "ladies deserve roses." Apparently I wasn't a lady for the six years before that, during the on-again-off-again game of *My Fair Lady* he called our "courtship." And I'm sure as hell not one now.

There's no need of me sitting here, baking in the heat like this. I should go back to the house, eat a cheese sandwich, take the laundry off the line, and curl up in bed. Start rehearsing for my future as a tumour-plagued shut-in. Instead, my jaw clenches, my eyes narrow, my spine is tugged up by an invisible thread of defiance. Or bravado. Or insanity. Or all three twisted together into something thicker than thread. A rope, hauling me upright.

"Fuck it. I'm going in," I say out loud, to the water, to make it more real.

Next thing I know, my clothes are in a haphazard heap. I'm standing buck naked on the wharf, my pasty flesh bathed in the warm rays of my noonday lunacy. Then, I'm in a quick sprint toward the end of the long cement path, with no space for second thoughts. There's no chance to chicken out when you're charging to the edge of that concrete cliff and catapulting yourself into the air for the six-foot drop. A moment of terrifying freedom. No ground beneath my feet. Nothing holding me, and nothing for me to hold onto. Utter uncertainty. The closest I'll ever come to flying.

The chilly, choppy water swallows me whole. A fast rush of bubbles flutters up and over my body. Minnows zip through the translucent blue-green, brackish fluidity that surrounds me. Eel grass brushes my toes as I reach the low point of the plunge. Then, a faint stinging sensation as jellyfish tentacles graze my arse on the way up. I bob to the surface. My head breaks the water's tension and the sun burns my salted eyes. A split second of feeling faintly reborn is followed by a gasp of terror. *Do I still know how to swim? Should have thought about that before I jumped. Should have checked for jellyfish. It is August, after all.*

Not even halfway to shore, I'm breathless. Back when I was young and healthy, and when this water was a part of me, I could swim this distance with two arms tied behind my back. The good news is, I make it to where my feet can touch bottom. The bad news is, a cop car just rolled up. I'm thrown into the clutches of another memory. The time Char nearly drowned here.

On Labour Day weekend, just before the start of grade eleven, there was a massive party at The Wharf. The kind where kids from Loch Bhreagh, Town, and even Town, Town came out to get wrecked and camp on the beach. Unsurprisingly, somebody called the cops. Probably Peggy's best friend, Shirl Short, because that's what Shirl Short does best. Calls the cops and wrecks the fun every time she smells "the dope." The cop car rolled up just after midnight. Sneaky bastards coasted down the road with the lights off until they were right at the edge of the crowd, then flipped on the red and blues. Two of them jumped out with their flashlights to nab anyone too trashed to bolt. Those of us who'd spent a few years drinking in the woods were pretty good at making cop escapes. Some of us had even become very skilled at jumping into various bodies of shallow-ish water to hide when parties got busted.

Me, Char, and Shirl Short's beloved saint of a nephew,

Duke, were standing at the far edge of the wharf, smoking a joint and staring at the stars when flashing lights and warning bellows of "Pigs! Run!" erupted from the shore. Char calmly turned around and jumped off the wharf, into the blackness below. Unbeknownst to me, not only was she on a hit of Paco Landry's bathtub acid, but she also had thirty squares of it in her pocket. She was selling it for Paco Landry at the party because, fully beknownst to everyone, Char was sleeping with Paco Landry. Within seconds, she started splashing and yelling because she was tripping hard, and sinking fast. Char could barely swim at the best of times, and the knee-high Dr. Martens and hoodie she wore didn't help.

I waited for Duke to jump in after her, since he was close to sober. And a provincial swim team champ. And a lifeguard. And also sleeping with Char. But the smarmy little prick didn't. Instead, he mumbled, "Shitty time if she drowns," before he jogged down the wharf and off into the woods. So into the water I went, getting close enough for Char to hear me, but not so close that she could pull me under with her panic. I talked her into treading water, then helped her doggie paddle over to the rusted iron ladder on the side of the wharf. Even the darkness, the chaos, the few sips of lemon gin, and the solid hit of THC were no match for what my body knew about navigating these waters. We clung to the ladder until we heard somebody yell, "All clear. Party on!"

The ladder is not there anymore. If it was, I'd be on the by wharf now, putting my clothes back on and wringing out my hair. Instead, I'm wading in increasingly shallow water, dragging my bare, jellyfish-stung ass to shore. Once there, I'll have to scoot over a patch of rocky beach, climb a little grassy hill, and walk another dozen metres on the wharf to where my clothes lie in a rumpled heap. In full view of the cop sitting in the squad car that's now parked a few metres in front of me. I should make some sort of attempt to cover myself. Feign a modicum of modesty, because Mama will kill me if word gets around that I was skinny dipping down at The Wharf, strutting my naked, shameless stuff in broad daylight when the cops showed up.

But what would Stacey Fortune do? She'd take a deep breath, smile wide, and revel in the power of her brazen big-city cougar glory. Give the poor small-town clown a story to remember. This *is* a moment to strut naked and shameless, while I still can. I throw my shoulders back, stick my B-cup boobs out, and give my saltwater-soaked hair a casual flip as I keep moving. Calm, cool, collected.

The officer gets out of his car and saunters toward me. I feel a flicker of pride when I see my reflection in the mirror of his sunglasses as he approaches the water's edge. Until a slow smile of recognition creeps across his mug, and he takes off the sunglasses, revealing just how hard he's leering at my tits.

"Crow Fortune?" Despite the intonation, it is not a question. He knows it's me. Constable Duke the Puke Clarke grins with a phoney incredulousness. "Nice to see ya. Again." His voice lingers too long on the word *again,* just as his eyes linger too long on my body. None too subtle reminders that he has seen this all before. Me. Naked.

I cross my arms over my chest, and let out a shiver. As if a chill from the summer breeze is the reason I'm suddenly trying to cover up. "Hey, grab my clothes off the wharf and toss them down, would ya?"

"Nah, don't think so."

Gone are the proud *Fuck It* attitude and Stacey Fortune sexy cougar swagger I had donned only moments ago. Utterly swept away by the surging memory of how this slut-shaming, reputation-wrecking arsehole helped drive me out of this place over twenty years ago. How Crow Fortune's story went from bad to worse at the tail end of high school, all because of one naked night with Duke the Puke.

A dangerous amount of Jack Daniel's at the post-prom bash at Loch Bhreagh River bridge seemed like a reasonable way to ease the despair of having been dumped by Weasel Tobin a week before prom. Who among us would not—under such circumstances—have felt flattered when the much-adored high school star athlete extended an invitation to "listen to some music" in his car?

I woke up in Duke's car the morning after the prom with a surprisingly clear recollection of what had happened during the night. We smoked cigarettes and listened to shitty gangsta rap. He complained about his girlfriend Angie, and how she was so jealous. He told me I had the cutest, perkiest little tits he'd ever seen, and wanted to get a closer look. Piece by piece, compliment by compliment, my clothes came off. I ignored the fact that I found him kind of revolting. That his skin was too greasy, his eyes too close together, his hands too rough and too pushy. I ignored the fact that I had heard he screwed Char and Allie and a couple of the metal-head skid girls, and that Angie once ripped a chunk of hair out of another chick's scalp in a fight. I ignored the fact that we didn't have a condom and that the aim of his thrusts was one orifice off more often than not. He ignored me when I said ow, stop, and please.

After a few too many wayward pokes in the back exit that were starting to feel intentional, I told him to get the fuck off me, right the fuck now. He was livid, grumbling about blue balls and cock teases as he pulled up his pants, got out of the car, and stormed away. I put my clothes back on. The new-fangled "lock-up" jeans that had been such a nuisance when I needed to pee in the woods felt like a godsend all of a sudden. I locked the car doors, locked my pants, wrapped myself up in my hoodie, and slept until Duke came knocking on the window at sunrise, sneering, "Get your slutty ass outta my car, Crow."

Had that been the end of it, it might have been okay. But it wasn't.

A week later, on the night of the Safe Grad fundraising dance at the rink, where—surprise—everybody got hammered, Allie and I were outside having a smoke when Char came ripping around the corner of the rink, brandishing a crinkled sheet of loose-leaf. A copy of the hockey team's infamous "Dirty Dozen" scorecard. Ratings and comments beside every girl's name. The challenge laid out before the Loch Bhreagh Marauders was to have sex with and rate a different girl every month. To nail the Dirty Dozen. They all kicked in some money, and anybody who completed the challenge would get a cut. The only guy who pulled it off was Duke. The slimy little prick was five hundred bucks richer, and this was his list.

"I'm a two! He called me a freak and gave me a fucking two!" Char howled. "I'm gonna rip his floppy excuse for a penis off and stuff it up his right nostril with the toe of my fucking boot. That copsucker."

Char had a way with words. And threats. She was also half

deaf in one ear, so she often heard—and repeated—things wrong. The first time she said "copsucker" in junior high, she was met with a chorus of jibes. She stubbornly argued that it was more offensive to suggest that someone sucked cops than cocks. Copsucker became our preferred insult.

Allie grabbed the piece of paper from Char's rage-rattled hand and carefully read down the list to see her name. Rated a four. Duke's comment? Weird nipples and old lady moaning.

I hovered over her shoulder, scanning for my name, praying I wasn't one of the Dirty Dozen, knowing full well that I was.

"Little Miss Perfect Ten," Char snorted at me. "Never would have pegged you as wanting it up the ass though, Crow."

As we started to make our way behind the rink to quell our collective rage and shame with a toke and a swill of cheap booze, Duke came outside. Char marched right for him, swearing and seething. He laughed as she launched into her tell-off. He reached into his pocket, pulled out a twenty dollar bill, and rammed it down the front of her shirt. Her cut for helping him win the bet, he said. He turned to walk away, but paused, turning back to face the three of us.

"Oh, and the numbers?" he smirked. "Not your skills, ladies. That's the Grudge Fuck Scale. You should be proud, Char. We like your snatch. Allie, you're in the middle. Bit of a pain in the ass, but not bad. Crow, though? You're the kinda stuck up little skank we all just wanted to slam the hell out of. Bang that bitchy grin right off your face. But you're all sluts."

"Get him!" I hissed in Char's pointy little attack dog ear. She leapt at him, swinging. He blocked the punch and knocked her to the ground. He spat on her, called her a ditch pig, and started back toward the rink doors. Char scrambled to her feet and darted after him. She jumped on his back and clawed the bejesus out of his face with her long scarlet talons. Just when everyone started flooding out of the rink after the last song, Duke went ghost-white at the sight of his own blood and started puking all over his preppy penny loafers.

As Allie and I dragged Char away from the scene, I yelled loud enough for everyone to hear, "Right on, Duke the Puke!" By Monday, his scratches had scabbed over, but the name Duke the Puke had stuck like shit to a woollen rag. In my fondest revenge fantasies, people still call him that. To his face. When he's in uniform. That would be a deeply satisfying piece of my legacy, at least.

I hustle up on to the wharf and into my clothes as quick as my soaked, exhausted, uncooperative body will allow, wincing as I pull my pants over the burning streaks of red where the jellyfish stinger got me. Duke stands there in silence. Grinning. Gawking. Finally, he speaks.

"Shirl said she saw you come down here twice today, but you know Shirl. Can't believe two words that come out of her mouth. Had to see for myself." He puffs out his chest and lets out a disgusting porn groan-sigh-*mmmm* sound. "Lookin' good, girl."

Every fibre of my being screams at me to walk over and smack the bastard. Instead, I pull out the best verbal smack I have at my disposal, the make-it-awkward card.

"I've got brain tumours. I'm home to die." I add a hiss of rage to the unvarnished explanation.

"Yeah, Shirl said that, too." His lumpy potato chin dips

into an exaggerated frown. "Too bad. Always thought you had a halfways decent shot at a normal life. For a Fortune."

"Nope. Guess not."

"I shoulda taken the boys up on that bet that you'd be back someday," he says, clearly amused as he slides his sunglasses back on, hooks his thumbs into his belt loops and leans back so that his crotch juts out in a pervy power stance. "Even after the... *you know.*"

Of course. How could I forget? He got me back for the nickname. And I had to get the hell out of this place after that.

Turned out that Duke was a disease bag of the sexually transmitted variety. I started pissing fire not long after prom night, and the test confirmed I had chlamydia. A course of antibiotics and everything would be fine, Dr. Gill said. But that's only because he didn't know what Duke the Puke was about to pull.

The highlight of the Loch Bhreagh graduation ceremony was always the yearbook committee's slideshow. The crowd of graduates, families, and local somebodies roared at the picture of Duke and his hockey buddies wearing dresses and wigs and gargantuan balloon boobs on Halloween. They groaned at Char posing with a half-dissected fetal pig in biology. They applauded Becky Chickenshit organizing university brochures in the guidance office. But the grand finale was a close-up of a white piece of paper with sharp black type on Dr. Gill's letterhead. My name, and the words *test positive for chlamydia,* circled in bright yellow. After what felt like forever, it faded to a picture of me in English class, giving a double thumbs up with my eyes crossed and popped, my mouth twisted into a lopsided grin, and my head cocked to the side. With the caption "Let's all 'CLAP' for Crow Fortune!" Nobody clapped. And nobody stood up to correct the glaring error, the thing I found myself screaming inside, as if it were the most salient detail: *gonorrhea is the clap, not chlamydia, you idiots!*

Everyone sat in stunned silence, then the murmurs began. The principal took the mic, blathered out a perplexed apology to my forty-nine fellow graduates, their families, their friends, all our teachers, the local MLA, three members of town council, and our special guest speaker, a writer for the newspaper. But the damage was done. I was done. I fiddled nervously with the tassel on my grad cap. My hands went cold and clammy. My face reacted with a flush of humiliated heat, and my eyes began to water, the tears unable to extinguish my burning cheeks. I looked around, suddenly grateful that I didn't have any family in the crowd that night. Everyone was staring at me. But the only face I could see through the blur of tears was Duke's, grinning from ear to ear.

I rose slowly and calmly, turned slowly and calmly, and walked slowly and calmly to the side of the stage, where I removed my burgundy graduation gown, folded it neatly and set it down. Then I turned to the crowd, smiled, bowed, threw my grad cap in the air with a thrust of mock triumph, and let out a long, loud, "Caaaaaaaaw." Slowly and calmly, I smiled and waved at the crowd as some arsehole in the back hooted and hollered and clapped, and then I walked out the gym doors and straight to the car I'd borrowed from Peggy. I got in. I lit a cigarette. I pushed my Meat Loaf tape into the deck, and I cranked up "Bat Out of Hell." I rewound and played it over and over again on the drive home, singing along at the top of my lungs, beyond certain that I had to get the fuck out of this place ASAP. And I thanked God, or Kurt Cobain, or whatever other sky-dwelling sadist might be up there, for the one tiny bit of grace afforded to me that night: that Mama was not there to see it. She was off at some *thing*. An emergency. Somebody needed her more than I did, apparently. Whatever. It ended up being for the best. And the whole humiliating graduation shitshow was the kick in the arse I needed to leave and never come back.

Except, here I am. Back. Face-to-smirking-face with the source of my long-buried shame and humiliation. *Quick, what would Stacey Fortune do?* Cry, probably. Stacey Fortune is out of her element here.

"Oh well, at least you get to have a little Three Amigos reunion before...whatever." Duke's voice yanks me back from memories of trauma past and into the freshly traumatic present.

"What?"

"Didn't you hear? Allie's old doll died. And Char's back, too."

"Is she now?" There will be no reunion with Char and Allie. Those two haven't been amigos for a long, long time. I can't even mention one's name to the other without triggering a tirade.

"Still crazier than a shithouse rat, Char is." Duke chuckles. "Anyway, tell your loser pal Gimp no smoking drugs in public, okay? I got better things to do than chase potheads in the boonies. And maybe think twice before nude beachin' it up in the middle of the day. Or at least give the ol' bush a Brazilian first. I won't fine you because your tits aren't too saggy. But this is a warning."

I stare blankly at him. *Copsucker.*

"Want a ride home? I'll let you have shotgun." A greasy delight oozes across his face.

"No. Thank. You." I say in a sharp, cold, stabbing tone. By now, I am seeing red. Literally. My wayward brain conjures up a colourful haze that seems to swallow Duke whole. Swaths of deep scarlet mingle with a brownish pinkish purplish mist. Puce. That colour is puce.

"All right. See ya around. If you're lucky." He struts back to his car, taking his red and puce cloud with him.

Lucky? Me? If it weren't for bad luck, I wouldn't have any.

3 THE WEIGHT OF THE EARTH

Mama's house looks like a pack rat hurricane bomb went off in it, and contrary to what she's claimed from the day I was born, the mess of this place is not my fault. There's twenty-one years of hoarding in here that is one hundred percent Effie Fortune, and she's got her reasons for it all. There's a cardboard box full of empty milk jugs in the corner of the kitchen where my ghetto blaster used to be. Mama's saving those jugs for the kids down at the elementary school for seed planting in the spring. The big bag of dryer lint and egg cartons that I have to hoist off the top of the deep freeze every time I go looking for frozen casseroles and ice chips is for Peggy's handy little fire starters. A godsend when the kindling is damp, Mama insists. And the piles of newspaper in every corner of the cramped living room? Well, there are good stories in them. History.

Then there's my bedroom. Stuffed animals jammed in the corner of the lumpy old bed, right where I left them. Axl Rose's, Kurt Cobain's, and Jim Morrison's sun-bleached faces still cling to the walls with rusty old tacks. My precious closet is now a time capsule that I can crawl inside whenever I need to wrap myself in a simpler reality. Mama could have turned my room into a den. Or a still. A storage space for the milk jugs, dryer lint, egg cartons, and newspapers. Instead, she left it all exactly as it was. No doubt she's got her reasons.

I've spent the last three days rummaging through the contents of the trailer while Mama's at work, ignoring the phone when it rings, much to the consternation of the pack of local nosy-holes who've taken it upon themselves to check up on me. The giddy lightness I felt when I pawned, sold, and chucked pretty much every piece of my Toronto life has been replaced by a heaviness. As my hands glide across the pages of the dust-caked photo albums I found in a milk crate, or tug on the seams of old pants to see if they hold, or even poke around in the clutter and mess that isn't mine, I feel more grounded in the gravitas. Surely to God the meaning of my life is buried in here, somewhere. But the weight of it all is a little more suffocating than I expected. Especially today. I have to go to a funeral.

"Ma, you could have cleaned out my room you know." As I walk into the kitchen where Mama's dribbling a dose of gin into her afternoon tea, I try to make those words sound like a simple statement. A permission, long overdue. She could have stuffed everything in garbage bags long ago, and I'd have had no right to piss and moan.

"Too goddamn busy cleaning up after people at the Gale to muck around in that pit of yours." Judging by Mama's response, I've failed to scrub that comfortably chronic teenage petulance from my tone.

Her hands are planted on her hips, and her steely grey eyes drill a hole through me. Her bottom jaw juts out, teeth bared in a cross underbite, just like Peg's mean German shepherd, Deeohgee, used to have. This is the face and posture my mother puts on if you happen to say the wrong thing when she's already in a bit of a mood. It's hard to tell what precipitated this particular one. It might be that she's getting too old and arthritic to be crouching over toilets and slinging piles of fluffy bath towels, day in and day out. It might also be that I'm making her come to Reenie Walker's funeral with me, and Peggy just called to announce that she's tagging along, too. Then again, it might be the photo album I left on the table this morning that turned her so sour so fast. It's still open to the one and only page that makes her spit sparks and slam the damn thing shut every time. The page I always jokingly referred to as the Hall of Shame, though Mama never laughed.

There are only two old photos on that page. One is of the Spenser family at a quaint little cottage on the Mira River, my father and his older sister—Saint Sarah as Mama always called her—flanking their parents, John Alexander and Rosalind. Their comfortable life as the Island's entrepreneurial upper crust is neatly rendered in tight smiles, tamed hair, and the saturated colour and gloss of a 1960s Polaroid. The other photo is a tattered black-and-white of Bernie and Lucy Fortune on their wedding day in 1951. My nanny is dressed in white and glowing like she doesn't know that she's already three months pregnant, clueless that that child will be the first of eleven, each doomed to the their own brand of pain and chaos. She's smiling like she couldn't imagine the man standing beside her ever grabbing her hair and driving her face into a plate full of dinner because it was too salty. Meanwhile, Black Bernie is rumpled and scowling, his hands and cheeks marred by the indelible shadows of grease and grime from the coal pit. Anyone can see that those narrowed eyes hold flashes of the smacks and squalor to come, and his dark hair storms from the top of his head in a wild mess of defiance. Everything about him is grim and unsettling, especially next to his bride's delicate beauty.

I park myself at the table and stare down at the photos on that page, looking for a trace of myself in the faces of family, when it dawns on me. Mama's reason. Why she never got rid of my stuff, and why she's hoarding dryer lint and newspaper and milk jugs. It's the same reason she keeps pictures of people who evoke in her either scorching rage or frigid indifference. Mama doesn't let go of anything. Not even things that cause her some measure of grief.

"Go get dressed if we're going to that funeral," she says, shuffling to the table and thumping the photo album shut. "And for Christ's sake, do something about that ungodly mop of yours."

[...]

Allie insisted that I didn't need to be at her mother's funeral, but I know I do. Not for her, but for myself. I need to see grieving in action, and put some thought into how my grand farewell will go down. I haven't been to a funeral since I left here. The healthy, wealthy Viva Rica chuggers and pushers I hung out with in Toronto don't just up and die the way people do here. Or as people in my family, particularly, tend to do. The last funeral I went to was for my cousin Mitch, who hung himself my last year of high school. That one ended with Mama breaking up a drunken family brawl, after my aunt Audrey's arsehole husband, Jeff, got loaded and told Mitch's father, Gordie, that they should have buried Mitch in a nice dress because everybody in Town knew Mitch was "a cross-dressing poufter."

Arsehole choice of words and timing aside, Jeff had a point. Everybody knew that Mitch wore dresses and makeup, and wanted to be a woman. That's why they all called him Mitch the Bitch. I even gave him eyeliner lessons and loaned him slutty clothes. But there were doctors in Montreal who felt he was too "mentally unstable" to have the hormones and the surgery, so Mitch gussied himself up one night, sashayed out into the woods on the Old Trunk Road, and hung himself from a sturdy oak tree. Peggy called Mama when she heard about it on the scanner. Heard a cop snicker about the "tranny in the tree" as they cut my cousin's body down. Peggy knew all the gory details, long before Uncle Gordie. She didn't spare us any of them.

"Phew! Smells like a French whorehouse in here." Peggy wheezes as she squashes herself into the back seat of Mama's car. "Cheap perfume. Always reminds me of Gordie's Mitch."

In fact, I am wearing the same black dress to Reenie's funeral that I wore to Mitch's. I found it in my closet, nestled beneath a near empty bottle of CK Eternity, *which I'll have you know, Peggy Fortune, was not by any means cheap perfume in its day.*

"Sure, everyone thought Mitch offed himself because of the cross-dressing transsexual thing, but I don't buy that," Peggy goes on. "Betcha he was hearing the voices, like Janice did. Woman voices. Telling them to do foolish things."

"Nothing we can do about that now, is there," Mama says curtly, eyes fixed to the road as she navigates the sharp bend onto the bridge and toward the foot of Ceilidh Mountain.

I turn around to remind Peggy how rude it is to speak ill of the dead, to remind her that I will haunt the fuck out of her if she talks about me like that when I'm gone. Then I notice the gaudy piece of jewellery pinned to her best funeral blouse. A glittering peacock brooch. From the Bargain Store. The one I tried to pocket when I was five and a half. The one I eventually saved up enough money to buy. It was supposed to be a present for my nanny, who loved shiny things even more than I did but never seemed to have anything beautiful of her own.

Nanny got sick and went into the hospital before I got a chance to give it to her. I was livid that nobody would take me in to see her. I knew from the hushed voices and red eyes of everyone around me that she was dying. Still, I wrapped the brooch up in a brown paper lunch bag and sent it to the hospital with Mama. Mama went on about how she adored it, how it made her feel better, brightened her right up. Nanny died two days later. They wouldn't let me go to her funeral, so I spent hours imagining it: Nanny looked happy and peaceful with the peacock brooch pinned over her heart for eternity. But now there it is, clinging to the centre of Peggy's gelatinous bosom. And it's pinned on crooked.

"Oh! 'Member this thing? Fortune family heirloom, what." Peggy laughs, chest heaving, fingering the brooch when she notices me staring. "Surprised none of them cheap little rhinestones fell off, even after all these years. Look, the gold paint ain't even peeling."

"How'd you get that?"

"Didn't try to steal it, like a certain someone who shall remain nameless. But I'll look at that party and whistle." Her painted sausage lips scrunch into an *O*, and she lets out a long trill as she pitches as far toward me as her seat belt will allow.

"Don't be a quiff all your life, Peggy. Take a day off," I say in my most pleasantly passive-aggressive tone, with the tightest of smiles.

"Listen, I'll leave you both here on the side of the road if there's any more snark." Mama's foot hits the gas pedal harder.

"For your information," Peggy says, "after Ma died, a nurse found a paper bag under her pillow and was about to toss it in the trash, but I stopped her. Thought you'd get a kick out of seeing it. You want it back?"

"No." I try to ignore the green-grey zigzags that are suddenly reducing my field of vision to pinholes.

"Good," Peggy snorts, "because it's the only thing holding my blouse shut."

[···]

There are two things I now know for certain I do not want at my funeral: family brawls and flowers that smell like cat piss. To be fair, the reeking chrysanthemums were not Allie's fault, even though she blames herself. Reenie's funeral plan was very specific in that there should be as many potted flowers as possible crammed into the church, and that they should come from Bridie at Nicholson's Greenhouse. What Reenie could not have anticipated was that by the time she died, her dear friend Bridie Nicholson would be in the throes of dementia and housing a dozen or so rescued cats in her greenhouse along with the plants. And that Reenie's sons would be too stunned to notice that the chrysanthemums smelled like cat piss when they picked them up and proceeded to pack them into the church. Thank God the minister lit up some holy incense.

"I thought only Catholics did the incense. What was Reenie, a Quaker?" Peggy whispers. "Them Uniteds will bury anyone, I guess."

Mama shushes her as Allie steps up beside her mother's casket, a guitar slung over her shoulder. Allie clears her throat, passes a thumb over the strings, and starts to play her mother's favourite Beatles song. The words of "In My Life" flow from Allie's depths, and ascend to the arched ceiling, filling the space, drawing tears from every eye. Except Allie's. Allie's voice and composure don't crack, even for a second. She's been practising this song, these words, these dry eyes for years. The rest of us are sniffling and sobbing. Allie just smiles in sympathy. With her soft face and nerves of steel, she can do things that other people can't. She can hold dying hands and sing sad songs without breaking. Maybe she'll even sing at my funeral.

"Oh Crow, it's so nice to see you." A dozen people pat me on the arm and offer some iteration of this phrase as the funeral crowd disperses.

I just nod and say, "Nice to see you too," to anyone who speaks to me. I have no clue who any of these people are, and my eyes have gone so wonky that I can't see much of anything anyway. What people don't do is let on that they know why I'm home, not in words at least. But it's written all over their faces, in their solemn tone, in the sympathy-laden arm pats that are heavy enough to make me cringe.

We shuffle through the receiving line, and Peggy stops to talk to everyone. Funny how the woman who can't work and has been on disability for twenty years because of her various "environmental sensitivities" has no trouble holding us all hostage in a crowded, confined space that stinks of cat piss, patchouli, and musty Bibles just so that she can glean some more gossip from this side of Ceilidh Mountain. Loch Bhreagh — and the surrounding communities snuggled in the misty green highlands, with their quaint rural dialects, their fiddlers and dancers, and their cursing in Gaelic — is Peggy's ex-husband Skroink's territory. Peggy wants to make sure she's seen and heard around here so it gets back to him. She lumbers around, shaking hands and chit-chatting like this is a grand social occasion.

"Good to see you, Marilyn. How did Ron's mother's surgery go?"

"Now, Donnie R., don't you look like a million bucks! What's this I hear about a new girlfriend you met square dancing?"

Oh, hello random Old Scratch! Would you mind telling me what colour shit you had this morning so I'll have something to post on the Facebook when I get home?

"Can we hurry up?" I say. "I'm not feeling good."

"It's a funeral. Nobody here feels good. A sin they're not doing a proper reception after. People need conversation here. To lighten things up." Peggy's jiggly elbow jabs me in the ribs.

I turn to Mama in the hopes that she'll put Peggy in her place and help me hustle things along. But she just stands there, ignoring us both, her hands clasped and resting over her belly, and her eyes closed. If I didn't know better, I'd think she was praying. I link my arm in hers as the receiving line begins to move again, and drop my head onto her shoulder when we come to another standstill. Mama reaches up, and I feel the heat of her freed hand as she tucks my hair behind my ear and strokes the side of my temple.

She pulls me closer and whispers, "So help me God, if you throw up in here, you're getting a boot in the arse."

When we finally reach the Walker family, I give Allie's brothers some quick hugs and condolences, then make a beeline for Allie before she's swallowed by another wave of semi-strangers.

"Oh honey, this must be so tough." There's not a hint of tears in her eyes or sobs in her body. I hug her tight.

"Could be worse." Allie's voice is distant and dreamy, the way it was during exams in university, before she had to drop out to care for her mother full time.

"You ate enough tranquilizers to choke a horse, didn't you?"

She finally hugs me back with noodle arms. "You bet your ass I did."

This is another good reason to have Allie by my side when I begin my painful descent into feebleness and whatever other oblivions await. She possesses a wealth of knowledge about the precise combos and quantities of prescription medications needed to render oneself comfortably numb yet meticulously functional. Or not.

"You have to come to the burial with me," she says. "You can stop me from shoving Dad and my brothers into the hole with Mum."

"Whatever you need, babe."

"K, c'mon. Before my tranqs wear off," she says through the corner of her mourner's smile as she slips past me to receive a few final sympathies from more strangers. I go tell Mama and Peg that I'm going to the graveyard for Reenie's burial instead of home with them.

"Feeling better, all of a sudden?" Peggy's voice is too loud and too light, and despite the fact that my nausea has passed, my vision is still as squirrelly as hell. Peggy's oversized head swims in a sea of yellow-green circles.

"Yeah, I'm fine." I feign clumsiness, and bump Peggy's tits right where the peacock brooch is pinned, as I move to hug my mother, before I go help my best friend bury hers.

[···]

Even at the graveyard, Allie remains perfectly stoic, while I'm doing my damnedest to be a good, supportive friend and not look like I'm ready to crawl out of my own skin. I squeeze Allie's hand and close my eyes while Reenie's casket is lowered into the ground. As the minister prattles on about her special place in Heaven, and God coming down to wipe the tears and heal the hearts of her children on Earth, a couple of scruffy guys come along and start pushing dirt over top the flower-strewn coffin. I forgot how much graveyards give me the heebie-jeebies.

It is not because of the stones and the bones and the myriad ghost stories I read as a kid. Not even because of my own circumstances, although I'd like to think I can do better than being boxed up and dropped into a hole in the ground. Graveyards remind me of my mother's youngest sister, Janice. In my earliest memories, she was my gorgeous, glamorous, teenaged aunt who'd come to babysit. She'd bring me Popeye cigarettes and root beer, doll me up with glittery eyeshadow and red lipstick, and let me prance around in her high heels. Everybody in Town called her Crash, because the mere sight of her walking down the Halfway Road was known to distract male drivers and cause accidents. But on a sweltering summer day when I was eleven and a half, Crash Fortune herself crashed. Or snapped. I was with her when it happened.

Janice showed up on our doorstep just after sunrise, insisting that she needed me to come on an adventure with her. I assumed that she had a long day of beach bumming and junk food scarfing planned, but instead she took me to graveyards. One after another, after another, searching for something. Someone. She wouldn't—or couldn't—say who.

"I'll know it when I hear her," she'd moan, as she writhed around on top of people's grave plots, grinding her ear into the ground so hard that her strawberry blonde hair got caked with grass and dirt. "I'll know it when I hear her."

By sundown, Janice had heard nothing but me complaining that I was starving, exhausted, and more than a little freaked out. She finally took me home, but when we got there, she leapt out of the car and ran into the woods. I told Mama what happened. We found Janice a short time later, just past the spot where I'd begun construction on what would become the world's most epic stolen road sign tree fort. She was on the ground again, curled in the fetal position, eyes red and teary.

When she saw us, her voice erupted in a manic speed and pitch, "I heard her! Among the coal black heart's tendrils! Crow, she sang to me!" Mama told me to go back to the trailer and call Peggy.

The next time I saw Janice, she was locked up in the Butterscotch Palace, which is what everybody called the old psychiatric hospital. She remained there for the better part of her life. And I say that not meaning "most of her life," but quite literally "the better part." There, she had three meals a day, a roof over her head, and couldn't get arrested for running down Main Street naked as a jaybird, and then trying to burn down the bridge with Molotov cocktails. She was kept in a comfy chemical straightjacket, a shell of her former wild child self. But at least she was safe.

When the Butterscotch Palace closed in the mid-nineties, Janice moved in with Peggy for a time, then abruptly dropped off the face of the Earth. No one knew where she was or what had happened, and after a while, no one even mentioned her name. Until I got the phone call in Toronto, five years ago. It was the police. They'd identified the body of an OD'ed hooker in my Toronto neighbourhood as one "Janice Fortune." On her paperwork at the shelter she frequented, she'd listed me as next of kin. Aunt Janice was three blocks away from me when she died. I'd probably walked past her in the street a dozen times on my way to the subway station.

Mama came up to Toronto, and the two of us sneakily spread Janice's ashes around the edge of a park in the ritziest part of the city. To this day, I like to think that the spirit of Janice "Crash" Fortune is directly responsible for all the fender benders that happen around there. Especially the one Dave got into with his precious Porsche a few days after we broke up. That would almost make it all feel okay.

As the last few shovelfuls of soil are laid over Reenie's casket, I get another round of queasy. I try to ease it by staring up at the clouds, as they grow ever more pendulous, grey, and start to spit. Or weep.

"Happy is the corpse that the rain falls on," Allie sighs, as water droplets dapple the freshly turned earth. She casually drapes an arm around my shoulders. "Let's go sit in the car. My mascara isn't waterproof."

Allie's father yells after us as the rain picks up and we dart toward the car, "Allie honey, you'll be home for supper, right?"

"Yes, Dad," she sings back. Then mutters to me, "They forget how to turn on the damn oven. I don't even know if it still works. The four of them lived off microwaved baloney and cold beans right out of the can after Mum moved to Halifax."

"So you're staying, I take it."

"Nowhere else to go."

"Good," I say, before registering the sting of my own selfish honesty. "I mean, not good, but, you know what I mean."

Allie nods and produces a tiny joint from the depths of the centre console, lighting it as she slides into a tired slouch in the driver's seat. She's handling all this better than most folks would expect. But I'm not one bit surprised.

"Picked up some of Gimp's Grade A medicinal," she squeaks, passing it to me. "Puts the 'fun' in funeral."

"Funerals. I need to have one of those."

"So, they're sure the tumours are…" Allie's voice trails off.

"Inoperable. Even if they're not malignant, I'm fucked. Just a matter of how fast," I say. "Plus, you know my family. No secret how this kind of thing pans out for us."

"Right." She slumps a little farther down. Allie knows better than to argue with my family's tragedy-riddled history.

She will not try to talk me out of my morbidity. Not like the silver-lining-obsessed Pollyannas I knew in Toronto. The ones who insisted that their "positivity," their faith in the benevolence of an all-powerful Universe, and the manifesting magic of blueberry juice would buoy them along through life. Finding myself alone, seizing, and helpless on a piss-stained subway platform was one thing. But the thought of having a steady stream of dewy-faced, #blessed socialites chirp at me, *Well, everything happens for a reeeeason. The Universe is guiding you to a deeper level of heeeeealing!* was more than I could bear.

"So what are you thinking?" Allie asks.

"Dunno, but something different. Maybe avant-garde. Or ancient. Or both."

"Irish wakes are kinda cool. Mum wanted one, but they're not legal."

"Oh man, if the police came and busted my wake?" I roar. "That'd be wicked. Dammit, I want to be there to see it."

Maybe I will be. Maybe my Irish wake can start while I'm still alive. And maybe my death and everything after doesn't need to be tinged with shock and sorrow and suffering. A little planning can go a long way.

In a traditional Irish wake, the women of the community are supposed to come prepare the corpse. But with a living wake, I'll bathe and dress myself, thanks. I'll do my own makeup too, because if Mama gets near me with a makeup bag, I will look like a corpse. The person being waked is supposed to wear white. White is not my colour though, so I'll wear black. A brand new, smokin' hot little black dress and red hellion high heels.

Irish wakes are pot luck. But no egg, tuna, or lobster salad sandwiches will be allowed at mine. And no mystery squares or funeral hams. My buffet table will groan with the weight of all my favourites, from the days when I didn't give a shit about factory-farmed meats and non-GMO organic kale and MSG hangovers and the mid-life spread: suicide spicy chicken wings, donair pizza, poutine, bacon-and-cheese-stuffed bacon-wrapped cheese balls. Deep fried. Dipped in butter. Foods that Stacey-Fortune-in-Toronto avoided because she was scared they'd kill her or make her chubby. But Dying-Crow-Fortune-in-Cape-Breton doesn't give a fuck.

My throng of family, friends, and fans can expect an eclectic mix of my favourite music. Nothing sappy. It's my party, and you won't cry if I don't want you to. Besides, it's bad luck to start the keening too early. I'll save the real tear-jerker tunes until the end, just before my wake transitions into the big sleep.

Once everyone is fed, libations in hand, the storytelling can begin. I want my life to flash before *other* people's eyes, not just my own, so I'll put my Viva Rica promotional video-production skills to good use by making a mini-documentary about my time on this Earth. A tribute. A testament to my life in all its knee-slapping, tongue-wagging, heartbreaking glory. I'll record Mama telling the story of her eight-month-old baby pooping all over Peggy's brand new sundress at the family barbecue. And how a mischievous ten-year-old Crow disguised sliced garlic as slivered almonds and slipped them into Peggy's trail mix. Allie and Char will laugh their way through the tale of the night they pinned condoms—and a note with my address on it—to my underwear before we went out to the bars. And how both those things came in pretty damn handy that night. Maybe Willy Gimp can finally pub-licly reveal our years of clandestine teenage sexcapades. The old people will squirm. The young people will roar. And it will end with everybody talking about why they love me, and what they'll miss most. I need to hear that while I still can.

Then, a party will rage until every soul either leaves or passes out, and I'm content with my send-off. After all that, I'll probably be tired. And hurting. And ready to go. So maybe I'll go back to Mama's trailer alone, and I'll take a little something for my pain. Maybe a little too much something. I'll make sure the living-room windows are open, so my spirit—whatever's left of it—can escape. From the comfort of the scruffy old couch, I'll watch the sun rise. Then I'll just close my eyes. The end.

My eyes were, in fact, closed as I described this daydream, the vision of my own end, to Allie. Now, I glance over at her. Her eyes are ringed in smudged mascara. She's sitting up straighter, her body frozen, her hands tightly gripping the steering wheel. My sick, ornery eyes promptly rebel against the new demands of light and shape, and add their own layer of blackness and blur to the details of her face and the space around her. I blink fast, trying to wipe away the sooty smudges in my vision, suddenly fumbling for something to say. But Allie beats me to it.

"Bitch, I told you this mascara wasn't waterproof."

I laugh, expecting Allie to do the same but she doesn't. She starts the car, cranks up the heat to clear the fogged windshield, and flips the wipers to hyper-speed, even though it's not raining all that hard. Before I can apologize, Allie jacks up the stereo and begins to wail along to some brooding Emo-pop boy band I've never heard before. She doesn't stop singing the whole drive. When she drops me off back at Mama's, I lean in to give her a hug and am surprised at how swift and stilted her end of the embrace feels with the tranqs and the pot worn off, and her patience for misery and company worn out, too.

"Sorry for messing your makeup," I say. "Call me if you need anything, okay?"

"It's fine," she says. "I'm fine. Go hug your mother."

But Mama's not home. I expect to find hot tea on the stove, a pan of her famous broc-o-glop casserole in the oven, and a note to say that she's gone to help Murdena Squires get a bird out of her chimney, or Shirl Short get her head out of her own arse. Instead, Peggy and my uncle Mossy are planted at the kitchen table.

Mossy was born smack dab in the middle of Lucy Fortune's brood. This was the pregnancy that Black Bernie nearly beat out of her because she was going through the coal too fast for his liking that winter. Mossy was born half deaf, blind in one eye, and roundly diagnosed by the nuns in the Catholic school and everyone in Town as "retarded." But to hear Mama tell it, Mossy's the closest thing the Fortune family has to a genius, a borderline criminal mastermind. With a tilt of his head and a pleasant, vacant face, Mossy Fortune could get away with pretty much anything. That face is why Mama and Peggy bore the brunt of an alder switch on their arses when Nanny didn't believe them that Mossy was the one who tied their starchy, uncomfortable second-hand Sunday school dresses to a tree and lit a grass fire around the trunk. And why the cops would arrest Snooker Burns and Billy Sockets but just drive Mossy home when the three of them got caught stealing.

Unlike the rest of the Fortunes, Mossy doesn't talk and he doesn't drink, although he used to do both. There's a sad story there, about a slow, quiet girl named Ruby Tooth, who Mossy supposedly knocked up. Mossy asked Ruby's father for her hand in marriage, but the old man said no. Called him a no-good drunken devil-spawned retard, and spit in his face. So Mossy hit the old man with a two-by-four, said he loved Ruby and would marry her anyway. But Ruby Tooth went missing. They found her body on the rocks off Greener's Cliff a few days later. Her father swore up and down it was a suicide. That she was driven to it by that no-good drunken devil-spawned retard Mossy Fortune. That was thirty years ago. Mossy hasn't said much, nor touched a drop of liquor, ever since.

"Where's Mama, and what are you two doing here?"

Peggy doesn't look up, just keeps languidly flipping through the photo album I left on the table. Mossy's eyes widen with a weird, youthful bemusement as a sympathetic frown deepens the lines in his faintly misshapen face.

"Effie's just down the road giving old Flossie Baker a hand, what with Flossie's hip being so bad. We found this rig here hitchhiking on the highway," Peggy says, with a quick nod toward Mossy. "So don't get your panties in a knot. We're not staying long."

She stops turning photo album pages, and looks to me with her mouth and nose pulled into a po-faced pucker. "What's that smell?"

Considering Allie and I were hotboxing a rental car in a graveyard less than an hour ago, I know that I reek of weed. *But I'm an adult now, goddammit, and I'll walk in this door smelling any bloody way I want, Peggy.*

"New perfume," I say. "It's called Eau d'Coping With Crisis. Hope you like it. It'll be my signature scent for the next while. And all my friends will be wearing it at my funeral."

"Got a hole for yourself good and dug already, do you?" she says, as she goes back to studying the photos in front of her.

"Oh, fuck no," I say, glaring at her with a woozy, button-pushing glee. "Getting buried in the dirt is for plebes. I want something a little flashier."

"Who's gonna pay for that, now?" Peggy pushes back. "Your mother on her hotel maid's pay? Maybe that fella you had in Toronto? Or that drug dealer you used to sleep around with, whassisname, Willy Gimp?"

"None of your business," I grunt, shuffling to the stove to find Mama's tea kettle cold and empty, then to the fridge, where there's nothing but a half-eaten egg sandwich and a jar of somebody's homemade green tomato pickle slime. An audible huff escapes my throat as I thump the fridge door shut.

Mossy is still gawking at me with an air of feeble sadness. Peggy keeps right on staring at Mama's photo album, her thick finger tracing the ridges and edges of a particular page.

"Maybe you should hit up the Spensers to pay for whatever fancy memorial you think you deserve, Crow," Peggy chimes. "God knows those people made a bomb on the backs of the rest of us *plebes.*"

I start down the hall to my room, to get out of this relic of a funeral dress and into something more comfortable. Like solitude. And silence. There's a loud tapping of Peggy's never-worked-a-day-in-her-life manicured nail on the plastic veneer that holds in place the photos before her, meant to draw my attention but I just keep going.

"Funny, I never noticed how much Crow looks like the Spensers, don't she Mossy?" He, of course, doesn't answer.

"Except for that hair. That's the Old Man on the spot, isn't it?" Peggy's voice booms, her fingernail taps harder and louder on the album page. Then her loud, guttural laugh echoes down the hallway. "Black Bernie Fortune and that silver-tongued Spenser fella will never die as long as Crow's alive."

4 IF YOU CAN'T TAKE THE HEAT, GET OUT OF THE KITCHEN PARTY

From the kitchen window, all I can see is the suffocating snarl of Mama's rambling rose bush, a yellowing sea of overgrown grass, and the skeletons of spruce trees that have seen better days. It didn't used to be like this. This land used to feel spacious and green and alive. But just like the inside of the trailer, the outside has morphed into a jumbled mess of things that should have been pruned, pulled, and purged a long time ago. Part of me feels compelled to feng shui the fuck out of this grubby little shack and start planning a landscaping makeover that I'll probably never get to enjoy, but that Mama will appreciate. Instead, I'm going to slash a path through the overgrown grass, find the old bonfire pit, and start burning stuff. Tree branches. Newspapers. Memories. She's all going up in flames tonight.

It takes me three hours, six minor injuries, and four hundred and fifty-eight curse words, but I do it. I find the old bonfire pit and yank away the tired, tangled vegetation that had swallowed the circle of hefty beach rocks. I lug a dead tree from a corner of the backwoods, and set it beside a pile of newspaper lugged from the corners of the living room. I tuck a wad of ancient dryer lint and yellowed grass inside a little stick teepee in the centre of the stone circle. Spray it with twenty-year-old hairspray, just for fun. I gently cradle

Mama's Zippo lighter in the palm of my hand. With the sun just beginning to set and Mama working the night shift, I'll have myself a merry little bonfire here. The first one since the summer I left. No s'mores and weenie roasting, but I've got a 1995 Shiraz that I bought at the snotty Toronto sommelier thing one of my Tinder conquests dragged me to, just days before Tumourpocalypse. I'm sure it will taste deliciously ironic when I slug it straight from the bottle in front of my Cape Breton backwoods junk fire.

I flick the Zippo and stoop, holding the flame to the lint ball until it ignites, then coax it along with a gentle stream of breath until a car comes barrelling up the driveway. A tinted-windowed Mustang blasting some schlock rock song, probably in an attempt to drown out the car's multiple rumbles of age and failure. It's Peggy, driving one of "The Twins," which is what she proudly calls the couple of crappy "classic" cars she took from Skroink in their divorce.

Except it's not Peggy.

The woman emerging from the driver's side is skeletally thin. Or at least, most of her is. Other parts seem to be outlandishly large. Her tiny, deeply bronzed frame is tightly wrapped in a lime-green sarong, which can't contain her wildly gigantic boobs. Big, round, leopard print–framed sunglasses crouch precariously on the tip of her elfin nose. Her twig-thin wrists and neck are weighted with layer upon layer of enormous red, yellow, and blue wooden beads, while on her head, dozens of thick platinum dreadlocks spring from beneath a zebra-print scarf.

Tendrils of blue smoke curl from the outrageously large blunt she sparks as she ambles across the yard toward me. I almost don't notice a spell of the squirrelly vision coming on. At first, I mistake the mirage of lights and colours for shades of sunset in the sky. Mama and I used to play a game at sunset and sunrise, where we'd each have to pick a colour from the ones we saw arching and flaring along the horizon. My eyes always found the patches where the cool blue of the ether met the warm glow of the sun, creating streaks of baby blue and bright pink tinged with wisps of an otherworldly violet. My brain has now plucked from my memory and conjured around this woman the impossibly real shade of sky-blue pink, which moves with her like a peacock's trippy plumage as she prances toward me on stupidly high platform sandals.

"F'eyed known there was a bomb fire, ida brung some bleedin' marchmellows."

It's Char.

Behind the giant glasses, beneath the platinum blonde dreadlocks and oversized bangles, and through a very bizarre and very fake quasi-British accent, it *is* Char. Because nobody else calls them bomb fires. Or marchmellows. The grammar though, that's Mr. Hillier's fault. He taught a whole generation of kids from Down North that it was "bring, brang, and brung."

"Bollocks! Hang on!" Char shrieks in my ear just as her twiggy arms coil around me in a hug. Mashing out the cherry of her mega-joint on the heel of her clunky shoe and stuffing the remainder into a fold of the zebra scarf, she boings back to the car, jettisons the driver's seat forward and wriggles into the back. When she emerges moments later, she's got one tit hanging out the top of her shrink-wrap sarong. Latched on to that tit is a tiny, squirming, naked baby. A tiny, squirming, naked, deep-brown-skinned baby with a giant orange afro.

She sashays back over to the firepit and smoothly drops into a cross-legged seat on the grass without even jostling the now still and peacefully feeding baby boy.

"Char, where'd the...is that your...you had a baby?"

"Got him down the Congo." She shrugs. "Those African tribeswomen, they don't care. They've got more babies than they know what to do with. Better me snatching the little fart than a bloody tiger, or him dying of ammonia."

"The Congo...you just took him? And came home?" I blink, still attempting to process.

Char's oddly coiffed head pivots back on her pencil thin neck and she howls with laughter. The baby doesn't flinch. A tiny trickle of bluish breast milk dribbles from the corner of his soft mouth.

"Jesus, Crow, ya dumb ass! Of course he's mine. How else would I get these giant milk-bag knockers he's slurpin' on? Usually, I tell people I stole him first and then whip out the tit, just to see the looks on their faces, but the little bugger was starving. God, you're some gall-able."

She barely slows down enough to breathe as she speaks. The phoney British accent has dissolved into a nasally Town brogue. Because even though Char grew up Down North, her mother was from The Mines, so she's Cape Breton bilingual. Those accents die hard. Or not at all.

"So, brain tumours, eh? That's the shits."

"Yeah. How'd you know?"

"I overheard."

"Overheard? Overheard where?"

"I dunno. Some old broad in the line at Shoppers. Or Needs. Somewhere, I was buying arse ointment. Word's out that you're home and you've got brain tumours."

"They sell arse ointment at Needs?" I say, staring at her in wonderment at how *that* part ended up sounding like the most salient piece of information.

"Depends on what you use for arse ointment, now don't it?" Char smirks. "So, what have you been up to since you got home?"

"Nothing. Writing. Remembering. Feeling like shit. Waiting."

"So, how bad are we talkin'? With the tumours."

"They can't cut them out without leaving me blind, partially paralyzed, and shitting myself every time I blink, kinda bad. Symptoms don't respond much to treatments, and they think it's a type that grows and changes and can get really bad in a hurry. Need a biopsy to confirm."

"Oh, man."

We instinctively avoid looking at each other while we let that sink in. I twirl another wad of dryer lint into a ball, while Char twirls a section of her baby's hair into a tighter coil.

"So, when are you gonna shave your head?" She is suddenly beaming.

"They only shave a little patch for the biopsy. I can hide it." I crumple up a piece of ancient newspaper and tuck it under a piece of wood to bolster the burgeoning fire. "And I'm not sold on the radiation and chemo thing."

"That's not why you have to do it." Char laughs. "It's one of those things. You always said 'I'm gonna shave my head one of these days.' But now you're staring the ultimate day-stealer right in the face. Shave your fucking head, girl! It says freedom. Fearlessness. Hair is deeply symbaltic, ya know."

Every time I went through a breakup, or had a crazy screw-the-world feminist/activist/anarchist spell, or when my roots got bad, my split ends got crunchy, and my bangs got straggly but I was too broke to get my hair done properly, I'd boldly proclaim, "That's it, I'm shaving my head!" Even just a few months ago, I stood in front of the mirror, ponytail in hand and scissors poised. But I always backed off, because head shaving was for women with nothing to *actually* lose. "One of these days," I'd say, "when I'm older. Wiser. Braver." *Put it on the Fuck It Bucket List.*

"I have cordless clippers in the car," Char says.

"I don't want to know why."

"Right you don't. But if it makes ya feel better, I clean them really, *really* good."

She plucks her nipple from the sleeping babe's mouth and stuffs the boob back into her sarong. With one hand, she unravels the zebra scarf from her head, sending a mess of Javexed dreadlocks splashing down her back, and deftly fashions it into a snug-fitting sling. She tucks the baby inside, and tells me the real story of her four-month-old son.

His name is Daktari Christ MacIsaac. His father was the twenty-year-old Congolese diamond smuggler. When he found out she was pregnant, he smacked her around a bit. But nobody smacks Char MacIsaac around and gets away with it. They found his body in a dumpster in Kinshasa. Of course, the guy was a serious criminal in an extraordinarily high-stakes, cutthroat, throat-cutting underground industry. He had enemies and rivals and friends ready to kill him at the drop of a hat. So, in all probability, Char had nothing to do with the fact that this dude wound up in a pile of napkins, goat scraps, and rotten cassava mush out behind the Sultani Hotel. Without a mark on his body. Poisoned, it seems.

By the time they found him, Char was in Halifax, where

she gave birth to sweet little brown-skinned, orange-haired Daktari Christ MacIsaac before meandering back home to Cape Breton to live with her folks. Wasn't long before they kicked her out, for reasons Char claims not to know, and now she's renting a room in her mother's ex-best friend's basement, and borrowing her mother's ex-best friend's prized divorce-settlement car—that ex-best friend being Peggy.

Char MacIsaac has always been a blurrer of lines. Daring or dangerous? Intrepid or insane? Fact or fiction? I still can't tell. It is part of her crazy charm. I never bother to dig too deep for the truth with her. It's more fun to do a little vicarious living through her wild, worldly stories while still feeling like I've got my shit together. Even though my shit is clearly falling apart now, and even though her wild, worldly stories seem more made up by the minute.

"Anyway. Nobody smacks me around and gets away with it." She flips off her monstrous sunglasses and winks an exaggerated wink with her makeup-laden eye. "Hey, got any good food? Havin' this little parasite on my tit does a number on my apple-tite."

"Suppose Mama' d boot my arse if you came to visit and I didn't feed ya. She was up making broc-o-glop at six o'clock this morning. Only food I haven't puked up yet. C'mon."

Broc-o-glop is Mama's finest culinary masterpiece. And the horrible name is intentional. A ruse. You bring it to a potluck, and people say, "What's that?" and you scrunch your nose in disgust and drawl, "Broc-o-glop." They won't touch it no matter how good it smells. And *boom*! More broc-o-glop for me. I'm not sure exactly what's in it, but I tried to make it for Dave once and it turned out a slimy, salty, broccoli mess. I begged Mama to tell me the broc-o-glop secret, but she laughed. Said Dave didn't deserve it, and refused to tell me. She won't tell anyone.

She's funny like that, just like she used to be funny about not letting anybody leave our house without being fed, whether they wanted to be or not. Whether money was tight or not. "Sit down," she'd say. "You look ready to eat a horse and chase the driver! I'll put another can of water on the beans." Which I always thought was weird because the people who came to our house never looked all that hungry to me, and we never ate canned beans. She even fed Weasel Tobin dinner the day she caught us screwing in the woods. He thought she was trying to poison him. I figured out that she was up to something even more devious: trying to make me think that she liked him, banking on the hope that I'd break up with him the second I thought he had her seal of approval. Mama's funny like that, too.

Two big bowls of broc-o-glop nuked and devoured. A good-sized fire roaring in the pit out back. The baby sound asleep. Half a bottle of posh vino consumed as we watch the sky become a blanket of star-dappled country dark. Char and I officially catch up on everything—real or imagined—that has happened since we last saw each other in the dingy basement apartment we shared in Halifax more than fifteen years ago. Before she bailed on our lease and ran away to join a psychedelic circus in Germany, which actually turned out to be a cult. But a fun cult, apparently. Not like the cult she later found herself in on the fringes of Shanghai. That one forbade booze, sex, and drugs, and encouraged members to renounce material wealth, serve others, and refrain from inflicting pain on the self, the Earth, or fellow beings. What kind of cult does that? Not a good one, by Char's standards.

Speaking of cults, the first thing I toss on that bonfire is the handful of *Viva Rica! The Essence of Inspiration! Stacey Fortune, Manager of Marketing* business cards, plucked from the bag of crap they handed to me when they cleaned out my desk at the office. The cards don't burn very well. They melt into a greasy, green, smoky glob of acrid pretense. The only other thing in that bag was a file folder I'm sure I meant to torch months ago. It contains a year's worth of weekly rose delivery cards, schmaltzy love-note Post-its, and a wedding "vision board" from my days with Dave the Douchebag, which also burn in an equally unsatisfying manner. They flare bright, hot-orange and golden for a minute or two, then abruptly become unrecognizable, black and charred. Twenty-year-old stacks of the *Cape Breton Post*, on the other hand? Those babies burn beautifully! Thick, heady grey billows of smoke and ash puff from the firepit as I feed armloads of newspaper into the hungry flames.

When the newspaper is gone, I see the last thing I had on my incineration agenda. The Hall of Shame page from Mama's photo album. I move to pitch it into the blaze, but Char snatches it out of my hand and examines it in the fire's glow.

"Who's that? Your grandparents?"

"Yeah, and my father."

"Dude, you can't burn those. Your mother will kill you."

"Well, she'll have to get in line. Brain tumours get first crack at me. Besides she hates those pictures. I'm doing her a favour. Exorcising some demons."

"Exercising demons makes 'em stronger, dummy." She peels back the plastic, tears out the pictures and stuffs them down the front of her sarong. "You'll thank me later."

The opening bars of "Stairway to Heaven" come ebbing out of the Mustang's stereo. Char reignites her baseball bat of a joint, rushes over to crank the song even louder, blows a kiss at the baby monitor when she hears Daktari momentarily fuss then settle from his car seat inside the trailer, then writhes back to the bonfire. She hauls heavily on the joint and juts it toward me. I pass, swigging from my bottle of Shiraz instead.

"Some people lose their memories with these tumours, or with the treatments." I shrug, my eyes fixed on the fire's mesmerizing dance. "But what kind of life is it if you can't remember your mother's face, or who you were? Or where you put your fuckin' pants. People are just a bunch of memories stitched together. When that starts to fall apart, what's left?"

Char stares up into the primordial breadth of the blackened sky.

"So d'ya start doin' Gimp again or what?"

"What? No."

"No as in 'yes,' or no as in 'not yet?'"

"Jesus, I thought we were having this philosophical conversation about memory and identity and me dying and shit," I say.

"You were," she laughs. "I was being stoned and staring at the sky and wondering when you were gonna start screwin' Willy Gimp again. I'd do him if I was dying."

"I dunno. Maybe. I'm kinda busy."

"With what?'

"With stuff. Dying stuff. I'm trying to write something, too. A memoir, I guess, about who I was. So none of them other arseholes can go telling stories about me."

"Well, I'd definitely do Gimp if I was dying *and* writing a memoir. Sex sells. Specially some bow chicka wow woaaaaw with a guy with cerebral policy. Handicapped is the new black, ya know."

Char jumps up and moves between the fully descended darkness and the firelight in a blasphemous marriage of belly dance and one-woman mosh pit as Robert Plant's voice howls from the car stereo, about winding roads and shadows taller than souls.

"You're a warped horn dog. You have ADHD. You're crazy as a bag of hammers, you're offensive as fuck. And you dance like a stripper. Nothing has changed."

"Actually, I am a foxy beaver. I eat Ritalin like candy. My craziness is a mute point. People being offended is *their* problem. And I *was* a stripper. In Columbia, where the *putas* dance like sexy raindrops!" She slithers her arms above her head, and flows close to me, cupping my face in her cool, electrified little hands. "Meanwhile, you, my sweet, brain-tumour-infested bitch, have athazagoraphobia."

"Moot point. And it's agoraphobia. And I don't," I say, brushing her off me.

"Like fuck. I mean Atha-za-gora-goddamnfuckin'-pobia. It's a fear of forgetting shit, and a fear of being forgotten. Or ignored. Being a regular old nobody. That's why you're obsessed with remembering everything. That's why you are writing your life down. And that is why you are secretly happy as a pig in shit that everybody is flapping their gums about the fact that you're home and you're sick. You are also a chicken. So you're right, nothing has changed."

"How am I a chicken?" I say, equally insulted by her insinuation as I am by the emptiness and overall mediocrity of my bottle of wine.

"Because you don't have the balls to drag Gimp out into the woods for a good ol' boot knockin' the way you used to. And you won't write a life story that *really* bleeds truth from your little gold veins if all you do is remember stuff and wait to die, without actually looking for more. And you won't shave your head unless somebody pushes ya. You're a chicken. You balk at everything."

She chicken walks around the firepit, going "Bawk! Bawk! Bawk!" for a minute or two, staring a hole through me with her mad, wide, sparkling, swamp-green eyes and sneering at me with her devilish grin before resuming her serpentine trance dance.

"Pass me that joint, go get the clippers and some scissors, and crank up the fuckin' Zepplin," I say.

Beneath a waxing moon, around a roaring fire, and under the influence of snaky chicken dances, wine, weed, and canonized rock riffs older than the hills, we dance and spin and play air guitar—Char dressed like a pop art Zulu priestess and me in a black yoga uniform that has never seen the upside of a downward dog, with a big frizzy ponytail thrashing around on the top of my head. It feels cultish or paganish. Probably looks like two messed up, middle-aged broads out in the woods pretending they have nothing to lose, while occasionally pausing to listen for crying through a crackly old baby monitor.

I hold scissors in one hand, thick cord of my hair in the other. I close my eyes as my chest fills with a strange sensation, a mixture of extreme detachment and profound presence. I am not thinking about the future consequences of being bald. I am not thinking about vanities past. All of that evaporates.

"Fuck it," I say, as I squeeze the scissor handles together and push the blades through the stubborn strands. Seconds later, I am holding my long, chocolate-brown-with-caramel-highlights ponytail in front of me. Two hundred and seventy-six bucks worth of salon colouring, right there. I toss it onto the fire, which unleashes the unmistakable stench of burning hair into the night and ruins the whole sacred ritual vibe I'd been riding.

Char flips the clippers to life. Her soft hands and the hard appliance caress my head. I feel the steady vibrations of every pass all the way through my skull and into my chest. *This is not what I thought it would feel like.* Moments later, my hands quiver as they travel over the unfamiliar terrain of my freshly liberated skull.

"Shit, Crow. That's rad. Like, GI Jane rad. Your head's not as lumpy as I thought it would be. You are totally gonna need some big honkin' earrings to rock that shit proper though." Char laughs.

I cry.

Headlights come ripping up the driveway. Too fast and too careless to be Mama. A battered old Monte Carlo sputters up alongside the trailer. This time it actually is Peg, ranting and raving the second she hoists her corpulence out of the groaning car seat.

"What in the name of Mother Mary, meek and mild, do youse think you're doin'? Your little bonfire is sending smoke all up the road. Them woods are as dry as an old nun's gusset! There's a fire ban on from Lands and Forests. Yas don't even have a bucket of water! And are those your mother's papers? She'll have your head on a platter!"

She stops ranting when she notices my head.

"What? Doncha like it?" I say, wiping away any trace of tears, sweet sarcasm tinging my words.

"If I can't say anything nice, I shouldn't say nothin' at all."

"That's never stopped you before."

"Fine. You wanna know what I think? You look like a skin-head. Or a cancer patient."

In the flickering shadows and light, out of the corner of my eye, I see Char tugging on her ear lobes with wide cupped hands and mouthing the words, *Earrings. Big honkin' earrings.*

I direct my full attention to Peg.

"Well," I say, "they have to stick needles into my brain to see if it's actually cancer or just tumours in the worst possible locations."

"Oh, don't be so dramatic. Anything for the attention, I guess," she says, her buggy eyes lurching back in a dismissive roll.

"Right. I came back to this shithole island with a head full of tumours just so you and all your nosy friends could spoil me with all your lavish attention," I spit.

A baby begins to holler over the monitor.

"Charlotte, go get the baby and get in the car. You, missy. Get a bucket and put out that fire before I call the cops."

Before my fury-forged, wine-sharpened tongue can tear a fleshy strip off Peggy, Mama's car comes clattering up the driveway. Char comes out of the house carrying a car seat, with her son nestled quietly into the zebra sling. Peg cocks an eyebrow at me, challenging me to say more. I shut up, just for spite.

Char obediently gets in the passenger side of the Monte Carlo. Peg strides over to Mama as she hauls her tired bones out of her own car, says she will come pick up the Mustang in the morning.

Mama comes to me, the deep, exhausted folds in her face uncomfortably emphasized by the bonfire's undulating flickers of shadows and light. She stares at me for a moment. Does the same eyebrow cock as Peg's, challenging me to say something.

"Ma, I just—"

"Go get a bucket of water and put that fire out. And while you're in there, put the tea on."

[···]

After much preening, I surmise that shaving my head was a terrible idea. One minute, I catch a glimpse of myself in the door of the microwave, with a little bit of soft light behind me and my chin tilted just so, and, *Ahhh, there she is. 1990s Sinéad O'Connor.* Then I go take a piss, and as I'm reaching for the toilet paper I glance up into the mirror, *Jesus Christ! What's Gollum doing in my mother's bathroom?*

Also, Char lied about the lumpiness of my head. The "cow licks" that Mama used to plaster down with a swipe of her licked fingers, that I artfully styled around, now nakedly protrude from my scalp for the world to see, along with the remnants of my Eddie Munster widow's peak, my mismatched ears, and the creeping neck hairline of an old Italian man. This is why head shaving was used as a punishment for loose women. This is why most women only ever talk about doing it. This is why a shaved head on a woman is a mark of complete IDGAF or all-out insanity. It's crazy hard to face yourself, never knowing if it will be Gollum or Sinéad staring back.

It wasn't long after things went down the crapper with Dave this past winter that I stood in front of the mirror in my pristine glass and marble bathroom, my hair clenched in my hands, thinking, *I'll show that bastard how much I hate his guts by hacking and discarding the part of me he loved most. Then I will. Be. Free.* My pseudo-friend Ami was there, egging me on, even though she was the one who set me up with her dear friend Dave in the first place. She was fresh off a yoga retreat in India and was all "let go of your attachments," and "re-align to your life's purpose," and "unleash the cosmo-licious power of your crown chakra" and shit. Which was ultimately what helped me make my decision that night: if Ami thought I should do it, there was no way in hell. This is a woman who'd glide around the Viva Rica office wrapped in a purple shawl, bowing with her hands in the sacred Anjali mudra, saying Namaste to everyone. But as soon as she put on her fur coat and started sashaying down the street, she was all flying elbows and nasty sneers at anyone who walked too slowly. A woman who loudly called squeegee kids and panhandlers disgusting. A woman who changed her name at the age of thirty-two, because Ahhhh-meee sounded more spiritual and exotic than Krista. Plus, she had professionally straightened fake burgundy tresses all the way down to her arse, and I didn't see her rushing to end all *her* self-cherishing and liberate *her* ego by hacking it all off in the bathroom with a dull, squeaky pair of scissors.

Now that it's done, I swing recklessly between feeling fierce, brave, and liberated, and ugly, shallow, and helpless. I want to call Char and tell her she's a liar. I want to Instagram Ami a picture of my best Nothing Compares to Sinéad angle and tell her it feels. So. Ahhhh. Mazing. I wonder if there are any earrings in the world big enough to balance out what my bald head is revealing.

And drinking an entire bottle of wine all by myself? That

was a full-blown terrible idea. I did, however, have the good sense to go to bed and not sit up with Mama drinking tea and gin, listening to John Denver sing about country roads and seasons of the heart. Which means I also missed seeing Mama cry. Whenever a few drinks inspire her to haul out the John Denver records, I know what's coming.

She pulls the old wooden rocking chair up beside the stereo, closes her eyes, and wraps herself in the stories of the songs. Her voice turns to velvet as she sings along. And by the time Denver gets to the chorus, tears are escaping from the corners of her still-closed eyes and she's rocking in rhythm. But there is never any mess to Mama's crying. Her voice effortlessly mops up any trace of non-musical emotion that might interfere with the tune. Her face absorbs the tears before they can spot her clothes. There's no sobbing. No snotting or sniffling. Not so much as an off-key crack of unrestraint. Just John Denver, his stories, my mother, her tears. Although I know that Mama's John Denver tears come from someplace other than West Virginia or windy Kansas wheat fields or Grandma's feather bed. Just like her Waylon Jennings and Willie Nelson foot-stomping, fist-banging, fuck-the-world-and-the-two-bit-horse-it-rode-in-on grin comes from someplace other than Luckenbach, Texas, and has nothing to do with red-headed strangers, blue eyes crying in the rain, or mamas letting babies grow up to be cowboys. Mama's tears and grins and memories come from here. From me. From my father.

While my head grapples with my usual morning malady, as well as the injury of a whole bottle of wine and the fresh insult of baldness, Mama's head is threatening to explode. She just realized that most of the fire last night involved the heaps of old newspapers she's been hoarding for decades, and she noticed the pictures missing from the Wall of Shame page in the photo album. She's pissed. Top volume Johnny Cash "Ring of Fire" at five a.m. pissed.

I get up before she has a chance to level the usual threat and brace for a dose of the maternal wrath. A little "who died and made you queen?" followed by the doling out of some arbitrary and unnecessary chores. Shoo the wasps away from the rose, but not the bees. Flip the cushions on the couch. Call Peggy and apologize for being an asshole. But there's none of that.

"You'll have to clean up your own vomit today, Missy," is all she says as she pulls on her worn-out work sneakers.

I try to tell her I'm sorry.

"Sorry is as sorry does," she grunts, busying herself with tiny adjustments to the frayed laces on her shoes. Still, she holds the sides of my newly shorn head in her hands and plants a kiss on my forehead before she leaves. On the counter, there's a fresh pan of broc-o-glop to replace the one that Char and I finished in last night's stupor. The tea on the stove is piping hot, made with three fresh bags.

When she's gone, I go outside with the giant bag of gnarly old flower bulbs that I found under one of the newspaper mountains last night. I dig little holes with a tablespoon, and tuck the bulbs into the cooling earth, all over the yard. Mama would always snort at me when I turned up my nose at the insect-buzz of that beast of a rose bush, or the aphid-covered lupins in the ditch, or the slimy sadness of daffodils and hyacinths and lilies when they die.

"Good Lord, Crow, who complains about flowers?" she'd say. "They're nothing but beauty-full."

So this is me, apologizing for burning her papers and letting Char make off with a couple of photographs I mistakenly assumed Mama'd sooner be rid of. My sorry is as sorry does. By the time these flowers bloom in the spring all of this will be forgiven, if not forgotten.

[···]

On the first day of fall, Mama and I head to the Regional Hospital in the dreary morning dark for a fun-filled day of head cages, foot-long needles, and robo-surgeons. Mama squeezes my hand too hard as we walk down the hall to the desk where a terse and cranky woman hands me stacks of paperwork, and begins grilling me about when I ate, what colour my snot is, and where I've been.

"Christ, this one's worse than Peggy," I grumble. Mama discretely pinches the back of my arm. I jump a bit, smile, and answer.

"Last meal was twelve hours ago, nasal mucus is clear, and the only travel was flying back here from Toronto three and a half weeks ago."

Then, a less cranky but equally terse woman leads me to the prep room and gives me a johnny coat.

"Why do I need to wear this if they're drilling my head?" I say.

Mama, again with the pinch that says, *Shut up. Stop being so contrary. These people are just doing their job. Put on the damn dress.* And I do.

Next comes a little paper cup full of drugs to "make me more comfortable during the procedure." Within twenty minutes of tossing those babies into my system, Mama's got fuzzy grey kittens playing hide and seek in her hair, the monochrome blue concentric rings that pattern my johnny coat ebb and flow in sync with my breath, and the nurse's words are the colour of Dijon mustard. Now I am definitely more comfortable, assuming "more comfortable" means "tripping balls."

"Gosh, I hope you didn't shave your head just for this!" the nurse says as she marks up my head with a ballpoint pen. "We only would have taken off a tiny bit of hair. The size of a stamp."

"Nah, I did it 'cause I'm such a badass," I hear myself trill. "And I needed a new do."

They rig the cage contraption to my head and neck, screw me down to the table, run me through the MRI, and then wheel in the fancy Skype screen, upon which the face of a friendly neurosurgeon in Halifax appears to direct the guy with the scalpel, the drill, and the big, long, hollow needles. But I'm not paying attention to any of that. I'm too busy blabbering on about naming my tumours. *Parry Homunculus lives way deep in my parietal lobe, where he fucks with my sensory processing. Ziggy Stardust is a wild one, dancing all over my occipital lobe making me see crazy shapes and colours. And the other one...fuck, I don't have a good name for that one. Let's call it Fuzzy. Fuzzy Wuzzy was a tumour. Fuzzy Wuzzy heard a rumour.* I hum loud and tunelessly to drown out the whir of the drill and the drone of the doctors—who are not nearly as jazzed about the tumour names as I am—and watch the fluorescent lights on the ceiling explode into billions of light specks that scamper madly around the room like baby spiders newly hatched from their silvery scale egg, then dissolve.

I don't know if time flew by or stood still, but before I can figure that out, the biopsy is done. As terse nurse removes the head contraption and gets ready to wheel me to the recovery room, the robot video neurosurgeon tells me that the results will be sent to Dr. Divyaratna early next week. The drill-wielding orthopedic surgeon tells me that I have the thickest, lumpiest skull he's ever seen. And Mama tells me that she could hear me butchering the bejesus out of "Take Me Home, Country Roads" all the way down the hall. Somewhere en route to the recovery room, I fall into something like sleep.

In my doped-up, post-procedure, post-nap stupor my eyes flicker, then fall on the carefully preserved old fossil of a woman in the bed next to mine. Tiny eyes peer out from beneath her pencilled-on shiny black brows and folds of alabaster wrinkles. Thinning coils of blue-tinted hair have been coerced into co-operation by too much Aqua Net. A frail frame is smothered in a burgundy velveteen dressing gown. Nobody has the heart to make the old fossils wear johnny coats.

I notice her giving me the hairy eyeball. Is it my relative youthfulness? My baldness? My quasi-stoned blaséness over the mouthful of yellow slime I just spit all over my bed?

"Whatever you were dreaming about certainly tickled your funny bone," she says in a voice dry and dusty, but not unpleasant.

"Damn drugs," I say with a groggy grimace.

"Cancer?" Her voice is still not unpleasant.

"Just had the biopsy. Probably."

"Shaving your entire head wasn't necessary, you know. They only take a patch about the size of a postage stamp. Nothing a little creative hair styling can't hide." Her craggy hands flutter nimbly to her own curls, reassuring them of their beauty with a tender pat. They spring back obediently. I fix my glassy gaze on her hair in a vain attempt to distract myself from the blackened grey and bile-yellow splotches now crowding my field of vision.

"Bald is my creative hair styling." Trying not to sound like her intrusiveness is starting to get on my nerves.

"It's unbecoming on a lady with your husky bone structure," she says, her brow furrowed and her mouth pulling into a puckered half-smile. "My friend Joan makes gorgeous wigs. With real hair. Blonde is quite fetching. Gentlemen prefer fair hair, especially once a woman has passed her prime. You should call Joan. She could even make it work with your ruddy skin tone." There's an unmistakable smack of scorn in her passive-aggressive benevolence, and my head can't handle anymore sage advice.

I turn to face the wall, and moan. "This sucks. I feel like a bag of smashed assholes."

"Mouth like a mine rat. Also unbecoming." The old bat sharply enunciates each word with the precision of an icy-eyed, strap-wielding Catholic school nun.

"Better a mine rat than a heartless old vulture," Mama's voice snarls from the doorway.

Even through my post-op distorted eyesight I can clearly see the old woman's face change. The tightly pursed lips part ways, the lower one slipping down in disbelief, drooping over the puckered chin. Her eyes are wide open and alive, crackling with something nasty as she stares down my mother.

The room starts to spin and my head starts to pound. Mama and the old woman are talking to each other, but I can't hear a word on account of the rumbles and clangs in my ears. The details of their faces and the space between them gets swallowed by a jumbled cloud of colour. Piney greenish-grey bands with streams of piss-yellow mash into jagged swaths of maroon, with intermittent black-red spirals shooting out in all directions. My stomach turns, my teeth start to chatter, and for a minute I can't remember who anyone is or what we're all doing here. Then the incision site on my skull starts to throb, the auditory cacophony subsides, and my eyes lay off on the technicolour trip just in time to see the stone cold fury on Mama's face as she yanks a wheelchair into the room, throws my coat onto my bed, and says, "C'mon. The nurse said you can go."

She takes a couple of quick strides toward me and pulls off my blanket.

"Ma, I'm still in the johnny coat —"

"Keep it as a souvenir. We're leaving. Now."

She hustles my coat over the hospital gown, guides my shaky frame into the wheelchair, plops my bag onto my lap, then breaks for the door. But she stops short, half-turning to face the dumbfounded old biddy in the other bed. Slowly, clearly, with glaring narrowed eyes and a feral smile tugging on the left side of her upper lip, Mama speaks.

"Hope the cancer gets you this time, Lady Rosalind. And may it hurt like the hot horrors of hell."

And out the door we go.

Rosalind Spenser. My father's mother.

[···]

Mama talks about my father with as much love and warmth as she can muster, which admittedly isn't a ton. The rest of his family, though? She says their names like she's spitting out shit: *Saint Sarah, Lady Rosalind, the Other Old Bastard.* My one and only memory of ever meeting them still sits vividly in my mind, despite Mama's insistence that I'd be best off forgetting they existed, because that's how they'd treat me and we'd never darken their door again.

It was Christmas Eve. I was eight. Mama wouldn't tell me where we were going, but she scrubbed my face and fingernails until they were raw because only streels went around with dirty faces and fingernails. She dressed me in an itchy, starchy green dress with red smocking and a big, floppy, white lace puritan collar. She wrestled my hair into too tight, too high pigtails, tied them with pieces of thick, fluffy red yarn, and jammed my poor duck feet into a pair of stiff, narrow Mary Janes that would leave gaping, bloody blisters on both heels. I remember looking at myself in the mirror in abject horror. I wanted my hair pulled back with a headband. I wanted to wear my orange corduroy jumper. I wanted my duck feet in warm, wide winter boots. But no. We were going *somewhere*.

Somewhere was a gigantic Victorian house on a hill, in the wealthy west end of the Northside, out in Town. Far removed from the dirty slushy streets in The Mines, where the air was permeated by the smell of gas and coffee and the sounds of people yelling, "Hey dere buddy, how she goin'?" Even distant from the nice parts of Town, the land of tidy split levels, with honeysuckles on trellises and stone bird baths in the yard. That was where the ordinary rich people lived. People who called the likes of Mama when they needed their house cleaned for a dinner party. But the *somewhere* we visited that night had a sprawling lawn edged in cold, naked oak trees. Rhododendron bushes wrapped in red and green lights. A life-sized nativity scene with hand-carved and painted wise men, angels, and animals, each under their own bright white spotlight.

Mama murmured, "Don't worry about paying the power bill here, now do they?" as we drove up the driveway. That was the first time I realized that Mama *did* have to worry about paying the power bill.

Inside, *somewhere* smelled like oranges and cinnamon and baked ham. An enormous ostrich feather fan hung on the wall. Glittering crystals dangled from a chandelier. Delicate horse figurines and tiny tea sets were carefully arranged on the shelves of two giant glass cabinets. Nothing here came from the Bargain Store. A fire roared in a big stone hearth, making the whole place too hot for my comfort, but clearly not for the small throng of unfamiliar adults. Men in blazers and sweater vests sipped amber drinks from little glasses, while women in velvet dresses held wine glasses in jewelled hands. Beneath the layer of chatter and guffaws, Bing Crosby crooned "I'll be Home for Christmas."

Mama marched me through the crowd until we stood in front of an older couple. The woman leaned against the man, clutching the sleeve of his suit jacket with her diamond-laden fingers when she saw us. Mama introduced me with ice in her voice and fire in her eyes, and said we didn't come to make a scene. We just came for some hot chocolate and a plate of cookies, like the boys got.

At a table in the corner sat two boys, both younger than me. A tall, thin woman with long blonde hair and a porcelain face ignored me completely, but dusted crumbs from the fronts of their navy blue suits as they nibbled cookies and sipped hot chocolate. The older man simply raised an eyebrow at me, shook his head, and walked away laughing to himself in a way that wasn't really laughing, and wasn't really to himself. The older woman stood, staring a hole through Mama for a long while. When it became clear that my mother wasn't going to budge, the woman flashed me a dagger of a smile, bit her bottom lip as she thrust out a furious "Fine," and waved us toward the table.

A waiter came out with a cup of cocoa and a plate with two star-shaped cookies. Mama stopped the waiter and said that my hot chocolate needed whipped cream. And chocolate shavings. And my cookies needed white icing and silver candy balls. Like the boys had. The waiter looked at the old woman. She nodded once, slowly, in a way that filled me with both glee and terror. But I wasted no time in slurping thick gobs of cocoa-tinged whipped cream from that cup, and letting the buttery sweetness of icing-slathered shortbreads melt on my tongue, while the thin blonde lady and two boys watched in horror.

From the corner of my eye, I could see Mama and the older woman standing almost nose to nose, speaking in tense, hushed tones. When I saw Mama squat in a mock curtsey and heard her sneer, "Yes, Lady Rosalind!" I knew my time in this weird Heaven was running out.

"Hey buddy, you gonna finish those cookies?" I asked the younger of the two boys. "Because I—"

Mama's voice boomed, "Crow. Time to go. Now."

I wolfed down the rest of my cookie, plus the one the kid in the suit had gingerly shoved toward me, and glugged the last half of my hot chocolate. Mama buttoned my coat, took my hand, and ushered me to the door. The old woman followed us, perching in the door frame as we walked down the steps, bidding us Merry Christmas and good riddance.

I smiled, curtsied, and said, "Good riddance to you too, ma'am," thinking it was some kind of rich person holiday greeting.

My mother turned to look the old woman square in the eye, then smiled so that every last one of her false teeth were bared, and said, "Lovely glass house you have, Lady Rosalind. Be grateful I'm not one for throwing stones." Mama hustled me down the walkway. And just past the spotlit nativity scene, my traitorous gut expelled all of that hard-won decadence, all over the walkway of my father's fancy family home. I've had a knack for a timely upchuck ever since.

[···]

I am too scared to turn around to see the precise quality of the look on Mama's face right now, but judging by the way she is steering my wheelchair at breakneck speed down the hall and turning the rickety bugger on a dime, the old doll is livid. Now is not a good time to ask questions about my father's family. Then again, there may never be a good time to go dredging through that toxic pool of old stories, even if there are uncharted islands of truth and revelation somewhere in it.

There's also never really a good time to get the results of a brain tumour biopsy, but within days, the call comes. *Congratulations Crow Fortune, you are the proud host of moderately invasive, extremely unpredictable, totally inoperable triplets, a trio of grade two-ish astrocytomas!* They grow long, nebulous tendrils that infiltrate surrounding tissue and are near impossible to cut out in any kind of clean way, especially when they have snuggled nice and deep into the grey matter of three separate brain lobes. Parry Homunculus, Ziggy Stardust,

Fuzzy Wuzzy, and I are bonded for life. And although they grow slowly and are technically considered low-grade and not yet cancerous, that could change in a wink. It usually does. Grade two astrocytomas are unpredictable little fellas. One day, they will just wiggle their little starry tendrils at each other and say, "Hey boys! Let's get our cancer on!" Then, *bam!* Brain cancer. Inoperable. Terminal.

The treatments sound worse than the disease, which will most certainly come back bigger and badder. If the tumours behave themselves, I've got a few years of pounding pain, whacked-out visual disturbances and generally feeling like I've been hit by the honey wagon. Radiation and chemo might give me a year or two more, but the side effects will probably make me wish I were dead. Once they start changing, I've got about eighteen months. And that's with aggressive treatment and a hefty dose of luck of which I've never had any.

Dr. Divyaratna seems delighted to tell me that this is not as bad as it could be. "We will just have to wait and see."

Which only makes me feel worse. I didn't come all this way to wait and see. To wither into helpless, snivelling clod-dom while my mother's hands tremble to hold my aching head and her own breaking heart together for years on end. To slowly disintegrate. I came here to say my goodbyes, sum up my life, and go down in a blaze of glory. Like a firework, screaming up into the backwoods darkness, shattering the night and the silence with my burning brilliance. If only for a moment. The idea of a swift and certain death held an odd comfort. The prospect of an uncertain life is far more unsettling. And even though on paper, I may now stand a faintly greater chance than that of an average ice cube in hell, there's a familial pattern and a gnawing feeling in my gut that says I'm still pretty doomed. It's just a matter of degree.

[···]

My Going Home To Die plan did not include a high school reunion on Thanksgiving weekend. But here I am, rifling through my old jewellery box trying to find earrings big enough to distract people from my bald and now slightly scarred head. When Allie picks me up, I wait for her to comment on the gaudy silver stars dangling from my earlobes, but she doesn't. The drive over Ceilidh Mountain to Loch Bhreagh is remarkable in its silence. Allie keeps her eyes on the road. I take in the scenery.

This is the part of my downhome tale where I'm supposed to gush about what I see from where I sit, and maybe be grateful I even get to witness all this. The land and the sea. The turning leaves and the glorious colours. How it is all just. So. Beautiful. I'm supposed to draw the reader into my world with vivid descriptions of the landscape and the natural beauty, and then somehow draw a poignant connection between the rugged beauty of the simple land and the rugged beauty of the complicated people.

Well, you know what I see now when I look at those trees with the colourful leaves? Death. We glorify the bejesus out of the dying leaves. We're all *ooh* and *aah* and gasping words like *gorgeous* and *majestic* while the poor leaves are just trying to eke out a few more sad weeks of being. By October, the leaves know. They know that one good night of wind, one lashing rain storm, and they're gone. Unceremoniously flung to the ground to rot. Fall is a season of letting go. Of grief.

Even though they manage to put on a bit of show for a while, what the leaves are really telling us is that those merciless, cold, dark days are coming. Pretty colours don't stop you from becoming a corpse. So the mountain isn't beautiful. It's coloured with a hundred shades of dying.

Allie and I roll into the postcard-perfect village of Loch Bhreagh, which is all decked out for the annual Celtic festival. More tartan and fiddles than you can shake a stick at. Throngs of tourists in search of an authentic Cape Breton experience. I should charge these visitors money to take them on a little tour out behind the rink and get them drunk, stoned, beat up, or pregnant. That's why I couldn't put my marketing skills to use here. If I had, you'd be seeing brochures that said "Cape Breton: Give Us Your Money and Git Out Before We Puck Ya in the Teeth." Or as they say in the fake Gaelic, "*Ciad Mille Fáilche Áielfs*: One Hundred Thousand Fuck Offs."

Over where the high school wing used to be there's now just a pile of rubble. They tore it down the day before yesterday. The elementary and junior high sections and the common gymnasium are still there, but the asbestos-ridden building where we spent our formative years is no more. The industrial arts workshop where Char gave impromptu table-dancing lessons is gone. The AV room where Allie gave a highly acclaimed and delightfully ironic performance of a Peer Education play called *Hugs Not Drugs* after eating a handful of magic mushrooms at lunch hour is gone. The janitor's closet where Willy Gimp found me hiding on Valentine's Day, crying over Weasel Tobin when I should have been in biology class, and where he held me and let me blubber all over his good shoulder, and where we had our first sober kiss, is gone.

Seeing the heap of waste and destruction that now sprawls across the space where the bricks and mortar of my memories once stood is a shock to my delicate system. A rush of grief gallops through my body, grips my throat, and starts to squeeze out tears. I chide myself before any can fall. I clear my throat, shoving away the choked-up sentimentality.

"What kind of asshole plans a high school reunion for Thanksgiving weekend?" I mutter.

The same kind of asshole who makes the reunion's theme "A Cape Breton Kitchen Ceilidh." An asshole named Becky Chickenshit, who is technically an arsehole, not an asshole. Anybody can be an asshole at any given time. But when you're an arsehole, you're an arsehole for life. It's part of who you are. Becky Chickenshit comes from a long line of arseholes. As Mama says, "If it's in the cats, it's in the kittens."

In the old gym, the fiddle music is a-blaring and there is tartan everywhere. Not even the Cape Breton tartan, but the garish blue Nova Scotia one, because Becky Chickenshit is a paper pusher for the provincial government. The banner on the back wall says "*Ciad Mille Failte* to the Class of '95 Cape Breton Kitchen Ceilidh." Every table has a lobster trap centrepiece stuffed with sprigs of fall leaves.

There is no lobster on the buffet table. Which is fine by me because as far as I am concerned, all seafood is revolting. Especially lobster. It eats garbage, for Christ's sake. There is, however, a mountain of cold cuts and rubbery cheese. Pasty white rolls with no name margarine. Coleslaw and potato salads straight out of the Presbyterian Ladies' Auxiliary cookbook. Pickled eggs on a bed of iceberg lettuce. Jell-O salads. Three of them: a yellow one with marshmallows and canned peaches, a red one with maraschino cherries, and a green one with black olives, ham chunks, and macaroni noodles. Allie averts her eyes and stifles a gag.

"What kind of a sick bastard puts meat wads and macaroni in Jell-O, and calls it salad?" I whisper. "And what the hell is a ladies' auxiliary?"

It's good to hear Allie laugh again.

The dessert table is worse. I've clung to many a plate of chocolate dipped profiteroles and fresh fruit in a sea of sushi and fried squid. I've been saved by the merciful grace of blueberry grunt and apple pie at lobster and clam chowder affairs. Rescued from previous stints in cold cut hell by heavenly cheesecake bites and ganache-topped brownies and butter tarts. But there is no sweet saviour here. Nothing but squares.

There's Shower Squares and Church Tea Squares and Funeral Squares and Bake Sale Squares. Everybody's got a secret family recipe lifted from a church cookbook or the back of a can. Despite the seemingly endless varieties, they are all the same. Gobs of margarine, a mountain of sugar, a handful of some flavour or colour or both, a mess of some kinda crumbs, and probably a can of sweetened condensed milk. Cooked, cooled, cut into rectangles, and spread out on the finest paper plates.

But oh, look, there's a bar.

Behind the bar stands the Ceilidh Queen herself, Becky Chickenshit, all decked out in a blue tartan skirt and vest with a Capers T-shirt underneath. Pewter earrings shaped like Cape Breton Island peek out from beneath her big yellow sou'wester. The selfie she's taking will probably be posted to Facebook and tweeted to her five followers with the hashtag #realcapebretonceilidh faster than you can say "*Sláinte*

Má Árse", or whatever wannabe-Gaelic nonsense it is she shouts every five minutes to make everyone clink and drink.

The urge to smack her rises swiftly and sharply. But there will be no Becky Chickenshit smacking. Not until she's done feeding me wine for the night. Or at least until Char gets here.

"Crow Fortune! You're here!" she brays, squinting, blinking. "We didn't think you'd make it...How *are* you?"

"I'm thirsty, Becky," I say, flashing my biggest, fattest smile in an effort to divert attention from my number two buzz cut, my fairly fresh surgical scar, and my ever-increasing gauntness. Judging by the way people are looking at me, I don't think the big star earrings are doing the trick. I smile even bigger, harder. This is a slightly new and improved version of the same big fat smile I'd use when I was concocting stories for Viva Rica! The Essence of Inspiration! team members, convincing them that they could transform their personal energy power to attract more health, wealth, and happiness in the form of steady customers. How they, too, could come across as strong, confident, and inspirational! How to not look like a desperate, overpriced blueberry juice–peddling multi-level marketing moron! It's all in the carefully crafted smile.

"Gimme a glass of red wine. And don't be stingy on the pour."

"Do you really think that's a good idea?" Becky says, wringing her hands and biting the corner of her bottom lip. "We have some club soda. Club soda is nice."

In my dim peripheral vision, I can see people stopping what they are doing, watching as whatever is unfolding here unfolds a little more. My hands plant on my hips. My head cocks to the side. My voice rises ever so slightly. Because I have something to prove. And now I have an audience. And I want a glass of wine, dammit.

"Tell ya what, Becky. I'll go home, curl up on my couch in a pink Snuggie, and sip some nice club soda like a good little shut-in, but only after I get hammered here tonight. So how about you gimme my wine? Preferably before I'm dead."

For a minute, she just stands there, eyelids fluttering a mile a minute at me through her glasses. Allie laughs so hard that the risk of pissing in her pants is becoming more real by the second. Allie is a notorious pants-pisser when she laughs. Which is why I'd never lend her my jeans. Char, on the other hand, was not allowed to borrow my jeans because she would draw penises on them, cut holes in the crotch, and sometimes light the pockets on fire. While she was wearing them.

"Well you just got told right the fuck off there, dinja, Chickenshit!" Char's face suddenly pokes in between Allie and me, her blonde dreads flipping and flopping as she gives an exaggerated side-to-side gawk around. Now things just got really awkward. And not just because Char happens to have both tits hanging out, with her baby snuggled in a sling and suckling on one of them.

Allie and Char have not seen each other since 1998. And I believe the last words between them were, "Fuck you, you psycho cunt face. I hope you rot in hell." At least, that's what the guy who lived in the apartment above us told me he heard somebody scream that night, before the door slammed and everything went quiet. I don't know exactly what happened, or why. All I know is that I came home from the bar to an empty apartment. The next day, Char told me she was bailing on the lease and booking 'er to Germany to join the circus.

A week later, Allie got kicked out of residence and moved in with me for a while, until her mother took a bad turn and had to be moved up to Halifax to be closer to a specialist. Allie said she and Char had a fight. That it had been coming for a long time. That Char was a crazy, backstabbing bitch, end of story. And all I ever got out of Char was a garbled complaint about Allie Walker and "all her melon-dramatic shit." I don't know what happened, but I knew enough to stay out of it. Never imagined I'd find myself standing next to the two of them again.

"Don't waste your money at Becky's little lemonade stand, girls. C'mon out to the car. I got a surprise for ya," Char says, kissing her teeth at Becky.

"I'll pass," Allie says, her spine stiffening, her eyes locked straight ahead, every trace of joviality wiped from her face. "A beer please, Becky."

Char smacks my arse.

"C'mon. You'll like this surprise. Promise," she purrs.

"Go ahead," Allie says without looking at me. "I'll get a table."

"Wanna hold my baby for me?" Char asks her, clearly knocking Allie off guard enough to make her eyes widen and look down at the baby clinging to Char's chest.

"No." Allie's cold composure is quickly restored.

"Dammit," Char mutters, her eyes suddenly speed-scanning the room. I grab her by the arm and usher her out to the parking lot.

The surprise in the car is a bottle of top-shelf tequila and a big fat joint being rolled up by none other than Willy Gimp.

"Hey, stranger," he says, sticking his head out the passenger side window. "Quite the haircut ya got there."

"It's her fault." I shoot a look at Char as she slides up beside me, having at least put away the boob that Daktari Christ MacIsaac wasn't using before sharply nudging me toward the driver side door.

"Most shit is her fault," Willy Gimp chuckles.

"Well, you two kids have fun." Char turns on the heels of her snakeskin stilettos. Which do not go with her hot pink peasant blouse and the Daisy Dukes.

I watch her prance away and wonder if I shouldn't go back inside, apologize to Becky Chickenshit, convince Char to leave before things get out of hand, sit and have a drink with Allie, smile and make small talk with a few fellow Class of '95ers, and then go home. Maybe stop and buy a pink Snuggie and some nice club soda at the drugstore on the way.

Gimp lights the joint and hands me a shot glass full of tequila, a lemon slice, and a salt shaker.

"If you play your cards right, maybe we'll hide in the boys' locker room and do body shots off each other after the dance starts," he says. "You can do one off my magically twisted arm." I can't tell if he's kidding or not.

An hour later, we waltz into the gym to see that Becky Chickenshit and the party squad have jacked things up to another level. The lights are dimmed, the fiddle tunes have temporarily given way to some quasi-country folksy stuff, and people are gathered around clapping and stomping and watching Becky fake step dance. I find Allie sitting alone at a table. I teeter to her side and start to apologize.

"It's fine. I get it," she says, glancing at Gimp.

"We were just hanging out."

"Whatever," she says. "No big deal."

But it is. She always did get pissy when she thought I'd

ditched her for a guy. Because I've ditched her for guys more times than I care to admit. I'm too buzzed and baked to argue with her, though, and the transition from the hallway fluorescents to the strobe-lit dance floor in the gym has set my eyes on a trip. I can't very well argue with Allie about the "no big deals" that clearly *are* and the "fines" that clearly *aren't* when she's got some kinda grey-blue dustball of pall parked over her head. I miss being able to focus on actually seeing people when I talk to them.

Meanwhile, there's Becky Chickenshit, her big tartan arse heaving and hoing all over the place in a dizzying display. Word is that Becky just got married to none other than everybody's favourite lecherous crooked cop, Duke the Puke. And there, my smug self-confidence is restored. At least my arse is small, I didn't marry a bona fide creep, and I don't fake step dance in public.

"C'mon, Allie, let's go show them wanker bits how to really dance. See if they'll play Salt-N-Pepa. Pretty sure I can still Pu-push it real gooooood—" I convince myself to ignore my wooziness, throw my arm over my head, and start to arch backwards, my chest and hips thrusting up as my lower back quickly begins to insist that I am too old and way too dizzy to do this dance.

"There've been enough scenes here already tonight."

I give her a quizzical look, as my eyes detect that the edges of her grey-blue dustball are tinged with the uneven reds of a fresh sunburn, or an old scar. I look around for evidence of a scene. Char is nowhere in sight.

While Willy Gimp and I were in the car getting a buzz on and talking about the old days, Char was inside doing what Char has always done best. Causing a scene of epic proportions. She went straight to the bar, but Becky wouldn't serve her because Becky didn't think it was appropriate for a breastfeeding mother to drink *alcohol.* Char got loud and mouthy. Becky blinked and stammered. Char got louder and mouthier. Becky started to cry. Then Duke showed up, and threatened to arrest Char for public indecency because by now, the baby was sound asleep in the sling, but Char had both of her boobs hanging out the top of her hot pink peasant blouse, just for fun. Char grabbed one of her boobs, gave it a squeeze, and nailed Duke right between the eyes with a stream of milk. Duke called her a nasty cow. Becky wailed hysterically. Char laughed like a lunatic. Duke whipped out his badge. Becky told Char she'd better leave at once before she ended up in jail. Char told Becky to go suck a pig dick, spun on her stilettoed heels, and traipsed out the back door of the gym.

"So where's Char now?" I ask.

"Dunno. Don't care." Allie takes a nonchalant swig of beer.

"Bah, she'll be back," Willy Gimp says. "I got her car keys."

"Where?" I lean in close to Gimp's ear, grazing his neck with my lips, hoping he can hear the heat in my voice over the caterwauling music. "Which pocket? This one?" My hands dance under the table and slide over his thigh. "Or this one?"

He laughs.

"You're wrecked, Crow Fortune," he leans in and whispers back.

"Yeah, so what. Wanna go do body shots in the boys' locker room?" I coo.

"We drank all the tequila."

"Not those kind of body shots." Beneath the table, my dancing hand makes my meaning clear. Just in case Gimp is not getting the hint.

I push my chair back. "We'll be back in a bit," I tell Allie. "We're gonna see if we can find Char."

"Whatever." Allie sighs, turning her attention to the dance floor hoedown. "You're lucky I love you."

I feel like a bad kid, looking over my shoulder, half hoping that someone is watching as I pull Gimp by the hand toward the boys' locker room. We awkwardly manoeuvre our clumsy bodies behind the heavy swinging door and into the blackness. He stops, his hand fumbling for the light switch. I keep moving and grab him by his plaid shirt, pull him close and kiss him hard. He kisses me back, but softer, more tenderly. I plant my hand in the general vicinity of Gimp's goods. He breaks away from the kiss and lifts my hand off his crotch and places it on his chest. His heart thumps along, smooth and steady.

"Listen, maybe we could do this like grown-ups, eh? Go out on a date or something."

"This is a date." I press my hips against him. "Don't wreck my dream of swaggering back out there with a freshly laid grin on my mug and my drawers in my purse. I might not get a chance like this again."

He flicks on the locker room lights. "I just...I want to be able to see you, is all."

"K, whatever, we can do it with the lights on," I say, pressing harder, trying to fling my leg around his waist, threatening to knock us both to the floor in a decidedly un-sexy way.

"Look, Crow, I don't think—"

"Dammit, Gimp, I don't have time for you to think. Are we going to do this, yes or no?"

Before he can answer, the chorus of "Smells Like Teen Spirit" comes streaming out of the place where I figured my underwear would be by now. I reach into my purse and answer my phone. It's Peggy.

"Get out to my place," she barks. "Char's up a tree with the baby and she won't come down."

5 YOU'LL WISH YOUR CAKE, DOUGH, BABY

November 19 is World Toilet Day. It is also the day I was born, and the day I damn near killed my mother, so you can bet I've heard all about that a few times. The doctor didn't know that there was a big slab of placenta blocking my exit when they jacked Mama full of Pitocin in order to evict me from her cozy womb. I was nearly three weeks overdue. The doctor chalked it up to Mama having her dates wrong, what with her being so young and poor and obviously stupid. They didn't listen when she told them that something was wrong after the first blast of Pitocin, so they gave her another one and added weak and whiny to their list of judgements about her. But she wasn't whiny or weak or stupid, despite being young and poor. She was hemorrhaging. A piece of placenta was blocking the exit and had separated, so I was trapped in a contracting uterus with nowhere to go.

Finally, a nurse had the good sense to see that my heart rate was dropping like a dirty bomb, and Mama was white and trembling. Still, the doctor said to "wait and see." Until Lucy Fortune got a hold of him. Lucy had given birth to every one of her children at home, and she knew that her daughter Effie—the toughest of them all—wasn't one to cry and moan and make a royal fool of herself over a simple thing like childbirth. So, with Lucy's persuasive hands gripping Dr. Dickey's collar, he agreed to look into the situation more closely. Within minutes, there was a frantic team of people jabbing my mother with needles to knock her out and give her blood transfusions, while another doctor told Dickey to get out of the way while he did an emergency C-section. And five minutes before *M*A*S*H*—Mama's favourite show—started, on what would be declared World Toilet Day some twenty-five years later, I entered the world. At which point, Mama almost left it when the hemorrhaging didn't stop.

Somehow, we both made it out of my birth alive. Mama came out of the ordeal with her midsection sliced from arsehole to appetite, a harrowing story to tell, and a low-key bitterness that the new *M*A*S*H* episode she missed was about her favourite character, Father Mulcahy—and I came out of it with a lingering sense of guilt over how much trouble I caused her right from the get-go.

[…]

I wonder if someday Daktari Christ MacIsaac will feel faintly haunted by that same spectre of guilt over what's happening to his mother. Char's been diagnosed with severe postpartum psychosis. What other explanation is there when a woman hitchhikes home from her high school reunion with her baby in tow after squirting a cop in the face with her breast milk? And then gleefully tells the trucker who picks her up that she's a celestial being who needs a ride to the edge of the civilized world, where she will merge into The Oneness and deliver mankind into the Cosmic Climax. And then, when she gets dropped off on the highway down by the gas station, walks to Peggy's house, where she goes into the yard, strips naked and shimmies halfway up a sixty-foot oak tree, proclaiming her barely five-month-old baby to be Icarus. With wings of light and love.

Allie was the only one sober enough to drive when Peggy called me. We got there just in time. Char had the sleeping baby in his sling, dangling from a branch, as she loudly, insanely sang "Rock-a-bye Baby." The first responders tried to appeal to her sense of reason. To rationality. To the risk. Things Char never gave a shit about at the best of times.

Gimp had a better idea. He told her that he was the maker of baby Icarus's wings, and that he'd made a mistake. The wings weren't ready. If baby Icarus tried to use them, he'd perish. Char appreciated this critical information. She let Gimp climb up a ladder to where she sat perched. She placed the baby in his waiting spastic arm, watched him climb down the ladder with her child, then climbed down herself. Gimp spoke to her slowly, gently, followed her into Crazytown, took her by the hand, and led her into the back of the waiting ambulance. Meanwhile, I was useless as tits on a bull, standing there trying not to pass out or puke at the thought of witnessing a baby killed by his mad mother. Allie stayed in the car until it was all over.

That night, after the crowd of emergency personnel and nosy neighbours had dispersed, after Daktari Christ MacIsaac was snuggled in his crib with Peg to watch over him, and after Char was sedated and en route to the lockdown psych ward at the Regional Hospital, me and Willy Gimp did the only thing we could think of to ease our rattled souls. The only thing that made any sense to burn off the jangled energy of circumvented tragedy. We went down to The Wharf, smoked a monstrous gagger of a joint, made up foolish new constellation names, and fucked in the bed of his grubby old pick-up truck while the stars of The Big Dicker twinkled overhead.

After that, everything went to hell in a handbasket.

Despite all the old dolls at the church down the road praying for me every Sunday, and the handful of pills I wash down with a bucket of sludge tea every morning, I'm getting sicker. There are days when I can't get out of bed, or see or walk or think straight. Days when all I can stomach is six Ritz crackers and a mouthful of applesauce. Char is locked up in the looney bin. Allie can barely eke out a coherent rejection when I call to see if she wants to come hang out with my sick, sorry ass. Willy has a fresh excuse every time I ask if he wants to go out for coffee. And he knows that coffee isn't what I'm really after. Mama is cranky, and still miffed that I have invaded her space and burned her papers. The best I get from her is a prolonged pat on the head, and orders to stop sooking.

Meanwhile, Peggy has become Mother Superior, beaming a warm, serene smile as she totes Daktari Christ MacIsaac everywhere she goes, espousing a steady stream of motherly wisdom she has no business pretending to have. A whole bunch of high school people also saw me at the reunion, heard about what happened with Char, heard that I'm sick, and think I'm seeing Willy. So now they've all found me on Facebook and I can't ignore their friend requests because I'm trying not to be an arsehole, in case one of them finds me half-dead in a ditch someday. The trees are naked, the water is angry, and it's cold as a witch's tit. Winter will clobber us soon. Mama says she can feel it in her bones.

Plus, somehow the student loan and credit card company

bastards have found me. I've always had a knack for spending money. Paying it back, not so much. That was Dave's job, and when we split I may have neglected a thing or two. Over the summer, I also may have racked up some new bills and overlooked some old ones. The credit card guy on the phone was none too pleased with my financial delinquency and wasn't interested in my sob story. I told the student loans people that I was dying. They didn't seem to care. Only a Form 37T filled out by a doctor, with triplicate signed copies faxed to their offices, allowing eight to twelve weeks for processing, can stop their now daily collections calls.

And Dave just texted to wish me a happy fortieth birthday. *It's thirty-nine, Fucker.* Happy World Toilet Day to me.

What the Jesus is wrong with you guys, I say every morning. *You need me. Without me, you're nothing. If you just laid low and didn't try to upgrade and make me so sick and shitty all the time, we'd all have a lot more fun.* But Parry, Ziggy, and Fuzzy do not listen. Tumours don't care that their shenanigans are cramping my farewell-tour style. They don't care that Dr. Divyaratna is talking about sticking laser blades in my brain, carpet bombing them with radiation, or soaking them in a chemo bubble bath. They don't care that it's my birthday. Probably my last. Maybe my worst.

I've had craptastic birthdays aplenty. On my fourth birthday, we invited a handful of kids from up the road. Mama made a chocolate cake and a Kraft mix weenie-topped pizza. There was pop. Cheezies. Balloons. I had a bubble bath and put on my birthday present from Nanny—my Elly May dress. It was a flouncy, frilly white number with blue satin trim and a sash. Like something worn by Elly May Clampett on *The Beverly Hillbillies.* It was reserved for the most special occasions, starting with my party. So, there I was all day—dolled up, waiting for my little friends to arrive with smiles and presents—when it started to snow. An hour before the party, a voice on the radio interrupted me and Dolly Parton singing the hell out of "Jolene" to say that the roads were a mess and the blizzard was big. Nobody wanted to be out in this weather. Wiener pizza, pop, Cheezies, and chocolate cake are not meant to be eaten alone, nor with a side of hysterical four-year-old tears.

"Stacey dear," Mama said plainly, "you'll have worse than that before you're twice married."

But I did get to wear the Elly May dress again, on the day of my Nanny's funeral a year and a bit later. The one I wasn't allowed to go to. Everybody else got all dressed up on that day, but the dummies wore black. Nanny hated black. She loved my Elly May dress. So I wore it for her, even though only the babysitter saw it.

There were other shitty birthdays, too. My seventeenth was spent in the trunk of Allie's car, hiding from Duke the Puke's psycho girlfriend because she heard I flirted with Duke in chemistry class, although Duke inflicting tit twisters on me was hardly my idea of flirting. On my twenty-first, I passed out on the bathroom floor of some guy's apartment, and woke up covered in puke that wasn't my own. Then there was my thirty-fifth, when I caught Dave kissing some skank at a restaurant. But at least I got diamond earrings out of that.

I'll call this one a win if I can get through it without a snowstorm, puke, or infidelity.

I go for a birthday walk down to The Wharf. Opening the windows to air the stench of Javex and boiled eggs out of the trailer just isn't cutting it. A rude wind shoves its way down from where the mouth of the lake yawns at the Atlantic Ocean. The bare trees on the mountain just stand there, rooted in dry apathy, waiting for winter. White-toothed waves bite at the shore, and there's no sun to soften and shimmer up the edges of their agitation. Banks of elephantine cloud lumber along, never leaving enough time and space for a crack of sky to appear between them. A half-dozen shit hawks scream overhead. And some jackass left a pile of puke and a used condom on the picnic table, even though there is a goddamn garbage can right there. Even so, this place still makes me feel better.

I caress the cool edge of the concrete edifice, legs dangling above the choppy waters, face lifted to the obstinate elephants above. I fill my lungs with the cool tang of salt air, and try my best to empty some bitterness from my soul. But all I can hear is the chorus of a song looping in my head. The song Peggy and Mama serenaded me with in the wake of my ninth birthday party, when I got a little melodramatic over the lack of Black Forest cake, and not being allowed to keep a loot bag for myself or have the first crack at the creepy Cabbage Patch Kid piñata. Except Mama and Peg took Lesley Gore's pouty party song to the next level, with flailing arms and stomping feet and fake boo-hoos. It takes me a minute to realize that "It's My Party" isn't simply looping with hyperrealism in my head. It's playing in my pocket. I wonder which smartass changed the ringtone to that.

On the other end is Willy Gimp, chatting me up. Like nothing ever happened. Like we didn't share in the trauma of Becky Chickenshit step-dancing at the reunion and Char dangling her baby from a tree. Like we didn't exorcise that trauma with orgasms under the stars. Like he didn't drop off the face of the Earth for five weeks. Casual as ol' hell, he wishes me happy birthday. And then asks me out on a date. A real one, that doesn't involve shotgunning enough liquor to choke a squid, or quickies in the woods. Tonight.

"What makes you think I don't already have plans?" I say, not too nicely. Because if there is one thing I learned from years of devouring *Cosmo*, it is how to play hard to get.

"Well, do ya?"

"Maybe. I'll let you know in an hour. Or two." I stuff my phone back in my pocket, and hustle my arse back to the trailer to shower off the eau de loser I've been wallowing in, and de-fuzz five weeks' worth of leg and pit hair. Then I call Gimp back.

"Fine," I say, "you can take me out tonight. But I'm warning you, I'm wearing the sluttiest dress I owned in high school, and no drawers." Because if there is another thing I learned from years of devouring *Cosmo*, it's how to play easy.

"God love your trampy little heart." Gimp laughs. "I'll pick you up at four thirty."

[…]

"You cleans up good," he marvels as I slide into the truck. Eyes traced in perfect almonds of smoky black, lips painted scarlet, big honkin' birthday infidelity diamond earrings to offset the inch and a half Monchhichi monkey doll hair that's glued down with green apple–scented gel I found in my closet. What is the worst thing that could happen from using twenty-year-old hair product? I live on the edge of danger.

"The b'ys at the Burger King are gonna be gawkin'," Gimp says. I note his dirty ripped jeans, plaid shirt, and grubby fleece jacket that says Northside Sharp Shooters Dart League on the breast.

"Where are we going, seriously?" I am afraid to ask, but do. Because I live on the edge of danger.

"Burger King," he says, straight as a pin. "The nice one. Out in Town, Town. Just a couple of quick stops first."

I flip down the sun visor and begin examining my fancy face in the mirror. I blot some lipstick onto the back of my hand and carefully dab away at the thick rim of eyeliner with the pad of my thumb. I fidget with the sky-high hem of my dress, and suddenly wish I'd worn cheaper earrings. And jeans. And a bra with a little less oomph. Maybe some drawers.

The first stop is Willy's garage. He goes in looking like a dart-chucking greaser and comes out fifteen minutes later looking like a guy who is not, in fact, dragging a whored-up fuck buddy to the Burger King for her birthday. His white button-up shirt is crisp and clean, and ever so slightly clinging to the sharply cut peaks and valleys of his chest and arms. His shaggy hair has been smoothed and swept to the side. He ambles back out to the truck, his awkward gait looking almost like a swagger. I stop lamenting my lack of underwear.

"Christ, Gimp, are those cufflinks?"

"One hundred per cent genuine cubic zirconia," he says, hoisting his wrists up onto the steering wheel. "There. We go together a bit better now, eh?"

"Parts of us anyway." I stroke his leg and nip my mascara-laden eye into a playful, seductive wink.

"You're a bad winker," he says, as if that's just an obvious fact. "Looks like you're taking a seizure. Or try'na let one rip."

"Shut up. Maybe I am."

"Stick to crotch grabs and kissy faces." He pats my leg, as I do my best to ignore the little orange sparks and electric blue squiggles exploding around his head. "One more surprise stop. Then, dinner."

"What's the stop?"

"To see Char. Nobody's visited her yet."

My face flushes with shame. She called me a few days after she went into the hospital and started regaling me with paranoid rants about whispering widows in spruce trees and gods in her instant mashed potatoes. After ten minutes of that, I told myself that the call dropped. But it didn't. After that, I dodged her daily dozen calls for a week, until I finally called the hospital and told them to tell her my phone was broken so she'd stop.

"It's your birthday and all, but I think we should give that poor soul a dose of love, wha?" Gimp smiles.

The lockdown psych ward at the Regional is probably better than the old Butterscotch Palace, but not by much. The narrow mint-green corridors begin and end with hulking doors that require three different security codes before they heave open with a shrill alarm. The soundscape arches from claustrophobic silence to haunted howls to unbridled laughter of the unsettlingly maniacal variety, as bodies are shuffled in and out of sight. It smells like Band-Aids and feels like limbo. Not quite hell, but you can see it from here.

It's the tail end of visiting hours. The orderly ushers us down the hall as a chaotic parade passes by. A young man goose steps along, yelling at the water fountain. An older woman tells me that she loves my hair, asks if I have a razor. The hospital PA crackles to life in the name of a code yellow, and a half-dozen newly electrified staff dart to the nearest grey leviathan door.

In the corner of the common room, Char is belting out an off-key version of "Hotel California" to a six-foot-tall ficus plant. She thinks it talks back to her and tells her to keep singing, which is certainly further proof of madness. Any plant in its right rhizome can tell that she's as tone-deaf as a telephone pole.

Despite being jacked full of every psychosis-busting drug known to modern psychopharmacology for a solid month, Char is still out of her mind. But she's elated to see us. I feel like I'm going to be sick, as a dizzying burst of blue-violet ribbons spring from her ears, bookending the alternating flashes of olive green and lemon pie–yellow emanating from the top of her head.

Gimp sees that I'm wobbly and white. He wraps his arm around my waist, and I relax a little, knowing that he'll catch me with his good arm if I drop.

"My saviours!" Char gasps as she dashes toward us with open arms. "I knew you guys would come. See that one?" she says, pointing to the nurse in the locked Plexiglas vestibule. "She has the papers you need to sign. I'm not sure who has the papers to get Horatio out. The janitor, maybe."

Horatio is the ficus plant. He, too, is being held against his will. The ignorant "sheeple" here only *think* he is a plant, but he is not. He is a philosopher king, and once he is exposed to fresh air, mankind will have a great "epissamee."

I smile and nod, lost as how to deal with her in this mess of delusion. I wince as she grabs me by the shoulders, staring at me with insane intensity. "Oh, Crow," she cackles, "Horatio said you'd be stumped!"

But there's Gimp to the rescue again. He tells her, with all the sincerity in the world, that King Horatio needs her to stay here and sing to him until the time is right. He tells her that she should only listen to the whispers that are helpful and beautiful and kind and wise. He tells her that we all love her. She hugs us both, telling Willy that she'll take good care of King Horatio if we take good care of each other. Then, in the middle of her green and yellow madness, a clear violet-blue flare forms. Stable, calm, and real. Like a flash of lucidity, born of my own tumour-induced delusion.

"Give my baby a kiss for me," Char says. "And tell Peggy thank you for doing her best."

Then, the lucid flare disappears and Char jumps head-long into an animated series of generic lunacy: illuminati are running the entertainment industry, 9/11 was a conspiracy, capitalist devils are poisoning us, and corporations are wrecking the planet. Crazy talk.

She shuts up all of a sudden, smiles, twirls, and dances away from us with a dismissive wave. But just before the nurse lets us out, she charges back down the hall toward us, stopping short at a hollering distance.

"Crow! Good news, bad news!" Char's arms and dread-locks flail around like the limbs of a psychotic octopus as she rushes toward me. "There's a brand new misfortune a-brewing," she says in an ominous almost chant. "With your cortex on a caper, you can *carpe diem*, rainbow warrior." A broad smile suddenly splits across her face, and I jump when her clammy hands grip my cheeks as she yells "Seeeees the day!" before she plants a rough, sloppy kiss on my lips and twirls away. Then, she turns back, the smile replaced by an earnestness that I've never seen on Char's face before. "Oh, and tell Allie to watch what she eats over Christmas. Sharp daisies can't release the past. Love flows better than blood. So tell her I'm sorry, too." Then she vanishes behind a giant tattooed bald man. And we disappear back out into the real world, where it's snowing like a bastard.

This isn't pretty snow. This is tiny little pills pelting down, stinging, bouncing, accumulating quickly. The grey-white immovable bully of a sky fires a bazillion tight little spit balls at us, and the sidekick wind roars in taunting laughter, driving them even more sideways. Still, Gimp manages to get a joint lit before we reach the truck, making the walk through the hospital parking lot more amusing than Char's cryptic craziness and this asshole weather stunt, combined.

[···]

Behind the derelict old bank building looks like a place where bad things happen. The windows are boarded up. The cornerstone, eroded and crumbling. Ample evidence that artistically inclined chaps like "Sk8r H8r," "Dickwad," and "FCKTHAPOLICE" come straight here after they lift a can of spray paint from the hardware store. And bad things do happen here. At least they did the last time I was here with Weasel Tobin.

We came to this parking lot on a "date" in the car he stole from his grandmother. While we were in the back seat fooling around, we heard yelling and screaming. Then we saw this big greasy old guy drag his big greasy old girlfriend into the alley, beat the piss out of her, and try to light her straggly bleached blonde hair on fire with a Zippo. The cops showed up, cuffed 'em, and chucked 'em in the paddy wagon. Just when we thought the coast was clear, an officer tapped on the window of Weasel's grandmother's car, told us to get dressed and come out for a chat. He asked what we saw. Not much, we said. The cop laughed, giving Weasel a wink and an elbow as he said, "Right on, brother!" and recommended a few alternative places to go parking before he left. Moments later, Weasel informed me that it was a good thing they didn't search the car, what with two pounds of hash and five hundred hits of acid in the trunk. The guy who beat up his girlfriend was Moose Matheson, who Weasel was supposed to meet at Pott's Coffee in an hour to make a delivery on behalf of Paco Landry. Willy chuckles when I tell him the story. I'm too stoned and too old to know if it's funny or sad. Or both.

"Nobody's getting beat or busted here tonight. Not even any drugs in the truck, except the medicinals." Gimp leans over and kisses my cheek.

Next thing I know, his hand is wrestling a tie around his neck. He drapes a black blazer over my shoulders when we step out into the weather, takes my hand and leads me to the rundown entrance. Part of me still feels like we're breaking into an abandoned building to drink and smoke and screw like dumb kids, which would still be among the better ways I can think of to spend my thirty-ninth birthday. Instead, the dirty old door opens without kicking or jimmying. We walk down into the basement of the old bank.

"Welcome to The Vault," Willy's voice purrs in my ear as we glide into Cape Breton's answer to high-end dining.

It's a swanky little place. The texture and depth of the original brick walls are accentuated by a deep red glaze. Ornate antique picture-less frames have been painted black, slightly scuffed, and hung on the walls in a laissez-faire way. Candles and strings of fairy lights create a warm glow where shadows and light play together. *Damn, Cape Breton, when'd you get hip and classy enough to spawn something like this?*

"And they make the best pizza in the world," Gimp says.

"How come you've been hiding from me since the whole reunion debacle?" I try to say all cute and coy, so as not to kill the mood before we get drinks and pizza and a chance to grope each other.

"Not you I'm hiding from," he says. "Just stuff. With Chrissy."

I can make a semi-educated guess about what he means by "stuff" based on the dirt I heard from Mama and Peggy. Chrissy got into the OxyContin again. Chrissy's brother Cracker is protective of his baby sister, and he wants her in rehab. And what Cracker Parsons wants, he gets. They call him Cracker because he's not afraid to breaks things. Laws. Windows. Legs.

Lucky for Willy, I'm not in the mood to press for details. All I want is pizza, wine, cake, and a birthday lay in the dark sketchy parking lot behind the old bank. Or, in the wheel-chair-accessible bathroom of The Vault, which we occupy just long enough to make it look suspicious when we wander back to our table. As if the ear-to-ear grins weren't enough to give us away. Happy World Toilet Day to me. Outside, it just keeps snowing.

[···]

Willy groans as he rolls over onto his back, stretching himself awake beneath the cool, clean whiteness of the king-sized hotel bedding. I languidly stroke the ginger-haired mer-maid inked into the sea of his bare bicep, thinking about childhood summers at The Wharf. And the time Ricky Dicks called me a whale, even though I was clearly trying to swim like a mermaid.

"So how was that for a birthday?" Gimp nuzzles in closer to me.

I want to say wonderful, because it was. The part where we walked out of the restaurant and into a full-on blizzard, and realized we were stuck here for the night. The part where we took a cab to the nicest hotel in Town, Town and the cab driver tried not to gawk at us in the rear-view mirror while we made out, and then let us smoke a joint in his car. The part where they almost didn't let us have this swanky hotel room because Gimp was so high and giddy that he kept giving them his Air Miles instead of his credit card. The part where Gimp and I *slept* together and then slept *together*, tossing and turning and drooling and dreaming like people who love each other do.

Instead of telling him it was wonderful though, I just mumble, "Not bad." Because all of it made me feel so alive. Which reminds me that I'm dying. As Gimp wraps an arm around me and pulls me even closer, my gut clenches with a claustrophobic guilt over letting him think he can love a dying woman. Or that a dying woman can love him. I push away and make a mad dash to the spacious, pristine hotel suite bathroom and unleash a gush of undigested urgency into the spacious, pristine hotel suite toilet.

I'd like to make this morning after feel as non-awkward and un-weird as possible. But, no dice. Awkward and weird ooze from my ungraceful stagger as I emerge from the can. Awkward and weird cling to my surprisingly unruly buzz cut bed-head and garbage breath. Awkward and weird roll in and settle like a bank of fog on the Bras d'Or when I crawl back in bed with him, and stare up at the ceiling because I don't want to see his face when I say, "So. What's the deal here? What *are* we?"

This is not the first time these words have been uttered between us. The summer before I started grade twelve, we were joined at the hip in public. In private, we were joined at other parts, but neither of us would fess up to that. One August night as we sat on the beach doing post-coital bottle tokes and trying to shimmy the sand out of our arse cracks, he stared up at the clear, ceilingless sky and said those exact words to me: "So. What's the deal here? What *are* we?"

And I laughed. Not to be mean, but because it just seemed so random, so out of the blue. We'd been doing this kind of thing off and on for years. It seemed silly that all of a sudden it needed to have a name. That there was even a "deal" or a "we." That there was anything other than a mutual desire to smoke and laugh and fuck. A wounded look sunk into his faraway eyes, and right then I knew there was nothing funny about it to him.

"I don't know." I shrugged. "This is perfect. This is what all the other wankers out there with their cheesy pet names and promise rings and four-month anniversaries of their first dry hump, this is what they really wish they had. Why fuck up something good with a label?" Then I sucked back my bottle toke, grabbed Gimp by the face and stuck my tongue in his mouth. Or something like that.

So now, I am lying here praying like hell that he won't say the same thing. Because while I was puking my tumour-riddled brains out in the bathroom just now, I had my own epiphany. I don't want to be alone on a hospital ward, with no one but my mother to bear full witness to my life and death. I need a steady, consistent supply of partnership, of love, of high-quality mutually orgasmic sexual encounters before I die. I want it carved in stone. Labelled for everyone to see. And I want it with Willy Gimp. I think.

"Ahhh, the ol' 'what are we' conversation." Gimp sighs. My eyes stay glued to the ceiling. Still, the room spins, my stomach churns again, and in my peripheral vision I can see pale grey clouds tinged with a sour yellow and royal blue gathering around Willy's head. And I suddenly wish I'd kept my big mouth shut.

"Crow, you know I can't —" and that's the moment his phone rings. "Shit. I gotta take this."

He yanks on his boxer shorts with one hand and presses his phone to his ear with the other while he shuffles to the bathroom and closes the door. Three minutes later, he is off the phone and pulling the half-buttoned white dress shirt over his head.

"What's up? Something at the garage?" I say, using Occam's razor to cut through all the wild assumptions and speculations I managed to jump to in the span of a three-minute hushed phone conversation.

"It's complicated. Want me to drop you off somewhere in Town, or stay here and I'll come back and get ya later because I gotta —"

"I want you to tell me what the fuck is going on. I'm a big girl. I can handle it."

Softening, slowing down, bracing for the wounded look he knows he's about to see in my faraway eyes when he tells me, he says, "You want the truth?" Like he knows the answer.

"No. Probably not. Lie to me." I stare back up at the ceiling, pouring my fractured attention back into observing the little swirls of plaster. Because for all the times I claim to want truth, it turns out I mostly want comfort. And comfort tends to come swaddled in lies.

"I gotta go rescue a sick and hurt old cat," he says as he gathers his cufflinks and shoes, and smooths his salt-and-pepper bed-head. "She's trapped under a pile of garbage, and I'm the one who accidentally left that garbage there so it's my fault. And the old cat's brother is a pit bull who will rip my balls off if I don't go help."

"Jesus, I said I wanted a lie. Not a stupid cat metaphor for the truth."

"It is complic —"

"It's always complicated," I sulk. "Go drag that nasty old pussy out of whatever dumpster she flung herself in."

"Do you want me to —"

"No. I can take care of myself."

So here I am, storm-stranded in a hotel in beautiful downtown Town, Town, feeling like I got dragged through a knothole backwards, with no underwear, a face full of sex-smeared makeup, and a little black dress that screams walk of shame. I may well be one year older, but I'm sure as hell none the wiser.

The cogent streams of searing hot water in the hotel shower makes for quite a sharp contrast to the lukewarm iron-smelling dribble dunks that I take at Mama's house. As the water pelts my skin, I come to a needling, precise realization: I need truth. Truth about my family. Truth about my father. Truth about myself. It's not going to find itself. It's not gonna drop from the sky. I'm gonna have to boot down some doors and drag all the family skeletons out to play, myself. Truth with a capital T is another item for my

Fuck It List, and I best not be burning daylight. I scrub my scalded skin dry, squirm back into my dress, and go ask the bright-eyed girl at the front desk to call me a taxi.

"Might be kinda tricky to get someone out on them roads today, ma'am," she says, laying on a thick commercial brogue. "Lemme call our handyman Roger, though. He's got a four-wheel drive. Get you wherever you need to go. He's right good like that."

"I have a few stops to make. And I need to get to the Northside," I say, hoping she'll just call me a cab and not subject me to more chit-chat about this Roger buddy.

I almost tell her that I'm from here. That she can drop the aren't-we-just-the-nicest-people-on-the-planet shtick and just biff me into the body-odour-scented, cigarette-burned back seat of a City Slicker Taxi Cab, driven by an ex-con named Rooster. And I can charge Gimp's credit card for the extra coffee pods and pillow case I tucked in my purse on the way out. But really, what good would that do? I need to get where I need to go.

"Thank you," I say, bringing my hands into a grateful-looking Namaste position, doing a half-assed little flakey bitch bow, and trying to sound like I'm from somewhere really exotic. Like Toronto. Or BC even. "All the brochures were right. This place is truly magical. Everyone is just. So. Friendly."

"Oh look, he's out there now! Just go hop in and tell him where you need to go." Then, with her grandest grin yet, she says, "Nice to see ya, Crow. Tell your mom that Corrine Burton's daughter Julie says hi, will ya?"

Behind the wheel of the big, beige Cossack that looks like a cardboard box jacked up on monster truck wheels, plastered with bumper stickers of "Why Be Normal" and "Magic Happens" and "Welcome to Cape Breton, Set Your Clock Back 20 Years," and with two massive spruce trees lashed to the roof, sits grizzled old Roger the handyman. He introduces himself as I try to hoist myself into the passenger seat without flashing him. His last name's Leblanc, but here it is pronounced "Lib-Long." His people were from over Chéticamp way. Shetty Camp.

Before I can ask, Roger Lib-long volunteers the story of the trees. "Christmas trees for the malls," he tells me. "Cuts 'em off me buddy Skip's land out in Mira Gut, and delivers 'em to the malls every year, for the Christmas Daddies Telethon."

"Appreciate the ride," I say as I pull out my phone to text Allie, hoping she'll pick me up in Town if the highway over the mountain's not too bad. Also hoping that my full immersion in my little screen is a clear signal that I'm not in the mood for conversation.

Roger Leblanc doesn't get the hint.

"You from here or away?" he says.

Trick question. Damned either way. If I say "away," I'm in for a grilling about where and why I came, followed by tales of somebody's sister's husband's first cousin twice removed who visited that place once in 1981. If I say "here," I'll get the classic "Whereabouts?" and "What's your father's name?"

"Family's here. I'm back from away," I mumble.

"Where ya back from?"

"Toronto."

"The big Shitty. Oops, pardon my French!" He claps a hand over his wrinkled clown smile, as if the word shitty fell out from between the gaps where some teeth should have been. As if a playful swear might offend the buzz-cut-haired, hooker-dressed, drawers-less human hangover in the passenger seat. "My brother's son lives up there now. Works on that there Bay Street. Stuart Lib-Long. Ever hear tell of him up there?"

"No." I smile politely, trying to ignore the good-natured twinkles of earthen orange and leafy green Highland flinging around Roger Leblanc's noggin.

"What's your father's name?" he says with a musical lilt.

Yep, here we go.

"Alec Spenser."

And that's when poor ol' Roger damn near puts us in the ditch when he reefs on the brake and lets out a belt of knee-slapping glee.

"Well, didn't I know your father, then!" he whoops. "Poor bugger woulda flunked grade ten without me lettin' him skiff off my sheets. Poor Smart Alec, God rest his soul."

"So which Fortune do you belong to then?" he starts up again after a short, awkward silence, his fingertips doing a delicate drum on the steering wheel.

"Effie," I say absently, retreating from the scenery and back into my cellphone screen, anxiously awaiting confirmation that Allie will come get my underdressed ass.

"Yes, yes. Crow, is it?"

"Yeah." My voice does not waiver from the curt side of friendly.

"Quite the rigs, them Spensers. Smart Alec was a good head, though. What brought you back?"

"Illness in the family."

"Sorry to hear that," he says solemnly, and stays quiet for the rest of the ride, like he somehow gathered that the illness in the family is mine.

Roger Leblanc wheels right up to the front doors of the Bay Flower Mall. As in, up over the curb. All the way under the awning at the main entrance, the trees on the roof scratching against snow-laden canvas as we get within spitting distance of the automatic sliding doors of the Island's grandest shopping mecca, currently a blizzardy ghost town.

"You got time for a little shopping while I get the tree set up. Hop out here, dear. Save you a trek through that snow," he says. "Meet you right in this same spot in 'alf an 'our."

The last time I set foot in this mall was when Char, Allie, and I went to Le Drapeau hunting for skin-tight shirts, platform espadrilles, and giant earrings to complement our grad caps and gowns. When a pock-faced rent-a-cop with a big gut and a tiny walkie-talkie started following us, Char got a little riled up. She asked him if he was following us because we looked like shoplifters or because he liked high school–girl asses. She pulled a wad of cash out of her purse and waved it in his face, before she marched over to the counter, where she demanded to speak to the manager. Char railed about her ample disposable income, her right to be respected as a customer, and her trend-setting influence among the sophisticatedly slutty high school set. Minutes later, Char strutted out with a smug grin, a heartfelt apology, and a twenty per cent off coupon. And in our grad pictures, all three of us are wearing shiny new Le Drapeau earrings that Char lifted from the store when the rent-a-cop wasn't looking.

There's no rent-a-cop in sight now. There's no "I Heart CB" souvenir T-shirt shop that sells loose cigs and hash pipes. No dark, dodgy arcade for the burnouts and the drug dealers. No old guys picking butts out of the ashtrays beside the benches down past the food court. No kids skateboarding inside. No big-haired mall rats. The mall isn't the glorious teenage wasteland of my memory. Now, it's just a place to shop. Le Drapeau is still there but no longer the bastion of cheap, tight, teenybopper crap it once was. Now it is "European-style" designer collections and two hundred dollar dresses. I make a beeline for it, thinking about Char the entire time.

Minutes later, I'm slinking out of Le Drapeau, embarrassed and empty-handed. Turns out that what was left on the overdraft of my bank account wouldn't buy the pack of drawers and warm gloves I spent twenty minutes picking out. I wander down to the far end of the mall, choking back hungover, flat-broke, post-birthday tears and lamenting the fact that my five-finger-discount friend is locked up in the Nouveau Butterscotch, just when I need her most. The scummy arcade has been replaced by one of those anything-for-a-buck stores. The lone employee who made it in for her shift on this stormy morning hauls a series of big cardboard bins out front, as if the hordes of little old ladies who dribble away their measly pensions on hair curlers and peppermints and plastic flowers there are still coming today. She scuttles out of sight as I near the storefront, and I pick up the pace for fear that the reek of sweatshops and chemicals will set off a wave of sick. Until something in one of the bins catches my eye. Something shiny. A pair of metallic-black gloves, the cuffs bedazzled with bright teal rhinestones. There's no rent-a-cop in sight. But there's now a pair of criminally cheap, gaudy, glittery gloves from a cardboard bin jammed into my purse, as I make my way to the mall exit.

I wait until I'm in a secluded corner outside Pott's Coffee before I pull out the gloves, and when I do, a crumpled twenty dollar bill comes tumbling out of my purse. I have no idea where it came from, until I do. Gimp must have stuffed it in there before he left me, and for a moment, I can't help feel a bit like a hooker. A shoplifting hooker who was too dumb to dress for the weather and eat the free continental breakfast at the hotel. There's a moment of moral quandary, where I think about going back to the anything-for-a-buck store to pay for the chintzy gloves. Or at least discretely dump them back in the bin and return to Le Drapeau to spend my new-found fortune on something to assuage my guilt. Like underwear. Instead, I stalk into Pott's Coffee with my crumpled twenty and stalk out with a burned bagel and coffee that needed four sugars to be drinkable. I catch a glimpse of myself in the mall mirrors. The ones I used to preen in, imagining I looked like the sassy girls in tampon commercials. Now, I just look old and sick, and like an arsehole for not buying a coffee for the guy who drove me here. Back into Pott's Coffee I go, to get one for ol' Roger Leblanc.

"Great minds think alike, and fools seldom differ," Roger says, holding out the coffee he bought for me, as I pass him the one I got for him. "But if there were no fools there'd be no fun!" He gives me another fatherly wink. "So, I'm to what's left of the mall down the Northside in Town with one of them stinky spruce. Yourself?"

The breath I draw through my nose rushes in deep and audible, inflating me with the kind of determined courage that would make Mama proud, if it weren't being used to do something that would make her have a conniption fit.

"You know the Spensers' place? Big house up on the hill?" I ask.

"Indeed I do," he says.

"There," I say.

"Good, dear, good," he says.

And God love Roger for not letting me go out in the cold in my pretty black dress. He gives me the Toronto Maple Leafs toque and the giant green cable knit sweater that he keeps in the back seat in case of emergency. They go great with my hot, sparkly gloves.

[···]

When I ring the ornate doorbell of the big fancy house on the big fancy hill, I am told by the golden-haired, sour-faced, beige-suited woman at the door that Rosalind Spenser is not here. She's dead. Just yesterday she succumbed to the cancer that had chased her for decades. I give my condolences. It occurs to me that the woman at the door must be my father's sister, Sarah. I tell her who I am.

"Oh," is her tight, flat response.

"I'd like to talk. May I come in?" I say, using my best professionally persuasive face to offset the air of lunacy surely exuded by the Leafs toque, oversized sweater, rhinestone gloves, and trampy black dress I'm sporting.

"If you must."

This is the woman who stood beside my father at the cottage in the Hall of Shame picture from Mama's photo album, with her long, pin-straight hair, her pressed and pleated baby blue sundress, and only the tips of her perfect teeth peeking out from between cagily parted lips. She was the lithe, glamourous guardian of the little boys in blue suits, who wouldn't look at me. She acted like I wasn't even there on that Christmas Eve when I was eight. Sarah Spenser is pushing sixty now but has done her damnedest to make sure that the march of years didn't leave any trail on her face. Her hair is carefully shaded with pale blonde camouflage. There is smooth, taut skin where her crow's feet and smile lines ought to be, and there's not enough fat on her to grease a skillet. By the looks of things, she's applied the same aesthetic ethos to the old family home. Erased its lines, its age, its history, and left only the bare bones. Crystal chandeliers and glass cabinets with expensive tchotchkes must have smacked of déclassé excess. Instead of an opulent hum of voices and music, cinnamon scents and warm firelights, the house is eerily silent, and engulfed by the smell of fresh paint and new plastic. Under Saint Sarah's watchful blue eyes, the Spenser house has been made smooth and modern, and I can't help but think she might have knocked back a bottle of celebratory champagne on the night her mother died. Alone.

Sarah gestures to a small, awkwardly angled leather chair. I sit, trying not to be rattled or distracted as my eyes conjure what look like patches of black ice on a slush-grey strip of highway weaving all around her head, her shoulders, her chest. She pours a single cup of tea into a delicate china cup and takes a sip.

Her meticulously pencilled sapphire eyes shoot little spitball ice pellets at me when I smile and say, "Some tea would be lovely. Thank you."

She dribbles some scalding, pallid liquid into another cup she has to leave the room to get, even though there are a half-dozen nice ones on the table right in front of her. From the first sip, it is clear that she can't brew a cup of tea worth a pinch of shit. But that's all right. I didn't come here for the tea. I came here for stories. For truth. I won't try to break the ice. I'll melt it instead.

"So, how are your sons?" I say, remembering the two boys I awkwardly had hot chocolate and cookies with here once upon a time.

"Stepsons. Ex-stepsons. Their father received a sizable settlement in the divorce, so I imagine they are fine."

"Oh. I didn't know that," I say, feeling sheepish. The Spensers have always been adept at keeping their stories out of the mouths of the chattering class, and God knows Mama can't even say their name without spitting venom, but still. Somebody should have tipped me off that Sarah got divorced and Rosalind died. It's hard to talk with a foot in your mouth.

"That's the essence of why I'm here, I guess." My smile is soft and warm, even as she glares at me. "I don't know much about my father, or you, or this family. I've been diagnosed with brain tumours and I might not have a whole lot of time, so I thought—"

"Thought what? We owe you something?" she sneers. "Money? A history lesson? The time of day?"

"A cup of tea and an honest conversation would suffice." I give my head what looks like a friendly tilt, but I'm really just trying to keep a lifetime of cynical questions from leaping out.

"Here's all you need to know." Her nails tap the edge of her teacup. "Your mother was a slut, my brother was an idiot, and this whole island is full of lazy, self-righteous have-nots like you who think that my family owes them something. It has been forever thus, from the day my great-grandfather invested in his first mine here."

"Oh. That the mine where two of my slut mother's lazy brothers were killed, or the one where they hired goons to beat the self-righteous miners, their wives, and their children

146

for wanting water and electricity?" I say, unable to tilt my head further or bite my tongue hard enough. "Maybe you're the one who needs a history lesson."

She stands up and gestures toward the foyer. "I'll see you to the door. I trust you've had your fill of tea and honest conversation."

I put down the half-assed tea in the second-tier cup and slowly hoist myself to stand. "Well, Mama was right. You are a piece of work, aren't ya, Saint Sarah?"

I steady myself against a table, as another dizzying bout of technicolour tumour-vision takes hold, this time spilling layers of jade green and sickly bubble-gum-pink around the periphery of Sarah's face.

"I have no interest in what any of you people think of me," she says through gritted teeth. "But if you want to know what really happened to Alec, consider that there might be something your mother and her family isn't telling you. Desperate people are capable of anything. And the Fortunes are nothing if not desperate." She strides toward me and sweeps an arm toward the door. "Now if you'll excuse me, I have a business to run."

I nod politely as she ushers me to the door.

"Before she passed on, Mother said she encountered you and Effie at the hospital." Sarah Spenser flashes a perfectly aligned smile. "She knew *what* you were just by looking at you."

"Really," I say as I clumsily wrench my shoes on, simultaneously trying to process what Sarah Spenser implied about my father and my family. "And what's that?"

"A troublemaker," she sniffs.

"Well that's probably the nicest thing she's ever said now,

isn't it?" I sniff right back just before she snaps the door shut behind me as I teeter down the icy steps.

Roger meets me on the path, waving around my phone as it whines "It's My Party" at top volume.

"This thing has been singing its brains out for a bit now. I didn't want to answer 'er for fear of gittin' you in hot water." He smiles and winks.

I fumble to answer it as he shuffles back to warm up the Cossack.

"Finally!" Peggy thunders at my hello. "Where the Joe Jesus are you?"

"None of your business," I say.

"What kind of a stunt was that, not coming home last night? Your mother was worried sick. Tell me where you are. I'm coming to get you."

"No, it's okay, Allie will—"

The phone warbles with an incoming text message. From Allie. Saying she can't come get me.

"Your mother worked an overnight, and now she's home in bed feeling like garbage." Peggy resumes her guilt trip. "I told her I'd find you and bring you home. Now, I don't know what you're up to, Crow, but you're old enough to know better. Where are you?"

With a fake sigh of fake acquiescence, I say, "In Town. Pick me up at the mall. And do me a favour? Bring me a coat and a blanket or something."

I end the call before she can ask me any questions. And just past the spot where the lit-up nativity scene would have been thirty-one years ago, I roll up the sleeves of Roger Leblanc's cable knit sweater, pull the Toronto Maple Leafs toque tight around my ears, and hurl a jet of bitter, weak tea and strong, sweet coffee into a pristine snowbank in the Spenser family's yard.

[···]

The first words out of Peggy's mouth when I climb in the car that sputters up into the greasy mall parking lot are, "Didja hear about Chrissy Parsons? Found her this morning with an overdose, barely breathing. And guess where she was?"

I don't have to guess.

"Front steps of your little boyfriend's dope shack," Peggy says, rubbing salt gossip into invisible wounds.

"He's not my boyfriend." I cocoon myself up in the faded floral of the cigarette-and-baloney scented comforter she brought.

"Good thing." Peggy nods stoically. "Because Shirl heard that Chrissy Parsons is having a baby for him. Crack baby, by the sounds of it."

"So if he's not your boyfriend, what is he then?" she needles into my silence.

"Nothing," I say. And I mean it.

[···]

"The other old quiff finally croaked." Mama beams as she soaks in her morning ritual of scanning the obits and sipping her G & Tea. "Good riddance, Rosalind Spenser."

I pretend that I haven't already known about Rosalind Spenser's death for days, just like I pretend that I never went to see Sarah Spenser. I'm less adept at pretending that I'm not sicker and weaker, going downhill fast. I throw up fifteen times a day. I sleep ten hours at night and take three or four long naps in between barfing fits. Exhaustion is woven into every fibre of my being. My headache is dull and constant, and only abates when it is supplanted by full-fledged explosions of intense agony. The novelty and amusement of the pseudo-psychedelic vision has thoroughly worn off, too. So now I pretend I don't see it.

Dr. Divyaratna calls it all "the expected trajectory of the illness." A sign the tumours are probably growing, because there is no real hope of getting better. Every time I see her and tell her what's happening, her pretty face stirs and crinkles with consternation as her black pen rips out a manic scrawl of notes. Due to the devious positioning of Parry Homunculus, Ziggy Stardust, and Fuzzy Wuzzy, she lists a whole host of new symptoms I can look forward to. More "sensory abnormalities": mood swings, personality changes, distortions of memory, cognitive gaps, confabulations. She recommends giving some new meds a whirl and starting an aggressive treatment protocol as soon as possible, which would probably give me a few more months of living, during which I'd still look and feel like death. I ask her about quality of life versus quantity of life. I ask her what she would do if she were me. She says she doesn't know. There are no easy answers. Just hard choices.

[···]

"Stop bein' such a sook and help me get the tree off the roof," Mama orders, letting the trailer door slam shut behind her as she tromps out into the crusty white wasteland of our yard.

Sure enough, there's a big, bushy, six-foot cat-piss spruce strapped to the roof of Mama's car with a half-dozen bungee cords. "Crooked as me arse, stinks already, but it was free. Beggars can't be choosers," she says, almost cheerfully, as she starts yanking on the cord clasps with her gloveless, gnarled hands.

Cheerful is not generally a word that describes Mama. Not even almost. So when I hear her humming a light and peppy tune as she irons her ridiculous Greeting Gale housekeeping frock, or when she wordlessly shuffles my head onto her lap and slowly, maternally runs her hands over my bristly head in the evenings as I lie on the couch yelling at the dummies on *Jeopardy*, or when she voluntarily calls Peggy, and the conversation doesn't send Mama into a fit of exasperated eye rolls...I get suspicious.

She's drinking more these days. Or drinking different, at least. Not getting as deep in her cups at night, but spreading her beverages out through the day in a more creative fashion. A shot of gin in her morning tea. A hot toddy after dinner. A flask of vodka tucked in the side pocket of her Greeting Gale housekeeping frock that she thinks I don't see. Despite her unsettling cheerfulness and her looser, more leisurely alcohol consumption, Mama looks tired. Thinner. Older. Or maybe that's just my eyes playing tricks on me. An extension of the other eye tricks that are growing more intense, more pervasive, more common when I look at Mama. More and more, I see this fog hanging above her head. Literally, a fog, thick as Peggy's creamed seafood chowder but somehow even more unsettling. Like the worst kind of fugitive from the steel-grey stratiform clouds outside has broken into the trailer and claimed squatter's rights to the space over Mama's head. Every now and then, a bolt of sangria red or dirty tequila gold comes leaping out of her fog, striking the ceiling or the floor. The bulk of it moves, shifts, but it never seems to really go anywhere. I squint my eyes just right, trying to make it dance and quiver like the other squirrelly vision spells. But this thing that clings to Mama doesn't budge. It just hangs there, smearing and smothering Mama's spark.

"God love your mother, she looks like death warmed over," Peggy says to me under her labouring breath as she wrestles with an ancient angel wrapped in toilet paper.

Regardless of how much of a brain-tumoury, self-centred sook I'm being, and regardless of how fake Mama's cheerfulness is, or how real her cloud shroud is, none of it's enough to get either of us off the hook for hosting Christmas this year. Hence the tree carcass now sprawled out on the living-room floor.

"For Christ's sake, Peggy, make yourself useful," Mama says, hustling into the room. She grabs the midsection of the supine tree and lurches it into upright obedience.

"Whaddya think I'm doing, unwrapping this stuff? You want these decorations or not?"

"No. I got new ones," I say, using every ounce of my bodily strength to hold the tree in position while Mama crawls underneath it to fiddle with the stand. "God, why are we doing this again?"

From under the cover of green spiky boughs, Mama snaps, "Shuddup, ya Grinch. It's Christmas."

Mama hates Christmas. She especially detested the years it was her turn to host the pack of nuts and delinquents she calls a family in our tiny trailer. But back in the day, the Fortune Family Christmas Eve party was one of the highlights of my year. You never knew for sure how the night would go down, but you could always count on a few things:

Uncle Ernie would get out a guitar and play old rock and roll tunes that Peggy would butcher, lyrically and melodically, until I joined in and set her straight. Uncle Mossy would "accidentally" trip and fall on my pile of presents, ripping the wrapping enough so that I just had to open them, right then and there. Mama would make double batches of broc-o-glop and chocolate almond crack. Aunt Audrey would get loaded off the smell of the wine cork and end up flat on her uptight arse in the middle of the driveway by ten o'clock. Uncle Gord would leave a bottle of something unattended somewhere, and Mitch and I would sneak a few sips.

Mama and her siblings — the remaining alive and functional ones — would sit around telling stories about themselves, about each other, about the ones who were crazy or dead. Sometimes one of them would whisper about Black Bernie, and muse about the curse on his bloodline because of his mother's rumoured sins and sorcery. Did old Black Agnes really read tea leaves and brew pennyroyal for pregnant Catholic girls? Did her people really ride out the Irish famines by playing mad and being sent to the bedlam? Did she really tell Black Bernie what she was up to the night she burned her own house and children to the ground? Eventually, those hushed conversations always shifted to a group gush about what a saint their mother had been, even though everybody in Town knew that Lucy Fortune had named all her children after characters in bodice ripper novels, like the worst kind of Catholic sinner. They'd laugh together about pit boots and payday drunks, and being beaten by the nuns for having dirty fingernails and unholy names.

Before the night was through, somebody would get in a fight. The fight was the most reliable of all Fortune Family

Christmas Eve traditions, the only one that Mama and I managed to carry on with any degree of consistency when she'd come see me in Toronto. But we only ever fought about stupid, nitpicky mother-daughter things, like how much money I pissed away, or what took Dave so long to propose, or why I wouldn't even entertain the idea of getting married out in Mama's backyard like she always dreamed I would, let alone come for a visit once in a blue moon. It was never as much fun as when the whole family was together.

The tree cleaned up good, with a fresh set of neutral white LED twinkle icicle lights and a few boxes of classy vintage-inspired glass balls in tastefully complimentary shades of chocolate brown and robin's egg blue. A bowl of fancy potpourri might even cover up its natural stench. This is probably the most valuable thing I learned from my life in Toronto, from Dave, from the gaggle of tony bitches who pretended I was one of them: how to take something sad and wretched and ugly and make it smile and shine enough to pass for almost pretty.

"Most boring tree I ever saw," Mama grunts every time she walks by it.

"You said I could buy new decorations."

"I know, but I didn't know you'd be so friggin' boring about it. Nanny's bubble lights would have been fine. And you didn't leave a branch for Dough Baby."

Right. Dough Baby.

When I was seven, Peggy gave me a lump of bread dough so I'd shut up and leave her alone while she babysat me one day. I made a wildly deformed "gingerbread girl" that Peggy baked, and tried to shame me into eating. Because there were children starving in Africa who would give their left foot for a bite of that dough blob. I told her to send it to Africa, because I wasn't eating it. But Peggy had a better idea. Paint it and give it to Mama as a Christmas present. So I did. It was ugly as sin. Weighed a ton. A coat of lacquer so thick it would be off-gassing for a decade. Every year, as I'd watch Mama wrestle it onto the thickest branch of the tree, I'd find myself wishing I'd just eaten the damn thing instead.

"You said you just wanted the tree to look good. Those colours are straight out of a magazine," I say. "And you always hated Dough Baby."

"Why would you say that?" Mama says.

"Because all you ever did was make fun of it and bitch about how it dragged all the branches down. It's an old glob of nasty bread dough soaked in shellac. It's no big deal." I shrug.

"Maybe not to you it isn't," Mama says, not even almost cheerfully.

[···]

The Fortune Family Christmas Eve festivities that we are hosting this year are a lot less complicated because Uncle Gord's off the wagon in a bad way, Aunt Audrey found Jesus, and neither of them is speaking to Peggy. Wacky uncle Cecil is hunkered down in his makeshift Armageddon camp behind the Pizza Hut with a new sleeping bag and a case of canned beans. And Uncle Ernie's in the clink again for shoplifting the new can opener he was going to give Cecil for Christmas, to go with the sleeping bag and case of beans he stole for his birthday. Instead of a house full of our chaotic relations, and a big spread of food and booze, we're down to a small family turkey dinner.

As such, the Fortune Family Christmas Eve festivities that we are hosting just got a lot more complicated because it will only be me, Mama, Peggy, and Char's baby. And Uncle Mossy. But he doesn't say anything, so he doesn't count.

Peg sits across from me with Daktari on her lap. She dips her bloated finger into a bowl of lukewarm gravy and pops it in his mouth. He slurps and coos, and the second he stops, she pulls her finger out, loads it up with more gravy and shoves it back in his mouth before he can protest.

"Char wants him vegetarian, you know," I say, before dumping back the last swallow of my first glass of wine in weeks. It's Christmas Eve, dammit. Probably my last. I should be basking in the joy of family and making merry with friends. But my family's too messed up to bask in anything other than its own long-standing dysfunction, and my friends are a little short on merriment themselves.

For weeks, Allie has responded to all my texts—friendly questions like *Any word on that job interview?* or *Your father and brothers smarten up yet?* or *Wanna come hang out with me?*—with a single-word answer. "No." Willy is still MIA with his cracked-out Chrissy Parsons drama. And Char, of course, is busy bonding with Horatio the ficus. So I'm jumping off the wagon myself. With bells on. We're only on our salads, but I pour myself another glass.

"Oh, it's only turkey gravy," Peggy scoffs as she picks up the bowl and lets a greasy rivulet stream all over her plate of California salad. I lovingly plucked that organic spinach from the plastic carton. Lovingly rinsed and sliced the organic strawberries and toasted the slivered almonds. Lovingly dotted it with bits of artisanal goat cheese that Peggy picked out with her fingers and dumped back in the main bowl because it was "one of them hippy cheeses" that is not fit for the turkey gravy she's dribbling over top of hers.

"Besides, if Missy Charlotte wants to have a say in how this baby is raised, she best smarten up," Peg says, as if medication-resistant postpartum psychosis is just another dumb choice.

"I'd like to know how you ended up with that baby," I say, even though I could probably make a pretty good guess at the answer.

Mama shoots me a dirty look. But Peggy seems pleased to tell me her version of the story. Turns out that Freddy and Dar, Char's parents, did not just kick her out because she showed up with what Freddy called a "Halfrican baby." They disowned her a few months ago when they found out she stole their credit cards and racked up enough debt to force them into bankruptcy, which cost them their cozy bungalow Down North. Freddy and Dar are now in a bachelor apartment in The Mines, living off canned beans and fried baloney. This was certainly not what they bargained for when they adopted her as a sparky, smiley, ginger-haired toddler. Now they don't want her anywhere near them, lest she do them more damage.

But there's more that Peggy doesn't say. History. Dar MacIsaac used to be Peggy's best friend because Peggy's ex-husband Skroink was best friends with Freddy MacIsaac growing up. And because they were both nosy big-mouthed bingo bags who grew up in The Mines, Peggy and Dar got along like two old birds. But then Peggy and Skroink split up and Dar told everyone that it was because Peggy was fooling around with Skroink's cousin Bonk. So it stands to reason that Peggy has been hankering to get a good solid dig in at Dar ever since. Char showing up with a baby and a ready-made sob story about how her racist parents put her out on the street? Peggy Fortune to the rescue. Now she doesn't actually have to deal with Char and still gets to parade around with the grandbaby that Dar and Freddy are too small-minded and petty to accept.

Mama puts a plate of turkey and a bowl of potatoes on the table.

"Jesus, Mossy. Don't sit there waitin' for me to wait on ya. Get yourself a plate," Mama says at about five times her normal volume and a third of her regular speed. Uncle Mossy smiles like the intellectual invalid he's always been assumed to be, and nods without making eye contact.

"Don't tell me he's deaf," Mama says, grinning sideways. "Selective hearing, that one."

Uncle Mossy shovels some meat and potatoes onto the good Blue Willow china plate, and smiles like the clever little Jeezer Mama always insisted he was.

Mama sits down, and in between bites comes the kind of familiarly awkward and awkwardly familiar conversation that makes me want to jump out of my skin and run screaming into the night. Or get good and goddamn drunk, at least.

"Willy Gimp's not around much lately. Were you two going steady or wha?" Mama says.

"Effie, nobody goes steady anymore." Peggy flutters her fat eyelids like she knows what she's talking about.

"Or *going together* or dating or whatever. You know what I mean," Mama says, waving the gravy boat around recklessly.

"They don't even do that these days. It's all with the *hookin' up* now. Right, Crow?"

I take a long, slow, convenient sip of wine.

"Hooking up? Like what hookers do?" Mama says.

"Oh, nobody gets any money for it," Peggy says with know-it-all bluster. "They give it away free. Girls these days. Casting pearls before swine."

"Well I hope they're using French safes," Mama whispers the last two words.

"Have to staple them to them girls' panties nowadays. If they even wear panties anymore," Peggy says. "Oh, Effie, is this turkey ever moist!"

If Uncle Mossy isn't really deaf, I bet he wishes to hell he was now. Maybe Uncle Ernie had it right back at Christmas Eve dinner, circa 1991. Maybe a fork in the eye is an absolutely legitimate response to our family dinners. But I stick with just getting wasted. Another filled glass.

"You'd eat shit on a shingle so long as it's salty," Mama's voice rises. "Peggy never met a meal she didn't like, eh, Mossy?"

"The other one over there, too busy draining wine bottles to finish her hippy salad. Willy Gimp not in the picture now, eh, Crow? He's back with the Parsons one, trying to get her off the drugs for fear of Cracker. That baby be born drug-wrecked, ya think?"

"You know..." I say, feeling saucy and sounding just a tad slurry. "That is none of my business. None of yours either, Peggy."

"I'd make it my business if I were you. I'd maybe lay off the booze too," she says. Then she looks right at me, her eyes glinting with several shades of trouble-making. "Heard you went to visit Sarah Spenser's a few weeks back."

"What? No. Where'd you hear that?" I sputter, amazed at how fast the instinct to lie like a busted seventeen-year-old comes roaring back.

"Tell the truth, and shame the Devil," she says.

"You calling me a liar?" I snap.

"No, but you are lying. There's a difference. And see, me, eh? I can smell a lie a mile away."

"Whatever. I had some time to kill so I went there. To introduce myself."

"To who? Sarah Spenser?" Mama says flatly.

"Yeah. Right after Rosalind died."

"There's nothing to be gained there, Crow. Unless you are looking to start trouble with them after all these years." Peggy cocks her head to the side so that her fleshy freckled jowls shift in an avalanche of ugly.

"Peggy's right. You'll get no love from the Spensers. You'd be lucky to get the time of day," Mama says.

"I'm not after love. I just wanted some ... perspective."

"Any perspective those people have is warped all to hell," Mama says. "They don't know their heads from their holes. Never did."

"Yeah, well I just got a little tired of only ever hearing one side of the story." My throat is squeezing and squirming, yet failing to constrict the emerging emotion. "Is it that unreasonable to want to know that side of my family before I—"

"Don't mistake your relations for your family," Mama says. "There's a difference."

"I'm just saying, I don't have much time so—"

"Oh, knock off the terminally ill bit." Peggy flashes a gum-toothed smile at me. "Your mother said the biopsy wasn't as bad as they thought, so there's no need for the 'Oh, I might die any minute' nonsense. You'll probably outlive us all."

Uncle Mossy just sits there, carefully plowing his mashed potatoes around his plate with the edge of his fork, not a care in the world. Daktari is slumped against Peggy's heaving, misshapen bosom, in a peaceful gravy-induced coma. But I can feel myself lighting up with some good old Christmas Eve Fortune Family Fight fury.

"Yeah, Peggy, I'm just being melodramatic, eh. What am I getting all bent out of shape for? The attention, probably." I take another swig of fuel. "I just need to smarten up. Right?" I fix a narrowed gaze on Peggy, tenting my fingers into a steeple, elbows planted on the table, leaning in like I mean business.

"Get your elbows off the table and stop staring your aunt down like a hooligan, missy. It's Christmas," Mama says.

I straighten up, pick up my wine glass, swirl the red nectar around, and knock back the rest of the glass. I fold my arms across my chest, lean back, and wait for someone to say something.

Peggy does not disappoint, even though her mouth is still half-crammed with potatoes.

"So what'd Sarah Spenser have to say?"

"Peggy, drop it," Mama says.

"You really wanna know?" But first I grab the wine bottle and watch as the red liquid trickles into the contours of my glass with a slow, controlled pour. "We had tea. She said that if I wanted to know what really happened to my father, maybe I should be grilling you two." I steadily increase the flow of wine from bottle to glass.

"Horseshit. How about passing me the gravy, Mossy. Anybody else find this turkey dry?" Mama says, her underbite jutting out, teeth pinching and scraping her top lip as she waits for Moss to steer the gravy boat toward her.

Peggy is uncharacteristically quiet, and has developed an unusual interest in rearranging the food on her plate. I stare at her, waiting, trying to figure out which of my buttons she'll try to push next. But I'm caught off guard when the air around her suddenly solidifies into thick bands of navy, dusty rose, and muted green. The colours seem like they're pressing down hard on her shoulders, making her slump more than usual. Like they're trying to push something out of her.

"Peggy, hand me the salt," Mama says, thunking the gravy boat down on the table. "I forgot to salt the water for these carrots."

I'm so mesmerized by the colours invading the space around Peggy that I fail to notice the wine kissing the edge of my glass. I stop pouring a millisecond after it starts to spill. I hunch over with pursed lips and slurp from the overflowing glass. Mama clears her throat, and looks around the table for the salt that hasn't arrived. Then, through the tension and the wine and the wobbling world of hallucinations, it hits me like a ton of technicolour bricks: *Peggy knows something.* And there are not enough sane, sober brain cells in my head to stop what comes out of my mouth, even as I sense Mama silently pleading with me to shut up.

"You know something." The heavy bands of colours shudder and shake, but my eyes stay locked on Peggy because now *I* know something. Those colours are a fortress of secrets built up around her, and *I can see it* starting to crumble like an old wall. If she tries to deny it, she'll probably pass out from the stifling shit stink of her own lies. And she knows that, too.

Peggy pulls her head up, her jowls quivering, eyes and nostrils flaring. She starts to speak but Mama cuts her off.

"Stacey Theresa Fortune, shuddup and eat your supper. Look, you're spilling wine all over hell and creation."

"No, Effie, I'm gonna—" Peggy starts.

"You aren't gonna nothin'. Shut up and eat your supper. Both of you."

"Mama, I deserve—"

"You deserve what? The right to wreck our last..." She stands up and grabs the salt shaker from its hiding place, six inches from Mossy's untouched wine glass.

"She deserves to know the truth, Effie," Peg says, an acidic undertone ebbing beneath the veneer of sincerity. The wall has not crumbled that much.

"Spit it out, Peggy. Just tell the truth and shame the Devil yourself for once!" I only realize that I'm almost yelling when Daktari starts to fuss.

"The truth, eh?" Peggy says softly, gently jiggling the kid back to sleep. "Maybe it's not all it's cracked up to be."

Little shards of her crumbling wall of colours fly around her head like antagonizing shrapnel. I wince. I don't have to take this. My voice is sharp, and tinged with rage. "Just tell me what the ever-lovin' fuck—"

"E-nough." Mama punctuates the word with a loud thump of her heavy hand on the table. "The next person who makes so much as a snide peep is getting grabbed by the scruff of the neck and biffed in a snowbank. Got that?"

Uncle Mossy looks dumbly up from his plate, puts down his fork, sniffs his shirt sleeve, and grins like a nut.

"Peep," he whispers.

Mama swats him upside the head as she picks up his plate before he gets a chance to lick it clean like he usually does, and she marches to the sink.

"Who wants pie?" she barks.

Not me. My head is spinning like a top, but it still tips back effortlessly as I pour the last of the wine down my throat. I make a point of setting the glass down with more than a gentle clink. I shove my chair back and sashay to the living room. And by sashay I mean stagger.

I hear Peggy scoff, "Look at the other one. Drunk as a skunk."

I'm just about to yell at her to go fuck herself when the world turns into a tilt-a-whirl. I close my eyes. The smell of cat-piss spruce tree swallows me, a million needles bury themselves in my skin, and my whole body is gripped by a heavy, claustrophobic panic. There's a musical clatter of glass, a chorus of voices, and the steady drumming of footsteps down the hall. I open my eyes. All I can see is tree. And the brownish orange fibre of the living-room carpet. Torn wrapping paper on the pile of presents, all of which are for me. Because I was too broke, too sick, too full of excuses to get anyone anything. And then there's that damn Dough Baby lying on the floor in front of me, its head cracked in two.

Mama resurrects the sideways tree. Uncle Mossy tugs at my arm until I'm sitting more or less upright, and starts picking up the hunks of shattered glass around me. Peggy stands at the living room entrance with Char's baby on her hip, pretending to stifle her laughter as it quakes through her body. And before it completely subsides, she starts belting out her own favourite John Denver classic, "Please Daddy (Don't Get Drunk This Christmas)," replacing *Daddy* with *Stacey*.

"Shut the fuck up!" I hear myself slur. "How do you know I didn't have a seizure?"

"Seizure, my arse," Peggy says. "You're piss loaded and ya fell in the tree. Just like the Old Man. What did I always say, Black Bernie Fortune will never die as long as that one's alive. Although I hear the Spensers were a bit of a wreck when they got on the booze, too."

"Are you gonna let her talk to me like that?" I say, lolling my head around to look at Mama. But Mama's not listening. She's sitting in the rocking chair, cradling the pieces of Dough Baby in her hard, heavy hands, not even trying to conceal the tears racing down her cheeks.

"Ma, I'm sorry. I lost my balance—"

"Go to bed, Crow," Mama says, her eyes fixed on the broken ornament.

"Effie, I—" Peggy starts.

"Go have your pie. Go home as soon as you're done."

And that is how I wrecked Christmas Eve. But Allie Walker managed to one-up me.

6 BLOOD AND WATER

One of the reasons Allie Walker did not die in the grungy bathroom of her father's house on Christmas Eve night is that her kid brother, Lennon, is a demanding, impatient little tool. Despite agitated huffing and puffing about how he needed to fix his hair before his girlfriend arrived, Allie still wasn't getting out of the bathroom fast enough. Lennon booted the door open. He found Allie in an empty bathtub, fully dressed, semi-conscious, with a broken Daisy razor beside her and an empty pill bottle in hand. The other reason that Allie Walker did not die in the grungy bathroom of her father's house on Christmas Eve night is that the bathroom wasn't even grungy. She scrubbed every inch of it with a toothbrush before dumping a mittful of Ativan down her throat, and trying to smash the blade out of a pretty pink razor.

[···]

"Allie, what the fuck?" It's all I can stammer when I see her propped up in her hospital bed at the understaffed, rundown General Hospital in Town.

Her golden hair is woven into a careless braid, fluorescent lights give her skin a dewy, ethereal cast, and her grey eyes a blue, mirrory shimmer. IV lines and leads tether her to the moment-by-moment realities of her blanket-draped body. She looks perfectly at home here, in the cool, sterile professionalism of the clinical world. There's an eerie elegance to her, like a porcelain doll in a glass case. Vulnerable and fragile, yet safe and secure. Allie would have made a kick-ass doctor. But she makes a beautiful patient, too.

"I didn't mean to," she mumbles, like she's lost in a rather pleasant daydream. I stifle a gasp, as around her head I watch a band of blackened blue wrap around a wobbling sea of cobalt waves. A greyish-white froth erupts and is swallowed over and over again, as that hallucinatory ocean bashes against the hallucinatory wall. Meanwhile, a sickly smear of thick soot has moved in and settled over Allie's midsection.

"Crow? You okay?" No mumbling now. Allie sounds concerned. On point. Like her practical, everything-is-under-control self.

"Me? Yeah. Fine. Why?" I say, pretending I can will away the surreal things I am sick of seeing. Still, the black blue band around her head bulges up in response to the thrashing and crashing. It's like a pimple. I cringe, feel my shoulders lurch up toward my ears. It looks like it's going to pop.

"You just spaced out completely. Petit mal seizures. Ask your doctor about petit mal seizures."

"No. Shut up. I'm fine," I say, bent on redirecting her attention to where it belongs, but where she was never good at putting it. "What happened, Al? I had no idea it was this bad..."

Which is utter bullshit. If I'd stopped to pull my head out of my own miserable arse for a minute, I'd have seen it. Her mother died. Allie wasn't there when it happened, like she always swore she would be. And just when she thought she might at least be free to do her own thing, whatever escape hatch she was banking on was taking too long to open even a crack. Long enough for guilt to creep in, for her to see that her father and brothers were eating frozen hot dogs and wiping their arses with pages from the phone book. They needed her now. Allie was pinned beneath that relentless old beast of family duty. Again. You don't need some sort of foolish tumour-induced psychic power aura vision to know that breaks people. But pleading ignorance is the best *mea culpa* I can muster.

"It was an accident." She smiles. The tumult of colour around her head surges and thrashes harder.

Bullshit.

I watch as the pressure builds in the bruise-coloured bulge, and the cobalt sea rocks and roils into whitecaps. In the bottom half of my field of vision, the black soot spot starts to swirl, making me dizzy and nauseous and slightly panicked. I can't look away. Something's gonna give. It just needs a shove, but I don't know how. Until all of a sudden I can see little pink daisies exploding into ribbons of blood-red, streaming from Allie's wrists, her stomach, her heart.

"I saw Char a few weeks ago," I squeak. "She said you should watch what you eat over Christmas. And some cryptic shit about sharp daisies and love flowing better than blood."

"What a psycho bitch."

"Allie, the pills? What were you trying to do with the razor blade?" The words push past my better judgement as I watch and wait for the air around Allie to respond. "Char wanted me to apologize to you for her."

Sure enough, she explodes. "She's a sick little sociopath,

you know that. I'm fine. They pumped my stomach and are sending me home tomorrow."

Then the daisies, the ribbons of red, all disappear as the blue-black dam bursts. The wall that stood between Allie Walker and her damage is swept away in a violent rush of spilling sapphire.

"You're not fine," I hiss at Allie, moving closer to her. "This wasn't an accident. This was a cry for help, and I'm here, Al. I'm listening. Tell me what's going on so I can help."

Her alabaster cheeks stay propped in a pleasant grin, un-eroded by the streaks of salted pain that are now streaming from her eyes.

"I thought I could escape, Crow. The right way. To something better." Her voice trembles, but her prim smile doesn't so much as flinch. "But they wouldn't let me in. Because of what I did. Even though it was long ago, and it wasn't my fault. So this was another way out."

Her hands hover over the sooty black hole on her belly. The black belly hole has been there since 1998, but I couldn't see it, and Allie couldn't speak of it. Until now.

It wasn't the abortion. It was what came after. It was all the stuff she didn't think of when she took Char's advice. Abortions were technically legal and available in the big city of Halifax then, but that didn't make them easy to get. Especially for a twenty-one-year-old university student who couldn't shell out the seven hundred bucks for the Morgentaler. Instead, Allie had to convince the stodgy old man doctor at the university health clinic — who also happened to be a prof in the pre-med program she was trying to get into — to refer her to the Termination of Pregnancy Unit at the hospital. And then wait weeks to actually get in for an appointment, and hope to God that everyone at that hospital would forget who she was by the time she was through school and doing her residency there. Allie was already nine weeks when she found out. Her courses were getting tougher to handle, especially the biology class that was covering human fetal development in excruciating detail. Her mother was getting sicker. The casual fuck buddy who knocked her up was a resident assistant in her dorm, and he was getting annoyed and impatient. She needed it over.

She asked Char to loan her the money, but Char had a better idea. "The trick," she told Allie, "is to just be a basket case. Say the word 'suicidal' and watch how fast they get that shit done."

So Allie pinned her hopes on Char's scheme. She'd play the basket case card, do what needed to be done, and move on with her life like nothing had ever happened. She went to the stodgy old man doctor at the university health clinic and told him she was pregnant, and suicidal because of it. Just like that, she got a prescription for Prozac and the procedure done, no questions asked. Which would have been more or less fine, had it ended there. But it didn't.

Within days, the stodgy old man doctor went to the pre-med program admissions committee and questioned Allie Walker's suitability for pre-med, what with her history of mental illness. Then, he met with the annoyed and impatient and now uncomfortable resident assistant in Allie's dorm and told him that the girl in room 307 was suicidal. This made the RA more annoyed and impatient and uncomfortable, since he was the one who knocked her up. So there were meetings about Allie Walker. Discussions about Allie Walker. Conclusions about Allie Walker.

The pre-med program admissions committee was not comfortable having such an unstable woman in the classroom. The Residence Life Team was not comfortable having such an unpredictable woman in their midst. What if she hung herself in her closet with a bathrobe belt? What if she slit her wrists with a bashed-up pink Daisy razor in shower stall number four? What if one of the bright, promising young students with wealthy alumni parents was traumatized because they found this bursary-dependant, loose-moralled head case from Cape Breton dead in the common room some morning? Allie Walker was a chance the powers-that-be just couldn't take. So they withdrew their recommendation for her pre-med program admission on account of her slipping grades. And they kicked her out of residence on account of "complaints" about her partying. When Allie found out, she marched right into the room of the uncomfortable resident assistant, and that's when things got very, very uncomfortable. Because Allie walked in on him screwing Char. It all went to hell in a handbasket right there.

Allie ended up being charged for destruction of property and uttering threats. Char ended up diving out the dorm-room window buck naked, and buying herself a one-way ticket to Germany the next day.

It was convenient that Char was ready to go within twenty-four hours of Allie charging into our place that night, calling her a psycho cunt face and wishing her a lifetime of rotting in hell. It was convenient that they left me out of all this because I had my own little dramas and traumas to deal with at the time, although none of them involved gut-wrenching choices and crushing decisions and showing up in court alone and scared to try to explain it all to a judge.

I listen as Allie recounts all of this. I choke back a gulp of guilt. I watch as the tide of colour around her head turns to a trickle. Except for this one little blob of blackened blue that sits squarely, staunchly, over her head. A fresher-looking bruise on Allie Walker's long unhealed soul.

"Do you know what I was doing when my mother died?" The corners of her mouth inch into a flat smile as the edges of her eyes swell with the clarity of expectant tears. "I was holed up in a slummy motel room at the border, drinking a bottle of vodka and making a pros and cons list for dying or just disappearing. There were fourteen pros for disappearing. I was about to count the pros of dying when Lennon called to say Mum was gone."

"But the job interview? In Boston?" I say. "You said it went fine."

"It didn't even happen." Allie's voice is cracking and choking, but her lips stay twisted in the smile of habit. "They wouldn't let me cross the border. Pulled some file, started asking questions about the peace bond from the university, my mental illness. Told me I couldn't enter the country. I'm a security threat."

I reach for her, to hug her, to hold her, to stop myself from seeing or hearing or feeling any more of the sorrow I should have seen and heard and felt with her all along. Allie recoils.

"So this is what I get" — her voice swells in volume and intensity, as the bruise on her soul deepens and darkens and spawns a new sea of cold blue anguish — "for trusting Char MacIsaac. It's like karma, right? I faked wanting to die, thinking it would help me get on with my life, and now I still can't get on with my life and I actually wish I was dead. Meanwhile, Char, Queen of Conniving, doesn't have to grow up. Screwing the same guy as your friend, Char? Oh well, just pretend you're helping her but wreck her life instead! Got a kid? No worries. You just keep being your crazy little self, Char! Somebody else will deal with it. Then there's good old responsible, sane Allie! Her mother's dead and she's stuck out in the woods, like Snow Fucking White in a house full of lazy entitled man-babies who can't even put down the toilet seat!"

She is yelling now. A nurse comes in, armed with a compassionate smile and a syringe full of calm. Allie juts out her arm with no hesitation. The landscape of pain around her dissolves in tandem with the rate of the nurse's injection into her rigid arm. A soft blue halo materializes, gently undulating around her head as she dutifully slides beneath the blanket and turns her face to the wall. The nurse assures me she will be fine. I tell the nurse they'd be wise to make sure she can't get her hands on anything sharp, no matter how fine they think she'll be.

As I make my way to the door, I hear Allie call out over her chemically unburdened shoulder, "Hey Crow, wanna know what Dad's last words to me were, while they were putting me in the ambulance?" Her voice takes on a deep tone of paternal concern, each word spoken with weight and bewilderment: "'Uh, Allie, sweetie? Do you think that turkey is done yet?'"

[···]

On Boxing Day, Mama gets called into work because half the girls at the Gale called in sick. I sprawl out on the couch, eating leftover broc-o-glop and watching *Golden Girls* reruns. Until Peggy shows up to drop off a couple of gifts, keen to tell me how she heard that Chrissy and Willy showed up together for midnight Mass at St. Pius' on Christmas Eve. And that Shirl Short saw Chrissy Parsons buy two tickets to the New Year's Eve dance at the KoC, them control-top pantyhose, those stick on bra-cup things that are supposed to make your boobs look perkier, massage oil, and — *ahem* — cinnamon-flavoured intimate lubricant, down at the drugstore.

I don't even have the energy to tell Peggy to fuck off, let alone absorb what the local trash talkers say regarding the movements of my former booty call and his newly knocked up rehab project. I have better things to concern myself with. Like stalking people I don't give a shit about on Facebook. Watching funny cat videos. Doing online quizzes and pretending that they give me deep insight into my shallow self. *What* Star Wars *character are you? Yoda. What Harry Potter character are you? Voldemort. What food are you? Pizza. What decade do you belong in? The '00s. What arbitrary thing are you? A hill of beans.*

So I'm just gonna lie on the couch and sulk for a while, licking the various wounds of body and soul that life seems hell-bent on inflicting. I probably deserve it. That's the real insight, right there.

Peggy seems genuinely disappointed by my lack of interest in the topic of Willy Gimp and Chrissy Parsons. So she ups the ante.

"How's Allie doing?" she says, as if she hasn't already heard one godawful tale or another about her.

"Fine. Took too many anxiety pills. It was an accident."

"How goes the little quest to dig up the family dirt?" she says.

"See me? Fresh outta fucks to give about whatever stupid secret you think you're keeping," I say, hunkering down under a quilt and taking a moment to lick the bottom of my broc-o-glop bowl.

Of course, I am lying through my broc-o-glop smeared teeth, and Peggy knows it. I can tell by the way she's scrunching up her snout. By the way her top lip curls and twitches.

"Oh well. What you don't know won't hurt you. Or your mother."

"That Betty White is a riot." I jack the TV volume up to stun.

Peggy plods toward the door. "There's a present there I forgot to give you. Merry Christmas." Then, from out on the step, she hollers, "It smells like a Dutchman's arse in there, by the way!"

I wait till I hear her car clatter down the driveway, then I grab the rectangular package she left. It is clumsily swathed in cross-eyed reindeer wrapping paper, the bejesus taped out of every seam, and "Crow" scrawled right on the paper in black marker. There's a faint *rattle clunk* when I give it a shake. *Every year, dollar store bubble bath. She knows I'm allergic. Dutchman's Ass scented, I bet. Or maybe a box of Nova Scotia tartan-print thank you cards with little fiddle envelope stickers, from the sale bin at some stupid tourist kitsch shop. Whatever.*

I shut off the TV and go to bed, chucking the box into the back corner of my closet on the way. But curiosity nags at me. I get up, fish it out, and open it to confirm the cheapness, the thoughtlessness of Peggy's gift. But it's not bubble bath or discount tourist schlock. Inside are photographs. One of me that I've never seen before, standing in front of the shocked and mortified crowd at my high school graduation, post-slideshow, my face flushed and my mouth wide open in that final "Caaaaw." The others are the Wall of Shame pictures of the Spensers, and Lucy and Black Bernie Fortune, which Char saved from the bonfire on head-shaving night. And there's a little tartan notecard etched with Peggy's heavy scrawl that reads, "If you don't come to grips with where you came from, you sure as hell won't understand where you're going." Which is worse — even cheaper and more thought-less — than I expected. So back into the box, back into the farthest corner of the closet, out of sight and out of mind goes Peggy's rotten excuse for a Christmas present.

I stay in bed, where I can piss away hours toying with the mindless voyeurism, amusing distractions, and faux self-awareness contained in my pretty little touch screen world. All the while pretending that the snow and the sorrows of the tangible world aren't piling up right outside my door. I have better things to do. Like combing the internet for ideas on what should be done with my corpse, for example.

Having my dead body put out on display in a box and then buried in the ground seems so old-fashioned, so pedestrian, so dull and depressing. There must be a better way. And what do you know, there is. My former high school classmate and new Facebook friend Sasha Marnelli has clicked "Like" on a share from my old arsehole enemy, Becky Chickenshit. Becky's comment reads "Here's one for vain egomaniacs..." Naturally, I click on the link. There it is. The most brilliant way to be dead I've ever seen. I want to be made into a diamond.

A company in San Francisco called Gem-Mortalize takes your ashes and squashes them into a big fat shiny diamond. They even do different colours. Mama's gonna hate it, but I don't care. It's my death and I'll be a diamond if I want to. Mama can have my sparkly stone self set into a tiara and wear me to fancy parties. Or she can just hold me in her hands late at night when she's drunk and alone and listening to John Denver, or lift me up to the sun, and revel in the light as it bounces through my coloured, crystalized facets. A new perspective when her world gets dull and flat without me. *Mama, make me a diamond when I'm dead. Strong. Brilliant. Beautiful. In-de-fucking-structable.* Who could say no to a dying wish like that?

[···]

Mama comes home from work looking more exhausted than usual. Thinner, too. They've been running her ragged at the Gale. One week she's on nights, the next week all days, plus staggered split shifts and overtime she won't turn down. If she wasn't so damn proud, a seasonal layoff would probably do her a world of good. Let her arthritic joints rest so she wouldn't have to be marching around pretending she isn't in agony all the time. And maybe she wouldn't have to sit by herself every night and get just drunk enough to fall into a relatively pain-free sleep. Mama, ever the pragmatist. Even in her vices. But there'll be no pogey for Effie Fortune. She would rather work herself to death than take the dole. And they know that about her at the Gale. So they take full advantage.

Still, this isn't ordinary toilet-scrubbing, bed-making fatigue on her face. This is different. The confusing clouds that have been hovering over her have finally started to break up, but not into anything like the brightly coloured fiesta of feelings I got used to seeing around her. Gradient, grainy charcoal lines scribble and scramble around her head in a shifting, static-filled silhouette. She pours herself a shot, heaves her tired, goofily dressed bones into the rocking chair, closes her eyes, knocks back the contents of the shot glass, and then minces no words.

"She's coming after the house," Mama says.

"Who? What house?" I say.

"The split level Cape Cod in Martha's Vineyard, ya dolt. Whaddaya think? This one." She pours herself another dose of gin. "Saint Sarah. Fallen on hard times, I guess. She needs the money."

Unbeknownst to me until just now, Mama never actually owned the scruffy little trailer and the swath of land that she and I have called home since I was four days old. All this time, we've lived here by the grand good graces of my father's people, the Spensers, who were known to buy up any scrap of land they could get their hands on, just in case. In case of what, God only knows. In this case, it was to keep Effie Fortune and an illegitimate grandchild out of their neatly combed hair.

"Not like they ever gave us a goddamn thing otherwise," Mama says, bitterly tossing out the familiar refrain. "This was literally the least they could do for their only grandchild."

But with Rosalind dead and Spenser Mining Inc. losing money hand over fist with some overseas mineral extraction company, Sarah can't afford to finish renovating the monstrous old family home *and* spend the rest of her winters at the condo in Florida *and* get her cheeks and chin pumped full of baby seal eyelash stem-cell extract, or whatever it is that makes her face look like plastic. The property went on the market on Christmas Day. We can stay until it sells. But as soon as the deed is done, we're out on our arses.

"What did I always say about them people? Never trusted

them as far as I could throw them," Mama says. "Selling for a song, too. Thirty grand for the trailer and the land. Some goddamn American tourist will be all over that like ugly on a codfish."

"Hey, maybe not. Maybe it'll—"

"Oh smarten up, Crow," Mama groans. "It's land. They ain't making any more. Somebody'll take 'er if she's up for grabs. Wouldn't be surprised if one of their sleazy business buddies already has designs on it."

The mere thought of some rich old American duffer buying this place to build a summer cottage that puts every house on the road to shame, or it getting snapped up by some finger-tenting tree-chopper keen to gut the land for a buck makes me intensely nauseous. Then again, everything makes me intensely nauseous these days.

Mama pours herself another shot of gin and tips it down her throat before heading over to the record player to rifle through her stack of moods and memories. "But see Sarah Spenser, eh?" Mama says, eyes narrowing, "That old tit-headed cow won't get rid of us that easy. Over my dead body."

Mine too, Mama. Mine too.

[…]

Once upon a time, New Year's Eve was magical. A time to reflect on the past while setting intentions and imagining the potential of the coming year. A time brimming with hope, and hors d'oeuvres, and opportunities for drunk sex in random rooms of other people's houses. Dave proposed to me on New Year's Eve two years ago. After I said yes, we did it in the Martha Stewart craft room at Ami's house. I left ass-cheek prints on the marble countertop of her glitter application table. Funny how all the lofty plans and aspirations that were born on the night Dave placed that ginormous rock on my finger and asked me to be his wife went straight down the toilet exactly one year later. That's when I stumbled into the bathroom at the New Year's Eve party hosted by Dave's nasty old cougar of a boss, and found her giving him a New Year's Eve blow job.

To my credit, I did not cause a scene. At least, not there. Not *right there*, in the bathroom. Instead, I calmly gave Dave a smile and a death stare, and walked away, closing the bathroom door behind me. Then I teetered out into the crowd of revellers in the spacious main room of the uptown mansion, perched myself halfway up the spiral staircase and smiled a gracious smile as I said, "Attention, everyone! Attention! I'd like to make a toast."

It was just enough time for Dave and the other one to make their way into the room. I smiled even bigger at them as they stood, paralyzed by their own stupidity.

"To our lovely hostess, Nicolette, who has opened her beautiful home so that we could all celebrate and ring in the New Year here." A round of applause and glass clinking. I beamed graciously and went on, "Who has opened her heart—not to mention her wallet—to start up Toronto's premier interior design magazine." More clapping. A few laughs and hoots and whistles. I smiled, nodded in agreement. "And, who—as I just discovered—has opened her mouth and let my fiancée, ad-man David Salyszyn, put his penis in it. That is, indeed, how you get *'ahead'* at *Sweet Home Magazine!*" The room got a little quiet after that. *Jesus, don't these people have a sense of humour?* "Happy New Year. Don't drink and drive. And go fuck yourselves! Or each other!" I bellowed. Then I slugged back my champagne, smashed the empty glass on the floor, and walked out the door to hail a cab.

Dave followed me. When he tried to get in the cab with me, I yelled "Get away from me, creep! I don't know you!" and the cab driver threatened to call the cops. I went back to our condo, gathered up a shitload of Dave's stuff—books, clothes, his laptop—and hucked it out the eighth-storey window into the alley.

By the time he showed up, I had already packed my bags, booked a hotel room, pissed on the memory foam king-sized mattress, threw up on the white suede couch, and jammed his Italian leather shoes in the garburator. Within days, I'd sold my engagement ring, found my own place, and slammed that chapter of my life shut.

But it must be Mercury retrograde or upside down Uranus or some other cosmic clap going around these days, because even the things I think I've slammed shut have a way of creaking back open. On the afternoon of New Year's Eve, my phone sings Green Day's "Basket Case." In the headspace I'm in, I shouldn't answer it, but I do. Because I'm a glutton for punishment.

"Hey, stranger. It's me, Dave. It's so good to hear your voice."
All I said was hello.

"How's the Motherland treating you? How are you? Everyone here really misses you."

It starts off cordial and small talky. A little annoying, but comfortable, which is how I'd characterize our relationship at its finest. Then it veers off into the douchebag ditch, our relationship at its core.

"I have news," he says, his voice soft and cautious, like

he's tiptoeing. "I wanted you to hear it from me. I'm getting married."

"That's nice. I'm sure you and Nicolette will be very amused." I gaze at the snowdrift which has crept up to molest the bottom edge of my bedroom window.

"No," he says. "Look, Stacey, Ami and I, we're—"

And then I just start roaring.

"It was all very organic," Dave sputters. "It's like the Universe just—"

"That wacky fuckin' Universe! It has such a knack for this kind of thing," I say, still half-cackling. "And talk about timing! Man, that universe of yours just nails the timing. Ami must be some proud of her manifesting powers these days. Betcha she stuck a picture of you up on her vision board, right there next to the big honkin' princess-cut diamond ring she's been trying to attract for six years."

"Look, I swear, nothing was going on between Ami and me while *we* were together, if that's what you're thinking."

"Know what, Dave? I don't actually give a flying fiddler's fuck either way. Thanks for the call. I wish the two of you all the happiness you deserve." *Which I roughly calculate to be not one goddamn iota.*

"Stacey, I—"

"My name is Crow," I coo. "Give my sincere disregards to your fiancée. Good luck with all that."

It is deeply unsatisfying to hang up on somebody with a tap of the end call icon. Cranking out a thunderous, maniacal "Caaaaaaaaaaaaw!" right into the other person's ear before biffing the phone into the back of the closet, on the other hand, is not without its pleasures. And I'll take whatever I can get right now. The friendless, homeless, hairless, end-of-life trajectory taking shape here is not the swan song I expected. And the only thing I have at my disposal for misery reduction is the chipped-off two-thirds of a joint stashed in my purse from my birthday.

In sheer spite of the weather, I go for a walk to The Wharf. Mama got me all new winter gear for Christmas because she didn't think my black leather pointy-toed high-heeled Gucci boots and my white three-quarter-length shearling coat — among the only pieces of clothing from my former life that I couldn't bear to sell before I left — were gonna cut it out here.

"You'll look some cute when they find you a week later, camouflaged in the snow like a friggin' polar bear, frozen dead in a ditch after snapping your ankle on a walk down The Wharf!" she said, when I told her I didn't need any new winter clothes. "And those flimsy little glitter gloves? What were you thinking?" I can't bring myself to tell her the story of how I stole those gloves from the bin at the mall after my birthday, even though we could both use a laugh. I throw them in the garbage instead.

Now I am the reticent owner of a gargantuan lime-green parka, a pair of silver moon boots, and bright blue snow pants. To top the ensemble off, Mama went to her friend, Betty Who Knits, and got me a red-and-white striped wool hat, a yellow and orange zigzagged wool scarf, and a "pair" of wool mitts, the left one pink with purple polka dots and the right one purple with pink hearts. She didn't need to spend money on me like that. I'll likely only get one winter out of the stuff.

"Shut up," she said, "or I'll have you buried in it."

So, here I am trekking to The Wharf looking like something Picasso threw up. But I'm warm and comfortable enough to not curse at every snowflake in sight. Warm and comfortable enough to stop for a little rest in a snowbank on the side of the road, where I spark up my doobie. It's not long before I'm deep in the throes of some wide-eyed stoner wonder. Enthralled by the way the piles of whiteness contrast with the tough, tenacious greenery. Mesmerized with how the blue shadows on the ground are edged with the sharp sparkle of sunlit diamonds in the snow. I notice the space. The silence. Until a big black crow comes flailing out of the woods and lands on the telephone wire that stretches overhead as he lets out a wicked string of clicks and caws. I click and caw right back at him.

They're not just noisy, beady-eyed scavengers with a penchant for anything shiny. They're better problem solvers than the average snot-nosed human kid. They learn the tweety dialects of other birds so that they know what they're saying to each other, and they mimic those sounds just to fuck with the neighbours sometimes. When one of their own dies, they have funerals. They gather together in the same tree, and holler in unison, and if the dead bird was important, other murders will come from all over to pay respects. And wild crows don't actually even steal and stash shiny things. They are too busy just trying to survive to be bothered with stealing anything they can't eat or make a nest with. They are practical creatures. It's only the young, foolish, spoiled ones that are thieves.

When I start thinking I can communicate with the woodland creatures, I am baked enough. Two spit-dabbed fingers pinch out the cherry on the joint. I awkwardly push and pull myself to my feet, stash the stubbed out spliff in the pocket of my new coat, and stroll down the road to The Wharf, as I consider my options for how to spend what might be my final New Year's Eve. I could go be depressed with Allie at the General Hospital in Town. Or go be nuts with Char and Horatio at the Regional, in Town, Town. I could join Mama for a meeting with Jacinta, the lawyer down the road, about how to screw Sarah Spenser's plans, before she heads off to scrub toilets. I could sit alone in my closet, wrapped in an old flannel shirt, eating one of the dozen pans of broc-o-glop that Mama hyper-efficiently assembled and froze on Christmas Day, before I even got out of bed.

Or I could try and hitch a ride into the KoC dance that everybody and their dog will be at tonight. I could go there and hang out with Willy and Chrissy. Probably run into Duke the Puke and Becky Chickenshit. Maybe even Weasel Tobin, or one of his kids, all named Weasel Tobin Jr. by their different mamas. I could go there and pretend to try to not make a scene, and then end up making the most scenic scene all these yahoos have ever seen.

Remember Crow Fortune and how she showed up, all bald and dolled up at the New Year's dance before she died? How she commandeered the DJ booth and got on the mic to give some toasts. A toast to Willy Gimp and Chrissy Parsons for her raging addictions and his man-whore martyr complex. A toast to Duke the Puke for keeping his secret identity as a clap-spreading creepazoid so well concealed for twenty years. A toast to Becky Chickenshit for marrying that guy, and playing a supporting role in wrecking her in public for no good reason. And a toast to Peggy Fortune, for being a conniving old bulldozer who managed to bury whatever it is she knows about the disappearance of Smart Alec Spenser good and goddamn deep. Then, good ol' Crow smiled and told everybody to drive safe and go

fuck themselves, and let out a wicked Caaaaaw as she swooped out
the back door. That Crow Fortune. She sure was a riot, wasn't she?

But I'm too sick for swooping and scene-making. I'm lucky to get out of bed, let alone out of the house. Since Christmas, my guts can't handle so much as the smell of booze, which is a most unfortunate turn of events because my whole plan of living out the rest of my days in a blaze of impulsive, outrageous, scandalicious, truth-bombing glory relied very heavily on considerable doses of liquid courage. That plan also failed to take into account how much energy Parry and Ziggy and Fuzzy would sap out of me. And I didn't think I'd be so alone.

My big silver moon boots plod through the foot and a half of snow piled up on the road down to The Wharf. Old Betty may have the gaudiest taste in colours known to man, but she knits some cozy mitts. And if I do happen to fall in a ditch, they'll find me pretty quick, in all my riotous rainbow glory. Mama, ever the pragmatist.

[···]

There is not a breath of wind, even down near the water. The brightly shining sun is almost enough to trick you into believing that it might not be cracking cold out. The wharf itself looks too snowy and slippery to be worth the risk of walking my stoned ass up on it today, so I walk my stoned ass down the beach a bit farther and settle for the lower view, closer to the shore. Long, salty spindles of ice cling to the concrete sides of the wharf, pleasantly distorting the graffiti letters beneath them, as the dark blue water gently sloshes around the swaths of opaque slush on its surface. Too early for any nice glacial clampers to have formed, or for any of the big bergs from the ocean to be visible out where the mouth of the Great Bras d'Or calls to the frigid ocean. Up on top of the wharf, out near the edge, a movement catches my eye, a bit of a burgundy blur. Then, a little splash. And another. And another. Snow and ice and stoned ass be damned. I'm nosy.

The man on the wharf is wearing a burgundy dress and chucking rocks into the water. Technically, it's a robe he's wearing. And those aren't rocks. They're live lobsters, which he quickly and precariously un-bands before launching them into the cold, sloshing water.

I didn't even know there was a Buddhist monastery tucked away on the edge of Cape Breton Island until I moved to Toronto and started hanging around with the Viva Rica super juice hawkers, who were always on a perpetual quest for the latest, greatest path to peace, love, and new trinkets to prove just how enlightened they were. Naturally, Ami knew all about it because some New Age shiny happy guru-type was on Oprah pushing a book about how she overcame all the negative vibes around her, and apparently, a key part of the process that fixed her entire life was spending a week in retreat with a Buddhist teacher at a monastery on some magical, healing, hallowed little Canadian island called Cape Breton. And *bam*! That monastery was besieged by throngs of flakes on a mad mission to find the bright white light of bliss up in the woods Down North.

Ami actually went to the monastery nestled deep in the hills of my homeland last year, but her retreat only lasted three days because they didn't have Wi-Fi. Or lattes. Or any hot young monks. And because the great Buddhist teacher that the Oprah chick gushed about wasn't in the habit of giving personal teachings to every random grinning ditz who showed up at the monastery. And, as it turns out, Buddhism is a bit of a downer, what with all the suffering and sitting and silence and such.

"You crusty little cocksucker!" The man grunts as he jerks his left hand back with a shake, and hucks a sprawling-clawed lobster over the edge of the wharf with his right. He bows a mechanical bow, mumbling something about merit and being of benefit and freeing all beings from the ocean of Samsara as he watches the crusty little cocksucker sink. He stands there for a minute rubbing his pinched thumb, hesitating to pluck another from the bucket.

I stand there, debating whether to engage him in some perfunctory chit-chat, like a good little rural busybody, or pretend he's invisible, like a good little urban sophisticate.

"You're welcome to help me. This gesture is meant to benefit all sentient beings," he says over his shoulder, as he gingerly plucks another lobster from the bucket, whips off the claw bands, and tosses it off the wharf. "But these guys aren't particularly appreciative of the liberation process. Not yet anyway."

Not appreciative of going from the balmy tank at the grocery store to the cold as a witch's tit Bras d'Or? Imagine that.

"Sure, what the hell." I've got nothing better to do, and being all grinched-up hanging out with a rather hot-for-an-old-guy Buddhist monk playing toss the lobster on New Year's Eve makes for an interesting story. More interesting than sitting in a snowbank squawking at crows, or hanging around the trailer by myself trying to figure out how to re-shave my own head. "I hate those crusty little cocksuckers, too."

Sure enough, the monk is from the hideaway monastery

that clings to the edge of a cliff above the jagged and merciless ocean shoreline Down North. He introduces himself as Brother Gyaltso, but I will call him Hottie McMonk Pants when I tell Char and Allie about him and his rugged Harrison Ford-ish charm. I tell him my name is Crow. A warm beatific smile offers up a stark contrast to his cool, devilish eyes.

"That's an interesting name," he says. "In Tibetan Buddhism, crows are a symbol of protection and great auspiciousness."

"Yeah, well I'm a cautionary tale. If it weren't for bad luck, I wouldn't have any."

I give him the Coles Notes version of the brain tumours. His lips scrunch up like he's got a mouthful of piss or wisdom, something that he wants to spit out, but can't. He turns toward the water and slowly fills himself with salt air and serenity.

"You are working with some very profound truths and teachings, then."

"Not really," I say, unsure if it's him or the water that's lulled me into confession mode. "I came back looking for some kind of grand farewell or deep truth or something. But mostly I'm just discovering that everything is a wreck. Including me."

"Ah. Sounds like you are studying teachings from the Kick Your Own Ass Sutra," he says, still gracing the water with his intense gaze.

"Are you guys allowed to curse?" I have to ask.

"Yes, but only after we've studied the Curse Your Fucking Head Off Sutra. The Cape Breton translation." He flashes a smile and winks at me, and I can't tell if he's trying to be flirty or fatherly.

With the last lobster liberated, I wait for my share of the

Buddhist benefits to come raining down. Instead it starts to snow. The monk picks up his bucket, gives me a pleasant nod goodbye, and starts to shuffle away to the rusted and duct-taped station wagon that somehow carried him over the string of icy mountains between here and the monastery.

"Hey, wait," I say, the words squeezed out of me by some impulsive urgency I didn't know was there. "Can you give me..." I don't even know what to ask for.

"Need a ride somewhere?" he offers.

"No, not a ride." I take a deep haul of breath. "Can you give me some, I dunno, guidance? The spiritual kind. I can't live like this. Or die like this."

He comes to stand beside me, and gestures toward the water, sweeping his arm to the place where Great Bras d'Or opens into the Atlantic.

"There is a Sufi chant," he says, almost in a whisper. "*The ocean refuses no river.* Look at these waters. It's choiceless. Shit and garbage and pollution flow in, and nothing is refused or denied. The ocean takes it in, and does its best to integrate and purify whatever comes. I offer that to you as a contemplation." He shifts his gaze from the water to me. "We are all dying. You're fortunate enough to know it."

"Yeah, lucky me," I say.

"May I give you something else that may be of benefit?" he says. Without waiting for an answer he does a slo-mo rummage through the folds of his robe and pulls out a pocket-sized book and a little black business card emblazoned with a white lotus flower. "My dear friend and colleague. You might find her offerings useful on your path." He presses the business card into my palm. "And this." He extends a tiny book with an overexposed picture of his own handsomely beatific face on the cover toward me, "is my first book." I look at the title, *Living and Dying: You're Doing it Wrong.*

"Gee, thanks," I say.

He smiles, does a weird little half bow, and shuffles off to the station wagon, chased by a wave of cloudy white curls and electric blue beads that only I can see.

I close my eyes to steady them as he drives away, then reset my vision by reading the card pressed into my palm: "Wendy MacDermid, Holistic Death Doula & Facilitator for *Crann Na Beatha* Eco-Burial Innovations."

The Wendigo.

In Native American myth, the Wendigo is a gaunt, hollow-eyed humanesque monster with a grotesque odour and a taste for human flesh. At Loch Bhreagh Rural High School, The Wendigo was a skeletal girl a grade behind me, who smelled like BO and gnawed at the skin around her fingernails until it bled. From her Down North rumoured to be part-something-exotic mother, she'd inherited charcoal black hair and eyes and a stare that drilled holes in souls. And from her American backwoods, crunchy granola, hippy father—who worked as both a veterinarian and a pet cemetery keeper—she got a pasty complexion, an obsession with dead animals, and a nerve-jangling laugh that was seldom contained by decorum. Rumour also had it that she collected roadkill from the side of the highway, and once ate a raccoon eyeball. All I know for sure is that she submitted a heap of "artistic" photos of the grade ten biology class fetal pig dissections to the yearbook that year. She also rode the same bus as Allie. By all accounts, Wendigo Wendy was a weirdo. Judging by her business card, she still is.

I stuff the card in my pocket, plunk my arse down at a

snow-covered picnic table, stare out at the grey expansiveness of the horizon, and decide that "horizon" must be Latin for "gaping maw of nothingness." I think about dying. About heavens and hells and the spaces between. About last breaths and good deaths and what it will feel like to slip from existence. For a minute or ten, I even wonder what it might feel like to drown. Or freeze to death. I hear both are pretty peaceful, once you get to a certain point. This is what Hottie McMonk Pants and my fake friend Ami and every other Woo Woo Guru hack would call "contemplation," I guess. Maybe the Universe is speaking to me. Maybe I met Hottie McMonk Pants here today for a reason. Maybe that reason was so he could give my dumb ass a ride home, so I wouldn't have to trek through the snow in my lime-green parka and silver moon boots.

[...]

By the time Mama gets home from work, I am in bed, and not dead. Without a knock, she lurches into my room, plunks down beside me, and reaches to stroke the side of my head like I'm a pitiful old cat. Her hand rests on the thick forest of mouse-brown scrub brush. She starts laughing.

"Ahhh, remember the time you shaved off your eyebrows and cut your bangs an inch long and they stuck straight out? So ya drew new eyebrows on with a piece of charcoal and glued your hair down with egg whites? What was that, the first day of grade six?"

Grade seven. My first day of junior high in Loch Bhreagh. Char and Allie were strangers, but they saved me that day when they overheard Marcus King call me Oscar the Spunk Can before the first bell rang. Despite the eyebrows, the bangs plastered down with what looked like dried semen, and the obvious social liability I represented, Allie came and sat by me. Gently, diplomatically, she offered me her new headband to make my bangs look almost normal. Then she led me to the girls' bathroom, where Char was waiting with a brow pencil and a copy of *Seventeen* magazine. By lunchtime, I'd begun to successfully fade into the Loch Bhreagh junior high scene. Until Char grabbed Marcus King by the nuts and told him if she heard anyone call me Oscar the Spunk Can again, she'd castrate him with a badminton racket and an emery board. It was harder to blend in after that.

I can't be bothered to tell Mama any of that now. I just want to lie here like a bump on a log and listen to her voice.

"Mama, sing me a lullaby, wouldja?" I mumble.

For a minute, she looks as if she has forgotten that Sarah Spenser is selling our home out from underneath us. That money is tighter than ever. That word is going around the Gale that she got caught drinking on the night shift. That her only child is dying. For a minute, Mama looks almost happy as her voice lilts into song, her foot gently tapping out the tune of the only lullaby I can ever remember her singing to me.

> *There was liquor on the barroom floor,*
> *And the bar was closed for the night.*
> *When out of his hole came a little black mouse,*
> *And he sat in the pale moonlight.*
> *He lapped up the liquor on the floor,*
> *and on his haunches he sat.*
> *And all night long, you could hear him sing,*
> *"Oh bring out the goddamn cat!"*

Her hands linger on my head for a few moments after she finishes singing, and I can't help but laugh at the fact that this is what passes for soothing comfort now. Gnarled, calloused hands on my throbbing, shaved head, and an off-key foot-stomped song about a drunk, fearless mouse in a bar.

"Now, get to sleep," Mama says. "So you can get your own boney arse out of bed. I'll be too knackered to kick it out."

[…]

Winter descends into a sort of perverted beauty. Once we chucked out the Christmas tree and burned the remnants of reindeer wrapping paper and made peace with the fresh evidence of our familial dysfunction, I settled into the desolation. The doldrums. The depression. The disappointment. All of the neurotic afflictions that start with the letter *D*. There is comfort in all that, and in the pristine whiteness that envelops the land. Everyone and everything is silent and slow now. There are also big icicles forming along the busted eavestrough of the trailer that look like penises. Perverted beauty. I want to snap one off and bring it to Char because I know she'd make a comical show of eating it, but I can't because she's too much in her madness. I want to smoke a joint and call Allie to tell her about the valance of phallic formations so we can both laugh and come up with other half-baked ideas for what to do with them, but I can't because they kept her in the hospital once she admitted that she was scared she'd hurt herself. And misery doesn't really love company. I want to talk to Willy so he can tease me and make me laugh, but I can't because he has his own life and drama that doesn't include me.

The fleeting appreciation of snow blankets and silence and dicksicles is no match for the quagmire of coldness and sickness and stuckness. I'm tired of trying to laugh but wanting to cry. I'm tired of hosting the relentless head-pounding, gut-turning, limb-numbing party that Parry Homunculus, Ziggy Stardust, and Fuzzy Wuzzy are throwing in my head. Mostly, I'm just tired.

February looms. I shuffle around the trailer looking for distractions. I stare out the window at the snow, at the trees, at anything my lazy eyes land upon. Which is pretty much limited to snow and trees. Every now and then, a crow or a chickadee or a blue jay comes along, scrounging for something to sustain its fragile winter existence. But when there's nothing to be found, they fly away, and I'm back to staring at the inertia of nature. Nothingness is a shitty diversion. So I stare at my phone a lot. Rereading old text messages. Scrolling through Facebook posts of people I don't care about, as if relationship statuses going from "in a domestic partnership" to "it's complicated" matter. As if sexy filtered pictures of Asian fusion ab-buster kale noodle salad bowls for breakfast matter. As if memes for "classy ladies who drink and say fuck a lot" matter. The noisy static of other people's fake lives in motion is a pretty shitty diversion, too. So I shuffle, stare, and drink tea. Shuffle, stare, drink tea. Maybe I'm already dead and just don't know it yet. This seems like the kind of shit a ghost would do in limbo.

[···]

While Daktari Christ MacIsaac learned to crawl and babble, his mother learned how to get herself thrown in solitary. She claimed that another patient was plotting to assault her in the dining room, and told her doctor that she could hear his children crying because of the things he says to their mommy.

Meanwhile, Peggy heard that they just punted Allie out of the General Hospital and into the fumbling hands of her father and brothers. "But don't worry," they said. A "Rural Community Mental Health Team" will be there to answer her questions and support her wellness plan for recovery on Mondays or Wednesdays from nine a.m. to one p.m.

Whenever my phone sings The Bangles' "Hazy Shade of Winter" at me, I brace for bad news. About Allie or Char or Willy or myself. Or maybe somewhere deep down in the abysmal pit of my winter-numbed soul, I'm wishing for it. Anything to break up the monotony, the bleakness, the darkness, the cold. But there are only ever two kinds of calls:

"Hello?"

"Hello, Stacey Fortune?"

"Sure."

"I'm calling on behalf of Allied Collections regarding—"

Click.

But I have to make the click sound myself. Which I do.

And the other kind of call goes like this:

"Hello?"

A rustle, a faint buzz, a pause, and then the sound of a foghorn blasts me in the ear.

"Congratulations! You've won a cruise!"

Click.

And when the house phone rings, there are only two kinds of calls: one is Peggy calling with the latest dirt I pretend I don't want to hear. Allie Walker, out of the hospital and spotted hanging around Down North with The Wendigo.

Duke the Puke and Becky Chickenshit's marriage is on the rocks over him being a philanderer. Sarah Spenser's picture in the paper, snuggled up next to some oily-haired suit from Alberta. Chrissy Parsons had a miscarriage.

And the other is Dr. Divyaratna's office, calling to schedule MRIs. Or cancel MRIs. Then rescheduling the cancelled MRIs. Cancelling the rescheduled MRIs, and looking to re-reschedule. Asking if I've made up my mind about chemo or radiation.

I still answer both those phones every damn time they ring, hankering for a scrap of something new, something nourishing. Something with a dash of flavour, even.

Be careful what you wish for.

My phone sings. I answer. But this time, it's Dave. Talk about nerve.

"Hey. Sorry to bug you," he murmurs. "You were the only one I could think to call."

Ami left him. Already. For her yoga teacher. And her yoga teacher's wife. Because polyamorous yogic orgasms are the new kombucha-flavoured artisan glass dildos, apparently.

"You were right. About everything," he says. And then he starts to sob. "I'm a pathetic piece of shit. Ever since we split up, my life has been a disaster. I never should have ..."

And on and on he goes about what an idiot he was to ruin our beautiful life. How, deep down, he always felt like he didn't deserve to be happy, to have a woman like me. How all his dysfunction springs from the distant superficiality of his own mother. And I just listen. By the time he gets around to asking about my shitshow of a life, a solid year of stony resentment feels like it has been dampened and softened by his tears. His honesty. His vulnerability. He asks me how I'm doing. I tell him.

"I'm getting sicker. I'm all alone. Everybody here's fucked. And there's a For Sale sign planted at the bottom of our driveway."

"Wow," he says, "that's awful. Do you think maybe you made a mistake going back?"

Like a sad, lonely, hungry fish, I take the bait. "I make a lot of mistakes. This was probably one of them. But whatever, it will all be done soon."

"Stacey, I can't do this."

"Do what?"

"Let you live like this. Or...or—"

"Die like this? It's okay to say the word, Dave. That's where this is going."

"Do you remember my buddy Wes? The doctor?" he says.

"The one whose wife curated the art show of placentas?"

"Yes! Remember that! God, we laughed so much."

Of course. I remember everything.

"I ran into Wes the other day," Dave goes on. "He asked about you, so I told him. Turns out, there's some clinical trial on a new tumour treatment here. Really promising stuff." Dave pauses. "Maybe Wes could pull some strings..."

"Dave, I—"

He jumps in before I can finish the thought, which is good because I don't know what that thought was going to be. "You could live with me..." He hesitates, then hurries, "have your own room. I'll hire a cook. Round the clock nursing support. Whatever you need. No strings attached."

"There are always strings, Dave."

"Then maybe that's the risk you'd have to take," he says. "I want to help. Make amends. Life is too short. What have you got to lose?"

I tell him I'll think about it. And maybe I will.

Two cups of tea and a dozen trailer-length shuffles later, Dr. Divyaratna calls, the smooth precision of her Indian accent cutting through my newest daydream: the one where I am anywhere but here, with anyone but myself. My MRI appointment was booked for next week. And now it's cancelled. My blood work from last week came back. There's something new to worry about.

"When can you come into the office to discuss the results?" Dr. D. says.

I tell her I don't know. Her office is over an hour away. It's frigid and icy and there's a snowstorm every second day. Mama's working like a madwoman to keep us afloat, I am not allowed to drive, and all the people who usually drive me places are currently busy being disasters, dickheads, or both.

"Can't you just tell me?" I plead, staring vacantly out the window, down the driveway at the For Sale sign as it clatters back and forth in the bone-chilling wind. I wonder what the weather's like in Toronto right now.

Dr. Divyaratna sighs, deep and heavy. Then she rhymes off an alphabet soup of blood test names and the elevated numbers that came back with them. All meaningless.

"Is this good news or bad news?" I ask.

She clears her throat. "It appears that you are pregnant."

Fragments of words crackle through the phone after that. Ultrasound. High risk. Decisions. Soon. But I can't piece it together coherently because the voices of everyone else are swelling in my head.

Every flock of old hens from here to Loch Bhreagh to Town, tsking and clucking: *There's Crow Fortune, havin' a baby for that other druggie fella, after him already gettin' the Parsons one*

in trouble. And her with them tumours. And her mother back on
the bottle. And the Spensers taking their home. Baby'll likely be born
handicapped, eh? What with the father and whatever made him all
gimped up like that. And the grass smokin' down there at The Wharf
all the time. Her, sick and pregnant. Tsk, tsk, tsk. Them Fortunes.
Makes ya wonder how much of it they bring upon themselves.

Willy Gimp, grilling me about how this even happened,
what he's supposed to do about it, and why I even bothered
telling him.

Char and Allie giving me various shades of dubious advice.

And then there's Mama's voice. Loud and clear and fierce
as hell: *You made your bed, Missy. You'd best damn well lie in it.*

When the phone rings again, I am too stunned to answer
it. The ringing stops. Then starts again. Stops. Starts. Over
and over. Finally, I pick up.

"What?" My social graces are gone.

"It's me," says Peggy, who never had much in the way of
social graces to begin with.

I just start laughing like a hyena. I laugh and laugh and
laugh. Laugh myself to tears.

"What's wrong with you?" Peggy's voice raised and rising,
tight and desperate. "Christ, Crow! Shut up! There was an
accident."

"What? Who? What happened?" I mumble. There's an
unmistakable urgency in Peggy's voice, snapping me into the
awareness that shit just got real.

"A car accident. Your mother," hushed and shaky.

"Jesus, is she okay?"

"No," choked and barely audible.

Not at all.

She's dead.

7 IN LIVING AND DYING COLOUR

Everybody always said that "letting go" was one of those things I had to learn to do. *Let go of grudges against people who are just born arseholes. Let go of needing to run the whole show, and just let other people do a piss-poor job and make mistakes. Let go of the cat's tail before she claws your eyeballs out.* But letting go is a lie. Nobody really does it, not in the way that all the serenity-stuffed blissers out there would have you believe. We usually just find something new to cling to. Something to fill whatever void is left by whatever we pretended to let go of, because voids make us twisted and twitchy. Letting go isn't liberating. It's a gruesome process of coming undone, especially when nothing can fill the void left by losing the only thing that held you together. The thing that was so precious, so deeply embedded in every fibre of your existence that you don't even know how to be in the world without it.

Still, on a frigid February day, I had to let Mama go. Literally. Despite the near weightlessness of ash, my hands ached and shook as all that was left of her slipped through my fingers.

For as long as I can remember, Mama made no bones about how she wanted things handled. No keening obit in the paper, no tiresome wake, no fancy funeral. She insisted that she be cremated, her ashes spread in a no-fuss manner down at The Wharf. By me. Because I was the only one who'd know how to toss her out properly. Poor Father Delahanty was a terrible judge of wind and water. Just ask the family of old Tully Crumb.

"Handsome young devil, that Father Delahanty," Mama would say, "but stunned as me arse. The service for old Tully Crumb down at Black Rock, he goes and chucks a scoopful of her ashes up into the air toward the water, and doesn't the wind catch it. Ashes flying back into everybody's eyes! One way to make people cry at your funeral, I guess. And knowing Tully, that was part of her plan all along. Getting in people's faces like that, just to be a prick one last time. But Delahanty is not to lay a hand on my ashes. Got that?"

Standing on the wharf, my lime-green parka over a long black dress that just grazes the tops of my silver moon boots, I test the wind direction with a spit-moistened finger. I watch the rippling water, and the cruising clouds up above. I chuck the little scoop the funeral home gave me aside because I need to touch her one last time. To hold her as best I can. My cupped hand gingerly scoops some of her ashes out of the plain black urn, and my fingers curl around her, squeezing her tight. I kiss her through my white, blotchy knuckles. Whisper goodbye. Then, one slow, heavy handful at a time, I let her go into the invisible current that will carry her onto the Great Bras d'Or. I let Mama go in waves.

[···]

A volunteer emergency responder named Fricker pulled her body from the car after they towed it out of the icy bay's depths. She was already dead, but Fricker didn't waste any time getting her out and wrapped in a blanket. He didn't let them put her in a body bag right away. He held her hand for a few moments, smoothed down her hair and closed her eyes. Mama would have appreciated that. She was always afraid that death would give her that freshly caught smelt look.

I can pick Fricker out of the crowd. I can't make out his face from this distance, but there are slivers of translucent blue and solid green that reach and pull all around him. When I shift my gaze to the group that has now inexplicably gathered at The Wharf, a dancing dome of colours is all I see. Every now and then, an electric indigo or incandescent white spark flickers, flashes, dissolves in the crowd of old churchies who are here to pray for Mama's soul, now that she's gone. *Because God knows they didn't have a spare prayer for Scruffy Effie Fortune while she was alive. C'mere till I give you an eyeful of ashes, ya pack of pious bastards.*

Oh shuddup, Crow, I can almost hear Mama say. *It won't kill you to accept a little kindness.*

If I squint at the world just right, my squirrelly vision could almost be beautiful today, and I can't help but feel an unexpected pang of gratitude for Parry and Ziggy and Fuzzy Wuzzy for giving me this gift of colour and light and movement in the midst of an otherwise frozen, dark moment. Like even the brain tumours are trying to show me some kindness.

Mama would be mortified that somebody put an obituary in the paper calling her "a blessing to her community." Mortified that the ladies' auxiliary pulled together an impromptu reception at the fire hall. Mortified that so many crying, sniffling people spontaneously found their way down to The Wharf today to pay their respects. But nobody got an eyeful of ash. So at least that went the way Mama wanted.

The investigation into the accident was quick. The treacherous turn by the bridge at the foot of Ceilidh Mountain is known for swaths of black ice. Mama lost control of the car. It went through the old guardrail, hit the big rocks on the bank before going into the water, then sank into the deep part of the Bras d'Or. The autopsy was quick, too. Mama was probably already unconscious from the crash when the car went under. It was the kind of accident people have been predicting for decades. *One of these days, somebody's gonna get killed on that turn, and won't that be a shame.* So there's no need to ask too many questions, and no need for Shirl Short or Dar MacIsaac or Bonnie Big Mouth or Peggy Fortune to make up answers.

Meanwhile, I've got a whore of a pile of funeral ham, because in Cape Breton the only way to offer condolences is with food, and there are only three kinds of foods that show you mean it: casseroles, squares, and funeral hams. When the funeral hams go on sale down at the grocery store for ninety-nine cents a pound, you stock up so you'll always have something to bring the family when somebody dies. Flossie Baker brought over the biggest slab of ham I've ever laid eyes on, cheerfully decorated with patterns of pineapple rings and maraschino cherries, all pinned to the meat with cloves. In fact, there's not a lick of room left in the fridge thanks to the gargantuan ham, two cheesy hash brown casseroles, and a tub of goulash. And the pan of deep-fried chicken wings and some kind of noodles. Clearly, there are some rebels down the Middle Rear Road these days.

"Here," Peggy says, shoving a pan of brown and pink swirly

squares at me as I prod the ham, trying to make some room. "From Audrey. She'll meet us down the fire hall."

"You take 'em. I don't eat squares." My flat voice is barely audible over the fridge's hum.

"Suit yourself," she trills as she jabs a finger into the red dye-drenched concoction. "Hunger's a wonderful sauce." She slurps the glob from her finger and grins. "*Mmm, mmm, mmm. I'd eat a horse and chase the driver right about now.*"

I bite my tongue as I abandon the fridge and instead fish one of the frozen pans of Mama's broc-o-glop out of the freezer. In my peripheral vision, I can see Peggy's head swimming in an odd pool of pale silver, shiny and concave like an empty spoon.

"Is that Effie's broc-o—"

"Frig off, it's mine and you can't have any," I say, looking up just in time to see the silver around Peggy tilt, tarnish, then disappear completely. I bury my head back into the depths of the fridge.

"Crow, listen, I know we haven't always seen eye to eye—" Peggy starts.

"Christ, that ham is a monster," I grumble, like I didn't hear her.

"Your mother would chew my face off for leaving you here all by yourself. She didn't want you to be alone."

"I can take care of myself. Not gonna be here much longer anyway."

I shove the fridge door shut, only to have it bounce right back at me because the stupid ham is sticking out too far. Two pineapple rings lose their clove pins and slop to the floor, while the electric red cherries escape into the filthy darkness under the fridge.

"Listen, Sarah Spenser is up to something with the land sale. I can smell it," Peggy says.

I expect to see the gleam of scheming and gossipy glee in her eyes, but instead her meaty hands are squashed together in an anxious clench. There might even be tears trying to sneak out from the puffed edges of her eyelids. The ham finally yields enough space for me to close the fridge door. I pitch the escaped pineapple into the garbage.

"Let's get this show on the rogue." Char sashays into the kitchen. Legs in thigh-high black leather boots. Dreadlocks contained in a tall black top hat. Daktari slung on her hip, dressed all in pink. Grinning, drooling, and waving.

"Christ almighty, Charlotte, tuck your tits into your dress first," Peggy sighs. "And try not to act like you're out on a day pass from the Butterscotch."

[···]

Everybody knows that you're not supposed to eat all the sandwiches and squares and drain the coffee urn at a funeral reception before the family arrives. But the pack of gannets who flocked from The Wharf to the fire hall for this one clearly forgot their manners, because all that is left when we get there are Lolly Ferguson's cucumber sandwiches and a plate of Helen with the Hairy Pits's gluten-free, sugar-free, taste-free cookies. *Poor Helen. She's a hippy and a Come From Away. New Brunswick, God love her.* Fine by me though. I'll just drink the tea, flash the requisite sad smile, and pretend I know who everyone is. Plus, there's a pan of Mama's broc-o-glop waiting for me at home.

The buzz of all the busybodies in the room evaporates when we parade through the door and into the midst of

Mama's mourners. Peggy steers Char and the baby toward the scant offerings left on the food table, then goes with Aunt Audrey to shake some old church lady hands. Uncle Gordie goes to the kitchen, rummaging for something to chase the pint of rum he has stashed in his funeral suit pocket. I make a beeline for Allie, who is standing by the tea, her arms outstretched and beckoning, her entire frame shrouded in a shaky teal haze. I lean into her hug and try to laugh as I whisper, "Fuck, would Mama ever hate this. Look at all these old bags, coming all the way out here like they give a shit."

She ignores my glib chatter. She squeezes me tight. She gasps in my ear, "Now we both have to learn how to be motherless."

I slip out of Allie's arms and bolt to the bathroom, where I crank the water on full blast in the sink so that I can heave and gag over the toilet bowl for a few minutes in relative secrecy. When I come out, Uncle Mossy is standing there, grinning from ear to over-sized ear. He takes a couple of quick shuffles toward me, squints his eyes, screws up the bottom half of his rubbery face, and cranes his stubby little neck until his face is just a few inches from mine.

"I sees it," he whispers, "dat little rainbow."

"G'wan, Mossy, stop hovering outside the ladies' room before somebody thinks you're some kind of pervert." Peggy elbows her brother over toward the dartboards in the corner. "Go smile and nod at Flossie Baker for a bit."

"You look like ten tons of garbage," she says as she turns to me. "Are you okay?"

"Fine."

She leans in so that for a second I think she's going to hug me, and I instinctively start to recoil. Instead, she takes a long, slow suck of the air in the space between my ear and my shoulder.

"Hmm."

"What?"

"Nothing." She begins to rotate her girth back to the busyness of the room. Then she stops. "You know what *petrichor* is?"

I give her a faint frown and a head wobble that barely indicates no. I hate admitting that I don't know what a word means. Especially to the likes of Peggy.

"It's the smell after it rains. That fresh, earthy, growing smell. Right fertile smelling." Peggy's voice is philosophical and dreamy, but then it shifts abruptly, sharp and pointed as she looks me in the eyes. "Weird to catch a whiff of that in the dead of February."

With that, she waddles off. My head spins, my eyes are bombarded by a slew of reddish-orange and dusty blue twinkles, and my gut tightens around an impossible, paranoid notion: *Peggy knows.*

Allie slides up beside me with a woman I don't recognize. Long coal black hair with a pale silver streak, nonchalantly looped into a knot. Intricately detailed birchbark earrings, a turquoise scarf, probably woven by a pack of goddess-blessed babies on the banks of a sacred Guatemalan river.

"Crow, you remember Wendy, right?"

The Wendigo.

She smiles softly and motions to give my arm a brush of sympathy. My body tenses up, as I smile and resist the urge to jerk away. Wendy's hand drifts back without making contact.

"My deepest condolences, Crow," she says in her slow, low, mournfully monotone voice. "Your mother was remarkable. I trust her passage was smooth."

"Nothing smooth about your car crashing into freezing water," I snort. "Getting incinerated in a thousand-dollar cardboard box doesn't sound so smooth either."

The Wendigo clasps her hands and bows her head solemnly. She flashes a gap-toothed smile, as the blue-green ripples around her head emit tiny tangerine bursts.

"If you'd ever like to plan a more personal celebration of your mother's life, or if you have things you'd like to explore with your own circumstances—"

Allie interjects. "Wendy is doing some really great work. Spiritual counselling. Grieving. Dying with dignity. Home wakes and burials. Sounds morbid, but she's amazing. They're doing a thing here at the fire hall in the spring. 'Rig Yer Mortis: Doing Death Right.' Clever, hey? I told Wendy we'd come."

I give Allie and her smooth, steady, blue-and-silver halo the side eye.

Before I can think, or tell them about my chat with old Hottie McMonk Pants down at The Wharf on New Year's Eve, I feel something pelt me in the back of the head. Then another. And another. A handful of pine cones are scattered on the floor. I turn, and see the emergency exit door of the fire hall flung wide open. Char stands in the doorway, her giant black hat in hand and filled with pine cones. Which she is biffing at me. Her eyes and her maniac mouth are wide open. She's howling with laughter.

"Little. Baby. Trees. Everywhere!" she shouts.

Before too many tongues can start wagging, Peggy ushers Char out the door. Into the Monte Carlo. Back to the looney bin. I pick the pine cones up off the floor, as Shirl Short and one of the nosy housekeeping broads from the Greeting Gale scuttle toward me. Shirl puts a hand on my arm. The other one has her doe-eyed, half-smiling head—tinged by a bubble-gum-and-mud-coloured halo—cocked to the side in some sort of half-assed condolence expression.

"Crow, dear," Shirl starts, all syrup and sympathy, with bile-and-tongue-coloured splotches clustered around her head. "I'm so sorry for your loss. A shame your poor sainted mother couldn't even be properly mourned without the likes of that one causing a scene. What was Peggy thinking, bringing her here? Silly twit."

There are a million things I could say to Shirl Short, and I know that whatever I do say is bound to get repeated. I smile politely. I try to picture Shirl Short as an innocent child. Or as an old woman on her deathbed. Aching. Vulnerable. Truly sorry for all the shit she couldn't help but cause. I open my mouth to let some saccharine platitudes flow.

"With all due respect, Shirley Short, go fuck yourself."

With a smile and a curtsey, out the door I go. To practise being motherless. Pregnant. And dying.

[···]

With the full moon throwing a sallow light across the icy whiteness of the yard, I bundle myself up in my snow pants, moon boots, and parka and go outside to sit in the snow. I plunk myself down just a few paces from the trailer and stare up at the pale old orb in the sky, surrounded by distant stars. I draw the frigid February night deep into my lungs and hold it there before sending a sigh's worth of my own exhausted, stagnant breath back into the world. As if the world needs more exhausted, stagnant hot air. I keep trying to suck in some peace, some relief. But all I get is cold and uncomfortable. With snot and tears frozen to my face.

Despite my broken heart and murky mind, it occurs to me that the path of least resistance is being fully illuminated by this moon and all the other cold, hard, glaring realities that hang over my head now. My mother is dead. My friends are fucked. My days are numbered. I'm about to be homeless, and I got knocked up by a disabled deadbeat drug dealer. Dave suddenly looks like a knight in shining armour.

He will give me a good-enough love. He'll hire some top-notch professionals to care for me when I'm blind and drooling and pissing my pants. Plus, Dave would be a stable steward of my little walking, talking legacy. Poor bastard always wanted to have a kid. I was always ambivalent, at best. Dave would make sure that this kid gets into the best daycare, the best alternative arts-based school, the best clothing and footwear. He would tell my child warm, charming stories about me without using the words *shitfaced* or *arseholes* or *sur-fucking-prise*. And he would most certainly be on board for having my ashes mashed into a multi-faceted gem of a memory after I die. Nobody around here thought getting Gem-Mortalized was as awesome as I did. When I told Mama that's what I wanted, she scoffed and said, "Oh well, pardon me, Your Highness." Even The Wendigo said it was creepy.

If I were inclined to believe that the almighty Universe is preoccupied with sending middle-aged, lower-middle-class white ladies divine cosmic messages about what they should or should not be doing with their existence, I might interpret the events of late as a series of none too subtle signs that my plan to live and die on this island was, in fact, a bad one.

You made your bed, now lie in it! I can almost hear Mama say. Almost. Except I can't hear anything over the rumble of the rig coming up the driveway.

Dulcie Cooper is almost a hundred years old, but she plows her old car up the dark, snow-drifted road like a reckless seventeen-year-old, and wobbles her old bones up the walkway, carrying a pan of squares, a quart of milk, and an envelope from the Drummond Presbyterian Ladies' Auxiliary. I don't know much about Dulcie Cooper except that she's old as dirt and drives like a nut. I didn't know there was a Drummond Presbyterian Ladies' Auxiliary. And I'm not going to eat the squares. But I do need milk for tea, and when I open the envelope, I nearly shit. Inside, there's two thousand dollars, cash. Which, as I realize all too quickly, is enough for a one-way first-class ticket back to Toronto. The Universe is not whispering to me. It's screaming like a banshee.

I'm supposed to invite Dulcie Cooper in and make her some tea, I think. But I don't. I stand there in the middle of the walkway with the milk and the squares and the envelope in hand, until she leaves. It's nine o'clock at night, and I just want this dizzying, surreal day to be over. As Dulcie's car clatters down the driveway, I drop back into my moulded seat in the snowbank.

I think about freezing to death. How easy it would be to do, right here, right now, if I just let my exhausted body fall asleep in the snow. I close my eyes, nestling a little deeper into the chill and the darkness. Until the lights of another rig come flooding up the driveway. *Dammit. I'm trying to die here.*

Moments later, Willy Gimp is standing in front of me, looking at me like I'm six slices short a whole roll of baloney.

A blood-orange and baby-blue fuzzball is poufed out all around his pained, tired face. There's a bottle of wine tucked under his bad arm and a gagger of a joint sandwiched between the band of his Nirvana ball cap and his right ear. I can't decide if I want to kiss him or kick him in the balls. So I just sit in the snowbank and cry. Mama is gone. Willy is here. And I can't drink that wine or smoke that spliff with him, and I should probably tell him why. But first, that bastard has some explaining to do.

Sure enough, Chrissy Parsons got back into the drugs, and it was all Gimp's fault. He gave her an ounce of weed to help her get through the vicious DTs she'd been having ever since she quit drinking. She started drinking to help her quit the OxyContin. She started the OxyContin to help her quit the gambling. And she started the gambling when she quit drinking the last time. The weed scheme was her ticket to hell because instead of just smoking it alone to ease the detox like she planned, she ended up attracting the keen-nosed attention of her upstairs neighbour, Weasel Tobin. The two of them were puffing their brains out in her grimy little basement apartment down The Mines when Weasel got an idea. What if they traded some of Willy Gimp's weed for something a little crystal meth-ier? Thus, Chrissy Parsons's highway to hell was paved with Willy Gimp's good intentions and Weasel Tobin's bad ideas, and she was on the meth and out turning tricks behind the Pott's Coffee on the highway.

Until her brother Cracker came banging on Willy Gimp's door. Cracker Parsons owns a shady construction company, and he has the strongest, toughest, most loyal guys on the Island working for him. He has a half-dozen dirty cops in his pocket. And he is a nutbar. So when Cracker Parsons comes round to say that he noticed you left some old gas cans and oily rags out behind your garage that could catch fire, and that he heard you gave his sister Chrissy drugs even though you knew better, well, you'll do whatever you can to get Cracker Parsons's sister out of the trouble he figures you helped get her into. Even if that means pretending to get back together with her for a bit. And pretending you were the one who got her pregnant. And taking her to the hospital when she has a miscarriage. And splitting the cost of getting her into a two-month residential rehab centre down on the Mainland. Then you can sleep again. Your garage won't mysteriously burn to the ground. And the cops won't hear your name or Chrissy Parsons's name when they bust Weasel Tobin and everybody else who didn't help Cracker get his sister off the streets and off the drugs.

"Sorry I didn't say something sooner," Willy sighs. "I couldn't. People talk. Sure you don't want a puff?" he asks, holding the joint out to me, as I sit curled up on the couch, underneath the one and only blanket that Mama ever managed to knit. "Or a sip?"

"About that," I mumble, fiddling with a piece of unravelling yarn in the middle of a grey-scale granny square.

"Weed's good for when you get the chemo and radiation. You won't feel as sick. I can hook ya up."

I reach over and snatch the joint from his hand and take a slow, deep drag. Just one. Just enough to give me the guts to say the words out loud for the first time.

"I'm pregnant."

He plucks the joint from my hand and gives me a wild glare as he stomps to the door and tosses it into the snow.

By the time he sits back down, his face is frozen somewhere between laughing and crying, while iridescent orbs and little gold sparks float and flutter around the brim of his ball cap.

"Well then." He clears his throat and straightens his hat, like he knows it might be knocked askew by the cascading sparks and bubbles. "Maybe this is just the kick in the arse the two of us need. Maybe this is a sign —"

"If you say 'from the Universe' I'll puck you in the junk." The only blanket Mama ever knit weighs heavy on my lap, my belly. I have successfully picked apart an entire granny square, and absently tied all the loose yarn up into one big knot.

"No, I was going to say maybe this is a sign that we need to grow up and stop pissing our lives away on what doesn't matter," he says, taking off his hat and setting it on his lap as a shield, just in case.

Without the hat on, I can see gold sparks popping out from the middle of Gimp's forehead, while the clear orbs shoot straight out from the top of his noggin, like one of those shitty dollar store automatic bubble makers made for kids too lazy to use their own air and effort for entertainment. I decide there's no way my kid will ever have one of those stupid things. *You want bubbles, baby? Blow them yourself. From your head. Like your Daddy does.*

"What do you want to do?" he says softly.

"Build a time machine and go back to the day I figured it was okay to skip getting my Depo shot. That seems like a reasonable first step." I stare at the yarn knot and roll it tighter so I don't have to look at him.

"Crow, this is kinda serious."

"No shit. Look, I don't know. I just found out, my mother is dead, and I'm not." A lump rises in my throat. My eyes squeeze shut, trying to lock up the tears.

His hand reaches to give me a caress of comfort, but I push it away.

"Everybody just fucks off right when I need them most. I always end up dealing with everything on my own." My voice, my face are contorting to accommodate my mess of tears.

"Want me to stay with you tonight?"

"No."

I catch myself imagining what Dave would do in response to such self-pity. Leap from the couch, throw his hands in the air, make a smart, snide comment about my self-centredness, and slam the door on the way out. Then he'd show up an hour later with a dozen red roses, chocolate brioche, and a bottle of acai berry juice pressed by the feet of Trinidadian Hindu yogis, and a million hollow words to validate my pity party.

Willy Gimp just hauls in a silent, steady breath and hugs me close, until I stop sobbing and ranting about how awful everything and everyone in my life has always been. When I fall into a drained silence, he quietly struggles to hoist himself off the couch because his bad leg is asleep and his bad arm has sunk too deep in the cushion to give him any decent traction. He drops his Nirvana hat on the floor six times while his unreliable limbs wrestle with his puffy coat. He kisses me on the forehead, shuffles to the door, and before closing it behind him with the utmost care, he looks back at me with his soft, spent wonder of a smile.

"Want to know what I remember most about your mother? Her 'pity party' song. She'd come into the garage, and the two of us would get to chatting. The second I'd start bitching about something, she'd grab my bad hand, give it a squeeze and then"—his voice drops to a gravelly sing-song— "'Nobody likes me. Everybody hates me. Guess I'll eat some worms. Big fat slimy ones, gross and greasy grimy ones, chubby little grubby little worms.' Made me roar every time."

I sit there sniffling and snotting into the tightly clutched corner of my blanket.

"If I was you, I'd eat some of Flossie Baker's ham and a few of them squares instead. There's more rock-solid love for you here than you think, Crow. I'll call you in the morning."

"Whatever," I sulk.

He blows me a kiss and a few extra shiny bubbles.

As his truck rumbles off, my fingers twitch and my heart inches up into my throat as I touch the little call back button on the screen of my phone. I'm staring at the digits of Dave's number as they pop up on the screen, when, without so much as a knock, Peggy barrels through the door with Mossy in tow. My shaky finger taps the end call button just before it starts to ring.

"Here," Peg says, "Mossy's gonna stay with you tonight."

"Look, I can—"

"Ain't got time to argue. Charlotte's back to the hospital, and the baby's asleep in the car. Don't be so contrary all your life, take a day off."

"I'm fine. I don't need anything from you people."

And right on cue, the room starts to swirl and spin. My head throbs, my limbs twitch, and my ears are assaulted by thunderous clangs, clatters, and grinding sounds. My vision blurs and my stomach lurches and then I throw up all over the floor, just barely missing the blanket on my lap.

"Mossy, clean that up and get her settled for the night, wouldja?" Peggy directs. "We know where your mother kept the Javex, and we know how to make a proper cup of tea. And Mossy here sleeps with his eyes open, don't ya, Moss?"

But Mossy doesn't answer. He's already boiling water for tea and rummaging for the Javex.

[···]

I look at Char's baby, sleeping soundly in the back seat of Peggy's car on the drive into Town, Town for my appointment. I look at Mossy, sitting next to Daktari, an amused smile plastered on his face as he stares at the smear of trees that zips past his window as the car cruises along the monotonous highway. I look at Peg, her eyes watching the road as it rolls out before us, her head swaying to the smooth cryptic croon of Leonard Cohen and his jazzy pop-a-sophical backup singers. And I decide it's all a little too peaceful. Time to officially get out in front of the story of my own stupidity before somebody hears or says something, and the whole thing is out of my control. Before Peggy officially figures it out.

"I gotta tell you something," I say slowly, carefully. "I'm—"

"Pregnant? I know," Peggy says. Casual as all hell.

Mossy giggles.

"I'm not stupid," Peggy says, glancing at me sideways. "You're barfing your guts up. You're starting to show. But I knew before that. Like I said the day of your mother's funeral, you smell like petrichor."

"Pregnant women smell like mud puddles?"

"No, petrichor. There's a difference. Mud puddles are more stagnant and mucky smelling. You smell like a mud puddle when you start bottling up feelings. Or like sour milk."

"You're nuts."

"Am I?"

No, she's not. In fact, she's radiating an intensely un-crazy teal halo, strewn with soft violet wisps. Peggy's nose. It knows.

"Now ask ol' Mossy how he knew," Peggy orders.

Mossy sits there, still staring out the window, grinning like the idiot everybody always pretends he is.

"C'mon Moss, spit it out. Tell Crow how you knew she was having a baby." Peggy cocks her head to the side, articulating each word in a half-shout.

"Answered da phone when the doctor called," Mossy says, the inner edges of his thick lips smacking together, cushioning the space between words. He giggles again.

"Smarten up, ya clown," Peggy says. "Tell Crow about the colours."

"Ohh," Mossy gasps. "The feels are the thoughts in colours, and babies makes the rainbows."

"Oh g'wan ya cryptic bastard!" Peggy groans as she flicks off the cassette deck, making me wonder if she's talking to Mossy or Leonard Cohen. She glances at me again. "How long have you been seeing stuff? Auras, or whatever the New Age hippy crystal rubbers call them."

"Well, with the tumours and—"

"It's not the tumours, Crow. It's like Mossy said. Emotions are colourful thoughts, and you two can see them. All this stuff, it's in the family."

"Right. The cursed Fortunes."

"I beg your pardon," she says, a sharp indignation in her voice. "You wanna see cursed? Look at the poor Willy Nilly Gilligans. Dozens of them all over the place, not one with an IQ over sixty-five. Or the Bonk-Headed Blacketts from Down the Point, who all look like they got beat with an ugly stick. Even the babies. Or your father's people, with their cold little hearts full of nothing but want and spite. Now that, Crow, dear, is cursed. The senses, these ways, have been passed down through the ages to people who've earned them the hard way. Not a curse. A blessing. If you learn to use 'em right."

An audible snort of skepticism escapes from my throat.

"Scoff all you want," Peggy says. "But it's true. Once you know what's what, you have a choice. Use it, or lose it. Your aunt Janice? She lost it. Couldn't make good meaning of what she heard, lost her mind in all the static, and died trying to make it stop. Same with Melly and Cecil. Or Gordie, being an angry drunk, or Audrey and her fanatical Bible thumping. If the stubborn bastards would just pay attention to what's right in front of them without getting all worked up, we'd all be better off. Now you and Mossy, you can see what people's minds are made of. Their true colours, and the shape of their lives. And once you got a clear bead on them, and what it all means, you figure out how to use it. For ill, nil, or goodwill. There's power there."

"What about you?" I wait for a plume of murky pink hypocritical do-as-I-say-not-as-I-do to puff up from her head.

"I'm doing the best I can with what I've got," she says, hands gripping the steering wheel tighter. "You know how you can't smell the hum of your own armpits? Well I couldn't smell my own hurt for the longest time. I used to watch my mother coo and coddle you, and I'd listen to Effie gripe about the trials and tribulations of motherhood, and you know what I'd smell? Warm cinnamon rolls with this hint of some other spice I could never quite place. Made me feel like a little beggar outside the bakery with my face pressed up against the window, drooling at the cozy sweetness just out of my reach. After a while, that smell made me sick. But your mother, she inspired me."

"What was Mama's freak show party trick, then?" I choke a little as I say her name out loud.

"You really don't know, do you?" Peggy says, as a host of incredulous purple curls spring from around her head and tickle the corners of her mouth into a soft smile. "What your mother did for people around here? Her, a first responder. Volunteer firefighter. Visiting the hurt and the sick and the dying at the friggin' hospital all them years, even though she was already spread thinner than the margarine at Lent. Didn't you ever notice those hands of hers? Or what she did with them every time you fell down and scraped your knee when you were little?"

She'd put her hand on it for a few minutes, before she'd even get a Band-Aid or peroxide.

"How'd she break up fights between your big galoot uncles?"

She'd grab them by the ear, and they'd stop without another word.

"What did she try to do to that head of yours after you moved home?"

She'd pat it like I was a friggin' puppy, every chance she got.

"Effie could lay hands on people," Peg says with a sad hush in her voice.

"Like reiki?"

"Lord, no!" Peggy huffs. "Effie's gift was more than that New Age energy jazz. She healed people, Crow. Didn't just make them feel better. Her hands did something special, but there was a part that she never let on. She absorbed the hurts. Physical, but sometimes mental, too. Those newspapers you burned in your little bonfire? She saved those because there were stories there, people she helped who went on to live good lives. She needed reminders of that because her hands, her whole body, didn't know what to do with the pain she took besides hold it. All gifts have a price tag. Christ, I wish she—" Peggy pumps the brakes hard as we merge off the highway and onto the main drag in Town, Town. A dusty little band of blue bricks begins to compact itself in front of her mouth.

Every time Mama dropped me at Peggy's while she went to visit some random old biddy on the road just to "be a good neighbour," I rolled my eyes. Every time I couldn't have the car because she was volunteering at the hospital or had to rush to a first responder call or had to go "give someone a hand," I huffed. And every time I curled up on my mother's lap with a skinned knee or a broken heart, and she'd hold me tight, I just assumed that I was strong and tough and able to will away the bulk of my hurt. All the while, Scruffy Effie Fortune was quietly, thanklessly, willingly taking on the burden of other people's wounds. Mine included. And for the first time since I heard the words "brain tumours" in the aftermath of my Toronto subway seizure scene, something that isn't overwhelming terror masquerading as Fuck It Bucket List, spit-in-yer-eye bravado washes over me. A wave of hope. *Maybe, just maybe, Mama's hands healed me.*

"So, we've got a genetic lineage of haywire senses with either half-assed impractical applications, or the potential to, I dunno, save people's lives. But we're also prone to going nuts and dying tragically before we ever get the chance to figure it out?" I say. "That's not a blessing. And it's outlandish as fuck," I say, pretending I'm not fazed by hope's fleeting flicker.

"Think what you want," Peggy says as we pull into the parking lot of the hospital. "For all I know, Black Bernie Fortune's blood was cursed but Lucy Dougall's heart was blessed, and there's a war between the two being fought in each of us. But I'll tell you this, trees grow best with a shovel of shit round the roots. That's not outlandish. That's nature's truth."

She takes a long, exaggerated sniff of the air. "And we best change Dakey's diaper before I bring him to see Charlotte."

[...]

Char will lose whatever's left of her mind when she hears Peggy call her child a goofy nickname like Dakey, and I'd like to be there to see it happen. Instead, I'll be under a paper sheet on a table in the diagnostic imaging wing of the hospital, waiting for the ultrasound tech to tell me which everyday item my fetus's size most closely resembles. Which, it turns out, is a fourteen-week-old lemon. This lemon has un-webbed fingers and toes. Its eyes and ears have moved into non-alien position. It can squint and grimace, flail its arms and kick its feet, drink and piss out amniotic fluid. I swore I wasn't going to look at the screen. I kept my eyes clamped shut. I put my hands over them when they tried to flutter open. But at the last minute, I peeked through a crack in the wall of tears and fingers, only to see a little embryonic arse float toward the ultrasound transducer and wiggle.

As she's wiping what remains of the now-warm goo off my belly, the ultrasound tech tells me that they just had the MRI machine free up because the old bird who was supposed to have hers this morning up and died. Ever alert to opportunities to get me a medical test because somebody else kicked the bucket, Dr. Divyaratna put me in the slot. Which means I also get to see what everyday items compare best to the sizes of Parry Homunculus, Ziggy Stardust, and Fuzzy Wuzzy. Last time, it was a June bug, a nickel, and a cranberry, respectively.

As the cold MRI bed slides in to the circular sarcophagus, it occurs to me that there's a race happening in my body now. Who can grow faster, my baby or my tumours? As the magnetic din of doom begins to whizz and whir around my head, it occurs to me that maybe Peggy had a point. Maybe my squirrelly vision could be useful. A bit of a blessing even, albeit well disguised.

When the MRI tech's voice comes over the internal speaker saying, "Miss Fortune, you're wiggling. Please try to hold still," it occurs to me that I should have pissed between the ultrasound and the MRI.

I wait for Dr. Divyaratna in a tiny closet of an office. When she enters, her nose is buried in a file folder, and she almost forgets to dispense her usual measured dose of bedside manner before getting down to business.

"Good day, Stacey." She places a steady hand on my shoulder as she makes her way to her desk. "I heard of your mother's tragic accident. Allow me to extend my deepest sympathies."

I do the sad smile and silent nod thing.

"So. Fourteen weeks pregnant. How would you like to proceed in light of this situation?"

"What are my options?" I squint as I fix my gaze on the space above her head, trying to read the coloured lines between whatever words come next.

"Moving forward with a fairly aggressive proactive treatment protocol could increase your odds of a more favourable outcome and quality of life, and in that case I would recommend terminating the pregnancy. But if you elect to carry on, we cross our fingers and hope for the best."

She flips through some papers and keeps going.

"The good news is that your tumours have not grown in size or complexity. Therefore, while carrying your pregnancy to term is not without risks due to your age and health status, it is not urgent that we pursue aggressive treatment options. We could wait until after you give birth, if you choose."

"Can I see the pictures?" I say, my body and brain so numb that I scarcely notice how tightly I'm gripping the pleather arms of the faux-cozy doctor's office chair.

"From the ultrasound?" Dr. Divyaratna smiles.

"No," I say, "the MRI. The tumours."

She tilts her head, and eyes me like I've lost it. After a quick rummage, she glides the big black sheet into place on a big white wall-mounted box. She turns on the backlight, and there they are, shining and leaping out from the greyness of their surroundings like wispy white explosions. Seditious little stars in a matter-of-fact grey sky. Parry Homunculus, Ziggy Stardust, and Fuzzy Wuzzy, fully illuminated. Before I know it, I'm parked in front of the light box, gently tracing the white lines that trail away from the solid centres with my fingers. Smiling and welling up with tears. Whispering the only lullaby Mama ever sang to me,

There was liquor on the barroom floor,
and the bar was closed for the night . . .

"They let you out?" I try not to sound weak as I emerge from Dr. Divyaratna's office with an armload of leaflets on tumours and pregnancies and ways to deal with both, to see Char standing there with Daktari perched on her cocked hip, gnawing on the tip of one of her neatly tied back dreadlocks.

"Yo, I be blowin' this pop stand. Back to tha muthaland," Char booms, with a crotch thrust, a fist pump, and kissing her teeth at the wall, before flipping some kind of switch, straightening up, and adding with a sweet shrug, "actually, moving into Peggy's with my baby. Doctor said that I'm right as rain."

"That's great." Though I doubt that it is. Then I watch as Char's aura or halo or whatever it is begins to materialize, gently pushing past her matted mane and into the emptiness surrounding her. An earthy, vegetative green base gives rise to little dashes of light purple. Like violets blooming in a bed of moss. Something new has taken root in Char. And it's starting to bloom.

The drive home is a slow, greasy one. Snow. Then sleet. Then snow on top of sleet on top of snow followed by a precipitous drop in temperature. Mossy and Char and the baby are all conked out in the back seat. Peggy is white knuckling 'er along the mess of a highway. I feel sick and cranky.

"So what did the doctor say?" Peggy asks.

The words "None of your business" race to the tip of my tongue out of pure habit. But I haul them back. "The tumours aren't worse. I'm fourteen weeks. Some decisions to make."

I consider telling her about Dave's offer. About how close

I was to calling him back the night of Mama's funeral, to taking the money from Dulcie Copper and the ladies' auxiliary and high-tailing it back to Toronto. But I don't. Because I still might.

"Are you going to keep the baby or what?" she says, staring straight ahead, her nose turned up ever so slightly like she's sniffing for something I'm not ready to give.

"It's not a baby. It's a fetus."

"You were a fetus once."

"Don't dare pull a guilt trip on me, Peggy."

"Guilt's not what I was after," she says. "Just sayin'."

"Do you honestly think I can raise a child?"

"Don't know. But you wouldn't be alone. People will help."

"Yeah, you with an orphanage for all the poor motherless snot monsters on the Island?" A split second later, I see that I hurt Peggy's feelings. Not by her face or her voice of course, but by the little red-oozing cuts in the foreground of her otherwise pale purple head cloud. I wonder if my words looked like tiny silver daggers as they left my mouth.

"There are worse things in the world than babies raised by other mothers." The little seeping slices in her aura zip shut.

"There are worse things in the world than abortions, too." I shrug.

"Indeed, there are." Peggy's eyes drift to the rear-view mirror, scanning the line of peacefully snoozing passengers in the back seat. The car fishtails just enough to yank her eyes back to the reality of the road.

"Becky Chickenshit's pregnant too, eh?" she says. A dose of gossip to take the edge off. "And Sarah Spenser just dropped the asking price on the property."

"Where'd you hear that?"

"Right from the horse's mouth."

"When?"

"Today. Me and Charlotte and the baby paid her a little visit."

"Ol' biddy was right bloody gobsmacked to see us!" Char erupts in Britishness from the back seat, making me wonder how long she has been faking sleep and exactly how many personalities live in that mixed up little head of hers.

Peggy and Char's faces are plastered with nearly identical shit-eating grins. Which makes me nervous as hell.

"This better not be something I read about on the front page of the paper tomorrow." I cross my arms and stare out the window as Peggy guides the car onto the faintly compacted tire tracks between the snowy ditches that are now the Middle Rear Road.

"Don't jump to convulsions," Char says, all cool and shady.

"You want Mossy to stay with you tonight?" Peggy says when we reach home. "Put him to work. He can at least shovel you out."

"No, that's okay. I need some time by myself. To think."

"Suit yourself," Peggy says. "Call if you need anything."

I turn on every light in the trailer in an effort to chase away the grey dimness of dusk and aloneness. I put the tea on. I watch the layers of fish-scale clouds in the sky grow darker as flecks of snow swirl and twirl and fall. I eat one of the godawful green-and-brown squares stashed in the freezer because one of the pamphlets from the doctor's office said a quick hit of sugar might make my baby move enough so that I can feel it. Then I call Dave to rhyme off all the reasons why I can't leave this place. When the sky is too dark to see the snowflakes anymore, and my head is too light for any remotely coherent thought, I go to my room and lie down in the cozy bed that I'm surprised to discover I actually made.

[…]

There's always a snowstorm around mid-March here. While Toronto is beginning to melt into a semblance of springy goodness, the East Coast is getting smacked by Sheila's Brush. The story goes that Saint Patrick had a mistress named Sheila, who happened to be his housekeeper. He kept her good and secret, and she kept him good and clean. But now in the afterlife, when Saint Paddy is being celebrated with a day of green drunken debauchery, Sheila takes it upon herself to purge and purify the land with one whore of a sweeping storm. That way, when spring finally comes, the Earth and the people are truly ready. And grateful as fuck. Last night, I dreamed about Mama. She was wearing her Greeting Gale dress but with her hair all loose and long and wild. She was laughing like mad and sweeping up a storm. A hard grinding rumble shoves me into wakefulness. I hoist myself out of bed, and slink into the kitchen to see what the hell.

There's a snowplow out there clearing ten tonnes of fresh snow from the driveway. A couple of young fellas are shovelling a path from the driveway to the trailer. There's an old guy pushing piles of snow off the steps. He gives me a big wave and a bigger smile. I don't have a clue who he is, so when he knocks on the door a few minutes later, I hesitate. It is eight a.m. I'm schlumping around, bleary-eyed, braless, and filthy yoga-pantsed. And I don't know the going rate for unsolicited snowplowing and shovelling services. The only money I have to my name is the stack of fifties in the envelope from the ladies' auxiliary, and I wonder if I'd be violating some law of the land if I asked for change. *G'wan, ya cheap bastard! Give them poor boys proper pay. And invite them in for tea, for Christ sake!* Mama would haunt me for being cheap. And rude. I pull on a half-clean hoodie and open the door.

"Hope we didn't wake ya, dear." The old man beams with a friendly familiarity.

I smile politely. "How much do I owe you?"

"Not a cent, love!" he laughs.

"Here, let me just get some—"

"No, no, no." The old man raises his work-gloved hands in protest. "It's the least me and the boys could do for you, Crow."

I look over at the three strapping guys finishing the pushing and plowing.

"They growed up, wha?" the old man says.

"Sorry." I offer a sheepish smile. "I don't recognize..."

"They sure remember you." He gives me a wrinkled wink and a half-toothed grin. "You and Effie, God rest her soul, yous two saved their lives."

The Alward boys. I didn't save their lives. I ruined them.

I was the one who told Children's Aid.

I was sixteen. Philly, Lukas, and Grubby Alward were two, three, and six years old when they moved from Town into the dilapidated old schoolhouse at the foot of Church Road, just a few clicks off the main road down past The Wharf. Their mother put up a barely legible sign in the gas station looking for a summer babysitter, and Mama made me call. Tishy Alward hired me over the phone. She paid me a flat thirty bucks per week—if she paid me at all—but she'd always leave me some hash and some liquor every Friday. Tishy Alward was, by my teenage estimation, a terrible boss and a worse mother, but her little Friday gifts were a good time, so I kept my mouth shut about what I saw and what I suspected.

I'd ride my bike down there for seven o'clock every morning. I was supposed to start at nine, but after about a week, I realized that Philly didn't get a diaper change and nobody got breakfast until I got there because Tishy slept late, and she was liable to backhand the first little face that woke her. So I'd feed them some toast and wash their filthy faces, maybe take a swipe at the table full of empty bottles and dump the overflowing ashtrays while they watched a bit of *Romper Room*, and then take them outside to play. By noon, Tishy would be gone. I didn't know where. She never said where she worked. She never left a number where she could be reached.

"If ya needa foind 'er, jus' call da cops," Grubby would sigh.

Poor little Grubby didn't even know that his name was Andrew. He only found that out when his grade primary teacher got after him for not responding during attendance. Grubby also almost got suspended that year for bringing beer to school instead of lunch. He tried to hide it in his desk, so his mother couldn't get at it.

Every day, I'd pack the boys up and walk them to The Wharf, then to our place for the afternoon. When Mama got home from work, she'd feed them supper, and drive them back home once Peggy reported seeing Tishy's taxi turn down the road. Tishy never asked where we were or what we did. She'd just smile and slur, "They're in good hands with you, baby doll."

Early one mid-August morning, I showed up and Tishy wasn't there. The front windows of the schoolhouse were smashed. The TV was, too. The kitchen table was on its side, bottles and butts everywhere. And Grubby had a black eye and a blood-crusted nose, courtesy of one of Tishy's "boyfriends."

Mama came and helped me clean up the boys. We packed little bags of their favourite toys and clothes. I called Children's Aid, and Mama waited with me until the social worker came to collect the Alward children. I never saw them again. Mama tried to update me on them from time to time, but I didn't want to hear it. It was bound to be another sad story.

"Harry Alward," says the old man who just finished shovelling the snow off my steps, holding out his hand. "Tishy's brother. That's Lukas in the green jacket. Phil in the orange hat. And Grubby at the plow." Grubby parks the plow, hops down, and gallops over.

"Crow!" he says, stopping short to doff his hat like some kind of gentleman.

"Oh for the love of God, Grubby Alward! Look at you! Ya grew up." I choke back tears.

"More by good luck den good man'gment." He grins.

It's scarcely past eight o'clock. But loud and clear, my mother's voice echoes through my mind, and before I know it, her words escape from my lips, "Well don't just stand there. Yas must be ready to eat a horse and chase the driver after all that work. Come in. I'll put the tea on."

The Alward men attempt to decline, but I'll have none of it.

The boys tell me all about their kids and the snow removal business they run with their uncle, who ended up getting custody of them. They tell me about how Mama would go visit all of them — including Tishy — for years afterwards, how she'd hug the bejesus out of them every time, and tousle their hair like she did when they were little. They said even Tishy eventually got herself together enough to see her grandkids at Christmas. Around each of their heads, sturdy red-orange flickers dance within soft blue ovals, the edges of which diffuse into the uncoloured space like watercolour robin's eggs.

Maybe I didn't ruin their lives. Maybe I'm not such a prick after all.

Then again, maybe I am. Because a few hours later, when Becky Chickenshit shows up on my doorstep, all my down-home "Come in, I'll put the tea on!" warm fuzziness goes right down the toilet. It takes every ounce of self-restraint in my still bleary-eyed, braless, yoga-pantsed body to not slam the door in her snivelling little shrew face.

Becky Chickenshit stands there, the awkward rhythm of her blinking eyes magnified by the thick lenses of her horn-rimmed glasses, face pulled taut by the bobby pins hap-hazardly holding her hair back. Her long red peacoat gives way to a gaudy floral broom skirt that hovers above a pair of beige pleather granny boots. She looks Amishly uptight and hippy dippy ridiculous at the same time.

"You must have been resting," she says, eyeing my ensemble, then shifting her gaze up to what I assume is my three-inch-long scrub of hair sticking up like a duck's arse, before she settles into comfortably condescending eye contact.

"Resting? No," I say, flatly at first, before I force myself to perk up and put Becky in her place. A hand flutters up to smooth my hair. Arms fold across my chest as I remember that I don't have a bra on. "Emailing Toronto...developing a framework...new marketing campaign. For my company. In Toronto. Having some trouble filling my shoes. No rest for the wicked awesome." I flash the biggest, fakest smile. Until I feel the crack of crusted sleep drool that gathered in the corner of my mouth during my mid-morning nap.

"How can I help you?" I say, my back teeth gritting with insincerity because frankly I'm more likely to bite her stupid blinky head off than I am to actually help her. Her chin sinks low to her chest, her gloved fingers clasp and wring in an anxious prayer.

"First, my condolences on the loss of your mother. She was a great woman. Secondly, I hope I'm not overstepping any boundaries here. But I heard you can see things."

"Yeah," I grunt. "Not blind. Yet."

"I'm sorry, I shouldn't have come." Her eyes begin to well with wetness beneath her glasses. She turns to leave, with a none too subtle sniff and a whimper. I watch as a jagged mass of forest green shards sputter out from a damn near blinding lemon-coloured gush of aura crap. I know that what I'm about to do will give the whole goddamn Island an open invitation to knock on my door and ask me to fix their lives with my psychic powers, and I know that means the risk of becoming a spent, sore, posthumous community saint, just like my mother. I know that I hardly believe all this is anything more than a figment of my own chaotic brain chemistry with a touch of ancestral insanity anyway. And I know that I really can't stand Becky Chickenshit, no matter how puppy-dog pathetic she gets.

Despite all of that, I take heed when I hear my mother's voice whisper, *Don't you ever turn your back on a person in need.*

Look at her. She's a mess. And you can help. Be somebody else's light when you get the chance, lest you find yourself alone. In the dark.

Yes, Mama.

"Becky. Wait." I step aside, making space for her and her sobbing mess of colourful thoughts. "Come in. I just put the tea on."

Her bawling slows to weeping and then subsides to a sniffle as I place a pot of tea and a box of tissues on the table. She takes one from the box, making a meticulously folded square with which to dab the corners of her eyes, and clears her throat with a silent sip of tea.

"Congratulations, by the way," I say. "How far along are you?"

She nearly chokes on her tea, her eyes wide with surprise.

"Only six weeks. How did you know?"

I tilt my head and smile enigmatically. "I just do." *Because Peggy Fortune is the Gossip Queen.*

The sniffling starts again. "I just need some advice. You may have heard through the grapevine that Duke and I are having difficulties."

The sniffling morphs into streaming tears, and the green shards in her aura crash and compact. Becky chases the tears with a precisely angled tissue corner, as they sneak past the thick rims of her glasses and onto her cheeks.

"Yeah well, he's a—" I stop short. Because she already looks damaged enough. "So where'd you hear that I can see things?" I ask.

"The Fortunes have...ways," she murmurs. "Everybody knows that."

"Well, it was news to me. Seriously. Who told you?"

"Char told William, and William told me."

"Gimp?"

"I don't call him that, it's insulting." She stiffens and shifts. "Look, I know you and Duke have some history. And I know I don't really deserve your help after what I did." Becky's voice drops to a whisper, as she rolls the tip of her Kleenex between her trembling, fidgeting fingers.

It is hard to be gleeful when you can see another person's pain so vividly. Even if that person is Becky Chickenshit.

"That crap in high school with the picture in the slide-show?" I say, as if I haven't held the sting of the whole thing in my heart and mind for twenty years. "Duke used you to get at me. It wasn't your fault, he was popular and you were...you. We're adults now. Water under the bridge, Becky."

I reach out to touch her hand, expecting to see a whole new spectrum of gratitude and relief blooming above her head at being forgiven. Instead, I get an eyeful of dirty brown guilt, accented with bottomless puddles of a deep, dark blue. But then I see something that makes me panic a little. A misshapen blackened red hole, like a burning garbage bag, creeps into Becky's colours. There's a greasy, sick sort of deterioration happening on the edge of her emotional orbit that I can only perceive in the peripheral vision of my left eye. I try to blink it away. And fail. My stomach churns.

"You don't know what actually happened, do you?" her words jolt me out of my uneasy fixation.

All through high school, Becky Chickenshit and Willy Gimp were close friends. All through high school, Becky wished that she and Willy could be more than friends. And all through high school, Willy confided in Becky about his feelings for me. So every time I'd be out chasing the arse off Weasel Tobin, then sneaking back to Willy Gimp when I got hurt, Becky Chickenshit knew. Every time I acted like he was invisible at school, only to go looking for him when I needed a shoulder to cry on, Becky knew. And every time I crowed indiscreetly about my nameless "friend with benefits," Becky knew.

"He loved you," she says flatly. "And you used him. You thought you were so cool, and he wasn't good enough to be anything other than a secret. Don't think that didn't hurt him. So, on graduation night? That was me. All on my own."

One day during the last week of school, Becky just happened to be on the other side of a bathroom stall door, when she overheard me telling Allie that I had chlamydia. While waiting for Dr. Gill to give her a check-up she didn't need, Becky found my file and snapped a picture of my lab report. She — a vigilante nerd mastermind who loved the guy I'd selfishly screwed over for too many years — put that picture in the slideshow.

With this confession, her colours clear and brighten. But the rosy sheen that envelops her freshly cleared conscience is no match for the eerie bruised shadow blob that still lurks around the edge of my awareness. It grows, smearing itself across her cheeks, her neck, her pregnant belly.

"Crow, are you okay? You are very pale. Was it something I said?"

"Yeah. No. Just tired."

Becky suddenly looks frightened. As though she can sense the unsettling creep of the invading darkness, too. "I should go." She gathers her coat tight around her neck, bracing for the chill outside. "Duke will be home at five, and he—"

And right there, I can see the blackened heart of Becky Chickenshit's rose-tinted life. Why she came here. What she wanted me to see this whole time.

"Becky, he hits you, doesn't he?"

"I'm not much of a cook, but I'm trying to—"

"Becky, don't go back there. Not tonight. Please. Here." I dart over to the cupboard and grab the cash-stuffed ladies' auxiliary envelope that would have bought my escape to Toronto. I press it into her hands. "Take this. Go stay at a hotel. In Town, Town. You can't go back there. He'll hurt you. The baby. Let me take care of Duke. You take care of you, okay?"

She takes the envelope, fingers trembling. Her eyes, her aura, fight to stay steady and sure.

"I knew you'd see it, Crow," she gasps. "Other people, they didn't believe me because he's so charming. He's always sorry after."

"Sorry is as sorry does, as my mother would say." And the next thing I know, I'm hugging Becky Chickenshit and imagining that my own aura is reaching into hers and filling it up with the guts and self-righteousness and curse words she's gonna need to get through the days and weeks and months to come. "And Duke? He'll be sorry, all right."

As soon as she's gone, I call Willy. To apologize for every moment spent not loving him the way he deserved to be loved. To tell him I want to spend the rest of my days making up for it. Or at least trying to. Right before I hang up, I blurt "Hey, did it ever bother you, being called Gimp?"

"I don't know," he chuckles. "Nobody ever asked me that before. Worked pretty good for me in the clink. Could have been called worse."

"Yeah, but if you had the choice?"

He is quiet, thoughtful for a moment. I stop myself from filling the silence with smartassery, even though a dozen flippant phrases teeter on the tip of my guilt-tinged tongue.

"They'd call me Mr. Crow Fortune. That'd make me some proud."

"G'wan ya fool. Come over here and say that to my face, why don't you. Also, I'm naming our baby Cletus the Fetus unless you can come up with something better." I hang up before he can say anything else. Because that's about all the lovey-dovey talk I can handle. Besides, I've got other fish to fry.

I call Peggy. I need her and Char to do me a favour.

[···]

Peggy's house is warmer and brighter than I remember, even in the scowling darkness of winter's last hurrah. Willy came with me to watch Daktari while Peggy and Char set out on a fact-finding mission, to get a sense of just how deep Duke's rotten streak runs. With Becky not home and no hot dinner ready at five o'clock, Duke decided to go on a bit of a rip. Duke got really drunk and went to a high school hockey game to jeer at the other team and leer at girls half his age. Duke staggered out back behind the rink after the game, looking for trouble. And he found it.

"Stargazer lilies," Peggy says matter-of-factly as she sits down at the table to pry her boots off her feet. "That was the hum off Skroink. Crow would have been about twelve at the time. I'd catch him eyeing her up and down like an old pervert, and *bam*! A wall of stench. Stargazer lilies. No one believed me except Effie, and everyone said I was the bitch for divorcing such a fine fella. But I could smell it. Couldn't even sit in the same room as him after a while. And see Mr. Duke, eh? You were right, Crow. He smelled like rotten meat and puke. Smells like sorry now, though, don't he Charlotte?"

"Dukie boy didn't know what hit him! And every single tree behind the rink was cheering you on, Big Mama." Char twirls and glides across the kitchen, sleeping babe in arms, and stands next to Peggy.

"Jesus, you two, you weren't supposed to beat him up."

Peggy laughs. "No? What were we supposed to do? Ask him to pretty please stop smacking his wife and chasing young girls? Cross our fingers and hope he doesn't do something worse? Or tell his cop buddies what he done and wait for the wheels of justice to start turning in the right direction? I think not. When the world is this goddamn cracked and broken, people like us have no choice. We take matters into our own hands. Speaking of hands, Charlotte, grab me an ice pack from the freezer would ya, dear? Best thing Effie ever taught me was how to throw a proper punch."

Char gently wraps the ice pack around Peggy's puffy pink knuckles, and kisses her on the cheek.

"Proud of you, Big Mama."

"Big Mama?" I smirk.

"Crow, you suck at this psychic thing." Char nudges Peggy's frame with her swaying hip. "C'mon, just tell her already."

My eyes flicker in and out of focus for a second, and nobody needs to tell me anything. The truth is written all over the air in the room, in sweeping strokes of deep, pure purple and ribbons of milky white that flow effortlessly between Char and Peggy, and wrap lovingly around Daktari's body as he nuzzles into his mother's chest.

"Holy shit, Peggy. Char is yours."

8 DOWN AROUND THE ROOTS

It's late, but Peggy puts the kettle on, and adds another tea bag to the remnants of the day's brew before she settles at the table to tell us the story. Six months after my mother nearly hemorrhaged to death in a hospital giving birth to me, Peggy gave quiet, uneventful birth to a baby girl, on a cot in a sparse room at the Home of the Guardian Angel on the Mainland. Four months later, when the baby weight was gone, and she'd stayed to see a few fellow unwed teenage trollops through their own entrance to and exit from motherhood, Peggy returned to Cape Breton, a heavy burden lifted from her belly, her conscience, and her family. Instead, she carried the weight of a slew of fictions about having "gone to an Aunt's."

Four years after Peggy's child was born, Freddy and Dar MacIsaac adopted a little spitfire of a girl from the Mainland. The kid with the wild red hair, snaggled teeth, and blazing eyes had already exhausted a few foster homes. She'd super glued fifteen caterpillars to a cat, and then the cat to a tricycle. Ended up with a forked tongue after sticking it in an electrical outlet. Smashed one car into the side of a house and another into the woods. The child was a well-documented, rip-roaring terror. But from the moment Peggy saw her friend Dar's new daughter, she could smell it. The smell of blood. Which smells like pine sap, according to Peg. So Charlotte MacIsaac is a bona fide cursed Fortune lunatic criminal, too.

Her eyes are wide and her smile is wild as Peggy tells the story. "Makes sense now, don't it? Cuss-int!" she croons, snake dancing around the room, sleeping baby in her arms.

"Yous are some messed," Willy says. "And God, I loves yas all for it."

"Shut up." I pinch his leg with my toes under the table. "You only love me for my money."

That was the other shocker of the day. While Peg and Char were out pucking the piss out of drunk Duke the Puke behind the rink, and Willy and I were playing happy family pretendsies with baby Daktari, Jacinta the lawyer from down the road called me, looking to deliver a copy of Mama's will. Mama had a life insurance policy. Mama died in an accident. Mama's will says I'm getting the fifty thousand dollars from her accidental death benefit. I didn't need to think too hard about my first order of business.

"Jacinta, how about you give your real estate agent friend a call, and make Sarah Spenser get her goddamn For Sale sign off my land."

It took a couple of weeks of haggling with Saint Sarah, and more than once I had to remind Char and Peggy that they were *not* to go trying to speed the process along. But now, the sign is gone.

This land is mine.

[···]

I probably should be inside hauling Willy out of bed, or Javexing the bejesus out of something in preparation for company coming. Instead, I'm parked on a stump seat near the firepit, staring at the little pokes of green dotting the yard. The mystery bulbs I found under the hoarded piles of newspaper have begun peeking out of the earth. The ones I planted all over the yard in an act of guerilla garden apology for burning Mama's proudest memories. The ones I assumed Mama would be here to see, even if I wasn't. Maybe they'll be blooming in time for the proper celebration of Mama's life, which Wendy and Allie are on their way over to help me plan. When they arrive, I tell them to ignore the mess and the rumble of Willy's snoring that's bound to be the backdrop of our conversation. But I did put the tea on at the crack of dawn, so it is good and strong.

"Death isn't the opposite of life." Wendy swirls her pointer finger around the edge of her nearly empty cup, as she gazes out the kitchen window at the just-starting-to-awaken rambling rose. "Death is the opposite of birth. They're like bookends. In between is the story we call life. My vision is that we relate to death in much the same way as we relate to birth. That we see it as a transition. A painful, yet normal and natural part of the human condition."

I glance over at Allie, expecting to see the roll and flutter of her lash-laden eyes, her head cocked in a sardonic tilt, traces of a barely swallowed smirk. Instead, I see strands of deep ruby and shimmery rose weaving their way through her wobbly blue halo, making it stronger. Brighter. Less wobbly. More beautiful. And when I finally pry my eyes away from Allie's colours, I see her looking at Wendy in a way I've never seen her look at anything that wasn't wine, chocolate, or super deluxe, high-tech medical equipment before. A look of profound gratitude. Of reverence. Of love. *Holy Shit. Allie Walker is in love. With The Wendigo.* And as Wendy drones on about celebrations of life and planning for death, I just sit there grinning like a fool. *Allie will have someone to love her and take care of her and help her make sense of herself when I'm gone.*

But the lovey-dovey shades of Allie Walker evaporate when Char comes crashing through the door and into my kitchen. Sweating, panting. Like she's run all the way here from Peggy's. Which she has. With her baby secured to her back with an elaborate scarf contraption.

"Crow, you ain't gonna believe what Bruce the Spruce said!"

That would be the tree in Peggy's yard. Char's new arboreal advisor. And no, I'm probably not going to believe it. Unless it suits me.

"Oops! Didn't know you had company." The words spill fast and furious in spite of her breathlessness. "Allie...Wendigo! Witches, right? Starting a coven? You need a fourth corner? I'm cool with the lezzie stuff, but no cousin lovin'." Char winks and elbows me, then plunks Daktari on the floor. Before he can fuss, there's a bippy in his mouth and a book about trees in his hand, and I can't even figure out where those things came from because all Char is wearing is a python print tube dress and Peggy's old sneakers. The mess of green and violet fanning out around her head is inversely proportionate to the size of her dress. Meanwhile, Allie's colours have gone all broody blue and bruised, and if there was ever such a thing as an amused shade of what-the-fuck-orange, well, it's wafting from Wendy like weed clouds from Willy's truck.

Allie's aura is headed for the door a few solid seconds before her physical body begins to move, but it snaps right back to the table when I say, "Stay put there, missy." I put another bag and another splash of water in the teapot. Because nobody's going anywhere.

"Look, I'll not go to my grave with the two of you carrying on a decades' old feud over who said what, and what screwed who. This foolishness is ending. Today."

"Jesus, Crow, you sound like your mother," Allie murmurs.

"Well, somebody's got to."

But unlike Mama, I order them both out to Willy's truck to smoke a gigantic joint, and to not come back until they've both laughed, cried, and begun building a bridge to get over all that has come between them.

"And believe you me, I'll see if you're faking it," I warn.

When they come back an hour later—eyes red from toking and crying, hair mussed up from both hugs and hollers, bodies soft from the release of tensions and secrets, big and small—there's been another shift that only my eyes can see. Streaks of the same violet that have been popping up from Char's new-found ground now dance and smear around the periphery of Allie's freshly brightened blues. And they both have the faintest flicker of a warm, golden fuzz in the centre of their chests.

"That one's still a grubby skank." Allie shrugs at me. "And I can't believe she's your cousin."

"Fuck you, Walker, ya melon-dramatic ice queen," Char drawls, thumping Allie's cheek with the most wayward dreadlock on her head.

"Shut up the two of you and give me some love." I waddle toward their glowy hearts and open arms. I pinch Allie's arse and wipe my snot- and tear-streaked face on Char's bare shoulder just to be a dick and remind them who is in charge of holding this world together, for now. I whisper, "Wait'll you hear what me and Wendy cooked up for Mama's proper memorial."

Look, there goes Crow again, causing a scene. Making some big dog and pony show out of me dying.

It's still jarring to have Mama's voice be the first thing I hear every morning when I wake up. Over the sound of Willy snoring beside me, over the racket of caws and screeches from the birds in the trees out back, over the symptomatic song of the Tumourific Trio that still pounds in my ears before my head leaves the pillow.

G'wan, Mama. There won't be any dogs or ponies there. No cat-piss lilies or drunken family brawls either. Just tea and squares and stories from all the people who love you and miss you. There's also a big bowl of rum punch, two pans of broc-o-glop, and a chance of an old country song sing-along before the evening's out. After the punch is gone.

The girls from the Greeting Gale went and Javexed the bejesus out of the whole fire hall, and every old scratch on the road is hauling out their potluck best. The ladies' auxiliary pulled together some raffle baskets featuring a weekend at the Gale, snow clearing from the Alwards, an oil change from Willy's garage, and a hat and mitt set from Mama's friend, Betty Who Knits. The money raised from the tickets will be donated to the various people and places Mama always made time to help out.

On the morning of Mama's Mother's Day Memorial Celebration, I drink my tea and watch the sun chase away every remnant of lazy fog, giving way to an endless umbrella of azure and light, and I'm not sure whether to laugh or cry. Because I realize that I'm not alone. In my grief. In my home. Even in my body. And my family isn't the pack of cursed pariahs I'd always assumed. The Fortunes use what they've got to do what they can, even if all they've got is a sizable mess or a dose of madness.

Then, looking out into my yard at the plant life that seems to have gone into overdrive overnight, I am struck by perhaps the most humbling, profound realization of all. The bag of shrivelled old mystery bulbs I rescued from beneath Mama's paper pile and planted back in the fall? The ones that I imagined would dapple the grass with bright beauty and provide a source of free Mother's Day flowers that I would childishly pluck and present to Mama today? I didn't know if the things I planted would grow, but lo and behold, they did. Onions. They are all goddamn onions.

[···]

There are too many people piled into the ramshackle rural fire hall to count, but I make a point of trying to shake the hand of every last one of them. Between sips of tea and rum punch and nibbles of squares and broc-o-glop, each has a story to tell about Mama. Stories I'd never heard. Like the time a Halfway Road stray cat named Dan Richard got its head stuck in a mayonnaise jar after little Effie Fortune gave it a whisker trim at her stray cat salon. Or the time that fifteen-year-old Effie clocked the pervy old priest who felt up her friend Wanda's arse after midnight Mass. Or the time she spent five hours straight at the bedside of a woman who'd been in a bad car wreck, absorbing her pain until the surgeon and anesthesiologist got there, even though it meant missing her own daughter's graduation. Wendy, God love her, trails behind me as I work the room, taking notes so that there'll be a written record of the stories people tell. For posterity. For celebration. For her grandchild, someday. Effie Fortune was full of surprises, even after she died.

I'm having such a time that I scarcely notice Willy when he shuffles up beside me, wearing a charcoal suit and a shit-eating grin. He grabs my hand, pulls me close, and whispers in my ear, "Turn around, ya goof."

I turn around and see the fire hall's prize possession—a forty-eight-inch wall-mounted flat screen TV—flicker to life as The Doors' "Hello, I Love You" struts out from the speaker. Pictures of me begin flashing across the screen. Me as an egg-headed newborn. Me, cake-faced on my first birthday. Me, beaming in my red velvet dress at the Christmas concert in grade three. Me and Mama at the beach, taken by Grubby Alward on his mother's stolen Polaroid. Me, Allie, and Char on the way to a high school dance. Me and Willy, shooting the shit down at the smoking grounds when we should have been in chemistry. My university graduation photo. The uber-serious professional headshot I had taken for the Viva Rica website just last year. And a selfie of me and Willy in the cab en route to the hotel, all birthday grinch-eyed and grinny, on the night that I got pregnant. As Jim Morrison wails out his final orgasmic hellos, the picture dissolves into words: "Crow Fortune, will you marry me?"

Willy's grin gives way to a nervous laugh as he flips open a small black box to reveal the biggest, gaudiest glittering rock I've ever seen in my life.

"It's not made of corpse ashes. But she's still a doozie, wha?"

And then, there's a sharp cracking noise and a blinding flash at the door.

Char, engulfed in a flare of searing red brilliance, is making the final few paces of a mad dash toward the man who just walked in. She hauls off and clocks him, sending a flurry of silvery blue sparks flying from the side of his shaved head.

"Christ Almighty, Charlotte!" Peggy wheezes as she bustles over to stop her wild child from taking another swing at the guy. He straightens himself up, smiling as his fingers pat the faint fleck of blood seeping from the spot where Char's fist met his mouth. He nods benevolently, assuring everyone he's fine as he smooths the front of his burgundy robe and scans the crowd with his cool, clear, azure eyes.

And then, through the rising tide of whispers and murmurs and curious colours, I hear Peggy gasp.

"Dear God! Alec?"

It's all I can do not to vomit on the shoulder of poor old Mr. Patterson's tweed sports jacket. In the commotion that follows, I almost forget to tell Willy that my answer to his proposal is a resounding maybe.

[···]

Some people escape the trappings of ordinary life or extraordinary pressure by slipping into shadows and dissolving into darkness. Others hide in plain sight. Over the last thirty-some years, Smart Alec Spenser Brother Gyaltso Hottie McMonk Pants did both.

On that October night in 1976, when Alec Spenser took to the water aboard *The Anastasia,* he figured everybody would think he was dead. Especially after he dropped his beer, gashed his hand picking up the broken glass, and left behind a blood splattered T-shirt. He knew he was leaving a wave of stories and suspicions in his wake. He knew that rumours would swirl in vicious circles for years, both from and about everyone in his life. He thought about his girlfriend, their unborn baby, and the big crazy cursed family she came from. He thought about his pompous old man, his cold mother, and his jealous sister. Then, he motored his little fishing boat down the coast as far as he could. Just before dawn, he ran *The Anastasia* aground and let her sink. He thumbed his way down into the States, where he hooked up with a bunch of glassy-eyed hippies on their way to a Buddhist shindig in Colorado. Six years later, Smart Alec Spenser was a brand new man named Brother Sharchen Gyaltso, who'd successfully transformed his personal hardships into spiritual treasure. Meanwhile, back on Cape Breton Island, Scruffy Effie Fortune was doing her damnedest to be mother and father to a little girl they'd just begun to call Crow.

While I was eighteen, loudly squawking about how stupid and confining this place was, desperate to spread my wings and fly away from this godforsaken island, Brother Gyaltso was making his way Down North, up into the highlands to run the small monastery overlooking the wild and spacious ocean. While I spent years flailing, trying to cleanse or drown myself in a sea of urban anonymity, Brother Gyaltso sat motionless on a cushion, staring out a massive window, watching the crows leap from cliff edges to play in the open air. And while I stood on the wharf, scattering Mama's ashes on the waves of the Bras d'Or, Brother Gyaltso was on the crowd's edge, preparing for the inevitable time when worlds and truths collide. Knowing that he'd have to emerge from the safety of his fake death's shadow, even if it meant taking a puck in the mouth. Which it did.

Charlotte knew who he was when he walked through that door before anyone else did. Bruce the Spruce whispered to her earlier that day. Something about righteous rage and sins of the father. See, Smart Alec Spenser made a few dumb moves. He went and knocked up Peggy Fortune, too.

[…]

"Well isn't this cute," I sneer at the two of them as they sit side by side at my kitchen table, as if time and space don't retain the sores and cracks of betrayal. Mama's not here to take them to task for their treachery, but I am. *And if there's one thing I know how to do, it is hold a grudge, by Jesus.*

"Crow, it's not how you think." Peggy's voice sways with a blunt edge of defensiveness. "Put on the tea and we'll talk."

"Did Mama know?" My lips purse into an O-shape, my eyes narrow. Because despite my new-found benevolence, I don't serve tea to backstabbing bastards.

"Just put the tea on and we'll talk," Peggy pleads.

"I want an answer."

"Put the tea on."

"Tea's made. Because my mother raised me right. 'Keep the tea on, and don't be a man-thieving trollop.' Pretty sure that's a direct quote from her." I cross my arms atop my blooming belly and cock my widened hips to one side.

Peggy smiles. I'm gripped by the urge to wipe that antagonistic grin right off her face, but no sooner does the bear hug of rage grip my chest, than a gentle ebb of fuzzy mauves and warm yellows materialize around Peggy. *Easy there, Jumpy McConclusionson. There's more to the story.* I uncross my arms and un-cock my hips, freeing my belly from the prison of that posture, that habit. My smirk disintegrates.

"Did Mama know about the two of you?" I soften the tone but not the insistence.

Peggy and Gyaltso look at each other, then back at me. Their heads bob in slow unison.

"She was the only one who knew I had his baby. There's more, though," Peggy says. "Is that tea good and strong?"

When Peggy went to Smart Alec Spenser on that October night in 1976 with news of her own pregnancy, she'd already paid a visit to his father to tell him that Alec had knocked her up. Old John Alec knew how bad it would make his family look if people thought his son had two back-to-back bastard babies with two different Fortune sisters. So Peggy agreed to do what my mother would not. Quietly, gratefully, Peggy took the money that John Alec Spenser gave her to pay for her very own trip to the Montreal clinic. But she had a different plan in mind for herself and Smart Alec. They both had to disappear. She, until after that baby was born, and he, for good. It would be for the best.

Because here's the thing: even though everybody knew that Smart Alec Spenser was the father of Scruffy Effie Fortune's baby, everybody was wrong. What everybody didn't know was that Smart Alec Spenser and Scruffy Effie Fortune were never more than friends, and not the kind with bedroom benefits. Smart Alec Spenser took responsibility for Scruffy Effie Fortune's pregnancy to protect her from shame and scandal. But when Smart Alec accidently fell in love with and knocked up Peggy, things stood to get complicated. So they decided to make it simple again. She went off to the Mainland and had the baby, and he just disappeared.

"Your mother and Alec were never intimate." Peggy gazes out the window, looking for something to make all of this less awkward. Probably wondering why there's a ton of onions planted all over the yard.

"Well, in the interest of right speech, there was that one time when Effie and I—"

"Lord thundering Jesus, man, she doesn't need details!" Peggy snaps her attention back to the robe-wrapped man. "Not right speech if it's wrong-headed, now is it? The point is, Crow, Alec isn't your father."

"Well then..." I trail off, distracted by the dance of tender reds and amber yellows that merge and mingle in figure eights around Peggy's and Alec's heads. I take a half-sip of my tea, which has grown lukewarm and too sweet since Peggy and Alec started telling their story.

Peggy sighs, shifting her weight from one arse cheek to the other as she looks at me, then at Gyaltso. She gets all still, stony, and mountainous for a moment.

"Your father was Old John Alec Spenser."

"Oh, for Christ's sake!" I thunk my head down on the table. "I don't have time for a goddamn identity crisis." Because at this stage in the game, it doesn't matter who my father was. I'm Effie Fortune's child, through and through.

The exact nature of Scruffy Effie Fortune's relationship with John Alexander Spenser is a detail that was scattered out on the wind and waves of the Bras d'Or along with her ashes. Despite decades of trying to sniff out the truth, the only thing Peggy could ever smell was her sister's ability to keep her mouth shut. It smelled like concrete and camphor. Smart Alec Spenser suspected that his father had taken advantage of Effie after they hired her as the housekeeper. But Effie never let on about anything until the day she came to Alec, after having told the old man to go to hell with his abortion money. Smart Alec didn't have to think twice. He got his father to agree to let Effie and her baby live in the trailer on this piece of land, and in return, Alec would be the public face of paternity for Effie Fortune's baby. To save everyone a pile of grief.

"Your mother was a wonderful woman," Brother Gyaltso says solemnly.

"And John Alec Spenser was a poor excuse for a man," Peggy grunts. "Which is why Effie never let on it was him who got her pregnant, and why she kept Alec alive in your heart and mind your whole life. He was the father she wanted you to have. The father you deserved."

"The father who faked his own death, ran for the hills, and left my mother alone and pregnant." I watch as the sharpness of the words, my tone, make a dent in Alec's rusty red halo.

"We were young. And stupid. Doing what we thought was best under the circumstances. Your mother wouldn't want your pity, or any sourness toward Alec. Effie always lived on her own terms." Peg's chin drops to her chest as the wall that was her auric defence collapses around her in a cloud of shimmering blue and yellow dust. "And maybe she died on her own terms, too."

"What's that supposed to mean?" I watch. Wait. Peggy squints hard, but that only forces out further the tears she's suddenly struggling to contain.

"Maybe Effie was sick." She straightens up, her eyes and her aura growing so wide and so open that for a moment I flinch, thinking they might have designs on swallowing me whole. "Sick with something real bad. Like cancer. All through her. Because her body held so many people's pain, and couldn't let it go. Maybe she didn't bother going to the doctor because she knew it by feel. Maybe I could even smell it after a time. And maybe her accident...well maybe there are no accidents."

The swampy swirls of Peggy's grief and relief and pride and shame pull me up and out of my chair. I wrap my arms around her in what would quite possibly meet the stringent qualifying criteria for the world's most awkward hug. My body—strangely steady and numb in the wake of it all—can scarcely contain her sobs and quakes. But I hold onto her until the seismic jolts of shifting secrets finally settle. Until Cletus the Fetus boots me in the bladder and I damn near piss myself.

"It is such an honour to witness this and to serve as a catalyst for a deepening relationship—"

"Oh spare me the holy Buddhist tripe, Alec," Peggy snaps. "You're a grandfather now, by the way. That child needs milk and diapers and proper hair care for that little red nappy head of his. And our daughter will live her whole life on the brink of cracking up because she's got ways that the world has yet to understand. So drop the ragamuffin-monk-on-the-mountain shtick. Mark my words, Saint Sarah is up to something with Spenser Mining. I smelled it myself. Sulphur and pork fat. You want to be of use here? Pry your share of the family money out of her bony little hands before she drives it all into the ground."

"My vows compel me to renounce the pursuit of material possessions," Gyaltso begins, each word imbued with an air of pious, methodical serenity.

But Peggy's neck is craned and her nose is wrinkled, as she interrupts with a loud sniff. *Sniff. Sniff.* "Bullshit and bubble gum," she says, tapping the side of her right nostril with her thick finger. "You're up to something, too. A wolf in monk's clothing, Alec." She pauses, drawing in another whiff of something that sends angry little flints of blackened red flying around her. "I'm gonna make a few wild guesses here, Alec, just from the smell of you. Tell me I'm wrong, I dare ya." Peggy leans across the table toward him, eyes fixed, face unflinching. "Sarah already knows you're alive, don't she? You came out of the damn woods when you heard this property was up for sale and tried to get her to give it to you, but she said no. You've got some little pet project on the go and you need help. That's why you showed up at Effie's memorial. To see if you could tap into the love for Effie here, and turn that love into money somehow. You're as bad as the rest of them."

"No, that's not why I—it is not just about money," he sputters. "It is a very noble enterprise, and could be a fresh start for us all, as a unified family. Unfortunately, the accumulated negative karma between Sarah and me prevented a fruitful conversation."

"Only fruitful conversation you'd get from that one is rotten apples biffed at your head in between insults. She always hated your guts, Alec. You being dead suited her just fine." Peggy's arms lock into a tight cross atop of tit mountain.

"The Spenser name is powerful, and could bring great resources to bear." He ignores Peggy's pouting, a calm conviction rising in his voice, his eyes. "If we could somehow convince her of the merit, of the business case, this could diversify Spenser's prospects and benefit the community in a sustainable, spiritually significant way. I can't help but think that my sister truly does have a loving, compassionate nature. It simply needs to be liberated."

"*Pfft.* All that meditation must have really made your damn mind go blank, then."

Meanwhile, I feel a grin creep across my face as I observe the little silver spirals twisting in and out of the fresh emerald-coloured cloud emerging around Smart Alec Brother Gyaltso. Peggy may well smell bullshit and bubble gum, but I see an opportunity for putting both my new and old skills to good use here, even if it is just a distraction from shock and sorrow and chaos. I've learned a thing or two about finding and freeing people's truths lately, and the impulse to make a living with a sales smile and a marketing pitch dies hard. What remains of the money Mama left me isn't going to last forever. It's no surprise to hear her voice quip ever so faintly in my ear, *Jesus saves, Moses invests.*

"Stacey," Smart Alec Brother Gyaltso says, as he sways to the edge of his seat, and spends a few too many moments gawking at me, like he's scanning for pieces of himself in my eyes.

"It's Crow," I say, like I mean business. Because I do.

"Right. Crow." His hands and fingers weave into what I imagine is some sort of sacred cross between a snivel and a prayer formation. "I realize that an apology is insufficient. But that day on the wharf, I feel we made a genuine connection. Perhaps, from that, a prosperous and mutually beneficial relationship could grow. My collaborator Wendy and I are hosting an event at the fire hall next weekend, entitled—"

"Rig Yer Mortis. I know. I'll be there." Because who am I to ignore what feels like a deep, insistent nudge from a faintly conspiratorial Universe? Or maybe that's just Cletus gearing up for another furious flurry of rib kicks and bladder jabs.

[⋯]

Turning a rundown rural fire hall into a half-decent space to host a celebration of life for a woman they all called Scruffy Effie was no great feat. But making that same spot into a place that can pass for an oasis of spiritual conversation and meditative profundity? It doesn't really matter how many pictures of lotus flowers you tack over top of the dartboards. There's not enough patchouli incense in the world to fully cloak the smell of a sewer that needs suctioning. And plunking a piece of red cloth and a Buddha statue on top of a rusty old dehumidifier just doesn't cut it either.

But that must be my big-city-asshole critical self talking, because nobody at the Rig Yer Mortis seems to care, or even notice. Gyaltso, Wendy, Allie, and four other people I should probably recognize—but don't—sit on cushions arranged in a lopsided circle. They take turns gawking at what sits just outside the ring, in between the tea table and the Buddha that guards the rusty old dehumidifier: a four-foot-tall, pale beige, translucent egg-shaped thing.

"Welcome." Smart Alec Brother Gyaltso folds into a deep bow from his spot on the floor. Everyone smiles at Willy and me as we stand in the doorway, hesitant and awkward as fuck. Because there is no way either of us can comfortably get down to or up from those raggedy little cushions. But God love Wendy, she goes and merges a couple of chairs into the formation without us even having to ask.

"Now, what? We bow to the Almighty Egg?" Willy cracks, loud enough to make me wince.

Wendy unleashes one of her infamously discordant peals of laughter. Allie and the strangers chuckle. Gyaltso smiles, all benevolently Cheshire Cat-ish.

"That"—Wendy's tone settles from jangly laugh to salespitchy chimes — "is a *Crann Na Beatha* Burial Pod. Anyone care to try it on for size?"

"Let's save the *Crann Na Beatha* conversation for the end, Wendy," Gyaltso says. "We will open with a group bow, to acknowledge the primordial wisdom and sacred intelligence in each of us as we embark on this journey into the unknown together." But nothing undermines a wise and sacred vibe quite like a three-hundred-pound buddy named Tooker letting a fart rip as he bows. Gyaltso, again with the Cheshire Cat face, "Wendy, open a window please."

We go around the circle to introduce ourselves and say what drew us to a community conversation about Doing Death Right. Allie talks about her mother, about her own frightening thoughts about death as an escape from pain and drudgery. Tooker talks about finding his own father dead of a heart attack in the backyard, how nobody ever let him talk about it, and how scared he is that his own son will find him the same way someday. An old blue-haired, droopy-faced scratch named Neilina is there because all her old scratch friends are dropping like flies. A young blue-haired, face-pierced, tattooed Townie named Kersti says her friends are ODing left, right, and centre. And an old backwoods rubber booter hippy named Barb says she came because she is just so intrigued by the mysterious wonder of it all. When it's my turn, I don't even know where to start.

I'm here because I feel bad about being such a shit friend to Allie, and to spy on The Wendigo and make sure she loves her the way she deserves. Or, I'm here to suss out what kind of business my newly undead fake-father real half-brother is plotting, and how I might be able to get in on the ground level and make a few bucks to pay for Cletus's diapers and therapy. Or, My mother probably killed herself and I miss her more than words can say, so I'm just here for the tea and squares. Instead, I blurt out, "Hi I'm Crow. How 'bout being nice to me? I'll be dead soon."

Loops of nervous orange and shards of wounded blue stop me from saying more, as they gush up into the air around Willy, Allie, and even a touch around Smart Alec Brother Gyaltso. Like what I just said is somehow news to them. Willy hauls himself straight up in his chair and gives me a bit of the side eye.

"I'm Willy. Some call me Gimp. Don't mind Crow. She's here for the tea and squares. I'm here because I can be. Tomorrow isn't a guarantee for any of us."

On that cheery note, Gyaltso dings a little bell and proceeds to take us — a sad pack of heartbroken future corpses — on a magically mystical meditative journey through an uber-serene Nirvana where all we do is sit and breathe for a few minutes. Allie is already bawling. Wendy breathes like a labouring moose with a sinus infection. Tooker breaks wind three more times because he had cabbage rolls for dinner. Me? I think about being dead. About Mama's ashes out on the Bras d'Or. About Parry Homunculus, Ziggy Stardust, and Fuzzy Wuzzy the astrocytoma trio having a knock-down-drag'em-out war with Cletus the Fetus, with my body as the battlefield. A version of Gyaltso's words from our New Year's Eve encounter down on the wharf rings in my head as he beckons us back with the bell. *We're all dying. But only the lucky ones know it.*

Over herbal tea and a plate full of vegan, gluten-free bird-seed cookies that leave me longing for squares, we talk. About all the ways we hide our grief, our guilt, our dying. How we are supposed to just bury the evidence and move on. The

way we aren't supposed to say terrifying things out loud—
especially when they are true—lest we make the fine folks
around us feel uncomfortable. The kid in the "Emperor's
New Clothes" story, who had the audacity to shout about the
dangling royal pecker and bare arse? Nobody liked that kid.
That kid never got to be in another fairy tale ever again. But
the emperor is prancing around buck naked.

We're all still dying.

And right before the whole thing whirls off into some
kind of nihilistic, nudist-shaming, existential depression
session, and right before I can articulate the profound truth
of how bad this tea and these cookies suck, Brother Gyaltso
intervenes by asking us to close our eyes and pretend we are
trees.

"Imagine yourself, strong, flourishing, and spacious," he
says, tilting his face and sweeping his arms up toward the
cobwebbed ceiling.

*How 'bout bent, crooked, and covered in fungus? Surrounded by
nuts. With an agitated chipmunk inside.*

"Now imagine any pain and suffering you perceive in
yourself, or in others, or in the world, as thick, dark fog. Like
air pollution," he says.

I can see it.

"Now breathe that in. Because that is what trees *do*." His
voice is urgent, insistent. "They take in what would otherwise
be destructive, and they use it. They change it. They let it
change them. And then, they put something useful back out
into the world. Oxygen. Life. This is what we can do. Pretend
we are trees when life feels hard. Breathe it in. Soften it. Let
it change you. Let your heart, your mind change *it*. Then
offer the world whatever it is inside you that is needed. Peace.

Courage. Light. A cup of tea and a good laugh. Don't hide from the sorrows of the world. Welcome them in. Watch them transform. Be a tree in your life."

"And now," without missing a beat, Wendy jumps in, "you also have the option of being a tree in death as well. We'd like to introduce you to the *Crann Na Beatha* Burial Pod."

She directs our attention to the thing in the room we've all been pretending not to see. The big old egg. The big old sales pitch.

The whole setup was brilliant. The cute, colloquial name of the night. Getting us here to think and speak freely about death. Feeding us gross cookies that might kill us. Then presenting us with a novel option for burial! My little marketing-stunt-loving heart bubbles with delight. As Wendy tells us all about it, Gyaltso busies himself by spreading for-sale copies of his book, *Living and Dying: You're Doing it Wrong*, at the feet of the dehumidifier Buddha.

Crann Na Beatha is Gaelic for "Tree of Life." Wendy wanted to call it *Ubh an Bháis*, meaning "Egg of Death," but Gyaltso put the kibosh on that one. The two of them ended up buying this demo model from a guy in Europe after Wendy's father died, and the local funeral homes went out of their way to harass Wendy about the post-death and burial plans. He wanted to forgo the chemical embalming, be waked at home, and buried on his land in a simple shroud. When *Ciad Mille Failte* Funeral Services Inc. caught wind of that, they came to Wendy armed to the teeth with threats and lies. *You can't do that. We're the only ones authorized. That's immoral, and that's illegal. Give us your money or there'll be hell to pay.*

But Wendy's no fool. She'd been studying with Gyaltso and the rest of the backwoods Buddhists Down North, and training to become a death doula. She knew the loopholes and laws, she knew her rights, and she knew how to say "Go fuck yourself" in Gaelic. Her father was waked in his own bed, with ice packs to keep him cool and rice bags to close his eyes, and friends and family by his side until they were ready to say goodbye. Then, they put him in a shroud and buried him in a clearing on the land he loved. Wendy and Gyaltso spent many a morning sitting at the site meditating, until one day, it dawned on them that other people would be ripped off and ripped up by the likes of *Ciad Mille Failte* Funeral Services Inc., unless somebody had the guts to offer something different. Thus, the Tree of Life Egg of Death plan was hatched.

"It's a nifty little thing, the *Crann Na Beatha* eco-burial pod," Wendy explains. "You curl a naked corpse up into it and you bury it deep in the ground, with no need for toxic chemicals or outrageous expenses. And in the top compartment of the egg, you place a tree. That tree is then nourished by both the biodegradable egg and the body it holds, as both return to oneness with the Earth. And instead of having a swath of land filled with embalmed bodies and crumbling gravestones, you have a sacred forest. Living memorials that take in the pollution of the world and turn it into fresh, clean air. Or fruit, even. That is our vision. A cemetery that is truly green, living, and dynamic as we wish our loved ones and our legacies to be."

Next thing you know, she's climbing in to give a demonstration of how a body fits into the thing. She wriggles her way in, knees hugged to her chest. "The way it softens the light. The warmth, the coziness. It's like a womb. In death, we are reborn."

Rubber booter Barb gasps. This is the magical mystery she's been waiting for. Even through the translucent shell of the pod, I can see Wendy's feelings streaming out in ribbons of crystalline awe, hopeful sunny yellow, and lavender joy. She pops her head out, smiles straight at big ol' Tooker and says, "We can order it in various sizes to accommodate all body types!"

Everybody *oohs* and *aahs* for a few minutes, and the room is crackling with the neons of novelty and the soft pastels of hope and faith. Sure, it's no Gem-Mortalization, but it beats the shit out of becoming a slab of chemical-soaked cold cuts in a Cadillac casket, or a pile of greasy soot in a glorified Mason jar. Plus there's the buy-local, eco-friendly, stick-it-to-the-capitalist-man angle.

But of course, the devil is in the details. Wendy and Gyaltso need a good piece of land. They also need ten grand in a trust fund, to make it over the first bureaucratic hurdle of setting up the business. And finally, they'll need a steady stream of bereaved renegades who can shell out to have their loved ones grow trees of life from eggs of death and are willing to tell *Ciad Mille Failte* Funeral Services Inc. to *Ciad Mille Fáilche Áielf.* Preferably in actual Gaelic.

They give us the soft sell, so as not to thoroughly taint the trail we've all just blazed through our own hardships and hang-ups. Proceeds from Wendy's death doula services and Gyaltso's book go to the trust fund. They ask us to keep an eye out for available land. And to think and talk to our loved ones about this exciting new option in the death and dying care services. And somehow, despite my ongoing preoccupation with my own ending, when I picture myself in relation to all this, it isn't curled up and buried inside one of those things. But rather: *Hihowareyatoday. I'm Crow Fortune. Marketing and Communications Director for* Crann Na Beatha, *Cape Breton's first and only eco-burial memory forest.*

Mama's voice eggs me on. *Remember Crow, those who get, get!* And I don't even know what the Jesus that actually means, but Mama always said it, and it sounds like encouragement. So, I'll take it.

[···]

"I'm good cop, you're quiet, not-acting-crazy cop," I remind Char as she fidgets and twitches in the shotgun seat of Peggy's car. I probably should have come alone, but I thought it wise to have a co-pilot. Someone to back up my story about why I'm driving without a licence if the cops stop us. Someone to witness the persuasion miracle I'm gearing up to work via a combination of business acumen and squirrelly vision insight. Or, someone to beat Sarah Spenser up if she's really nasty to me when I diplomatically lay out the case for Spenser Mining Inc. partnering up with *Crann Na Beatha.* Or when I tell her I'm her sister.

By the time Sarah Spenser answers the door, Char is off caressing the tentative green buds of rhododendron bushes on the lawn and singing to them. Loudly. Off-key. In Gaelic. Which she doesn't speak. Sarah Spenser says nothing, but her cold gaze sweeps past my face, and lands squarely on my belly bump, where the ice in her eyes morphs into disgust. Still, I smile my biggest Viva Rica smile, exuding an air of *professional. Sensible. Convincing.* Not even wearing a slutty dress, morning-after makeup, and an old woolly toque like I was last time I stood on this doorstep.

Char comes galloping over, all grinny and wide-eyed, still

humming the melody of the tune she'd been singing. "Man, they totally dig that Gaelic music shit. 'Kill 'em Maroon,' or whatever they wanted me to sing."

"What?" Sarah sneers.

"The song old Rozzy liked to sing in the garden, *duh*." Char's dreads do a serpentine flop dance as she juts her face forward.

"'Gillean Mo Run.' It was Mother's favourite song." Sarah's face is harder, stonier than when she opened the door. "Nice of my brother to share some of our family's history with you. That's all you'll be getting."

"Yeah, well, the bushes are pissed that you won't even sing to them" — Char's voice drops to a whisper — "so they told me all of the things."

I elbow Char in the ribcage and hiss, "*Not*-acting-crazy cop, remember?"

"What do you want?" Sarah glares.

"I have a business proposal you might be interested in. One that could revive the Spenser brand, financially. And socially." I extend my hand, but it might as well be a toilet plunger the way Sarah Spenser grimaces and recoils. Still, I can tell she's intrigued, at least enough to humour me. Money and status are irresistible lures for the likes Sarah Spenser, even when dangled by the likes of me.

"Fifteen minutes." She opens the door just wide enough for my belly and Char's dreadlocks to squeeze inside. I follow Sarah through the hallway, where the old bones of the Spenser house have been caked and covered with gleaming, sleek, off-white modernity. Her office is decked out with a mahogany table, leather chairs, and crystal whiskey decanters. On the way there, we lose Char. Sarah has a white-knuckle grip on her nerves as the two of us sit, face to face. Despite the terse grin, the proud posture, and the tented fingers, I can see it. A thick grey mass heaves and hovers over the anxious flurry of blood- and bile-coloured sparks that spit around her head. Gripping. Containing. Controlling. I look for a way in. A way to soften her. A place to begin the bridge we need built.

"As you know, Alec is alive and well." I watch for signs of a thaw. "We're working together on a new initiative. A one-of-a-kind cemetery comprised of eco-burial pods that grow trees."

"And?" she says, eyes shifting down to the screen of her little gold-cased phone where a timer counts down our fifteen minutes of grace, her French manicured talons dropping down to impatiently drum the table surface in rhythmic displeasure.

"I'm considering dedicating a portion of my land for this purpose, but we need partners with more substantial business experience. I know Spenser Mining is having some challenges. Understandable. Times have changed, and mining isn't what it used to be." I do my damnedest to meet her suspicion with sincerity. Or at least blow some hoots of sycophantic smoke directly up her clenched old ass. "*Crann Na Beatha* could be a great opportunity. Diversify your business. Give something lovely back to the Island and the people. An innovative legacy investment for you. Really positive PR, strategically speaking."

She taps her carefully shaped nails on the table, looks at me, and again settles her gaze on the spot where a new generation of her own family is evidently growing. She smiles, tight and stiff. "My family has given you people enough already," she says through gritted teeth. Her hands go still. Her eyes, spine, and voice harden in tandem with the darkening wafts of murky grey around her head. "And what do we get in return? Indignation. Ingratitude. Entitled have-nots with too many kids and not enough sense. Gutter snipes stretching out filthy hands, asking for more."

From somewhere in the bowels of the groaning old mansion, Char hollers in a fake punk rock Londoner brogue, "Oy! Auntie! Biscuits? Thas what we want! Bloody biscuits!" Crashing and thumping ensue, until Char emerges with a handful of Fig Newtons. She plunks down beside me, lips smacking, crumbs tumbling all over the pristine Moroccan rug. The concrete edifice around Sarah Spenser's head clamps down on any trace of emotional ether, hiding the little flecks of humanity I was hoping to draw out. I have seven minutes or less, and one final card up my sleeve.

"You do know that Alec isn't really my father, right? That your father is my father. That we are sisters."

I wait for the cracks. For a gush of raw green feeling. I wait for her to realize with crystal clarity that I'm trying to reach across the gulf between the Spensers and the Fortunes, the divide within myself, with some truth and intentions that might let our family tree grow into something beautiful and new. Instead I'm slapped with a red hot bolt of rage.

"What is this, more blackmail?" she snaps, her perfect jaw clenched and her voice, low, seething, slicing. "I suspected as much. I just wasn't sure what kind of salacious rumour you and my brother had concocted."

"No," I say. "But maybe telling the truth about our families is the first step to building something better for us all. For future generations."

"Unless blackmail is what you prefer?" Char says.

"Shut your mouth and eat your Fig Newtons," I growl, again scanning for a trace of vulnerability, emotion, empathy, anything even remotely human in Sarah Spenser's face or space.

"Hear me when I say this, Mizz Fortune," she says, everything about her, mean and stony now. "I don't know who impregnated your slut of a mother, but it wasn't my father. It probably wasn't even my idiot brother. And I don't give two sweet figs about the next generation of lazy ingrates being spawned by the likes of you. Your fifteen minutes are up." She stands, sweeping an arm toward the door. "This has all been amusing, but my patience ends here. If you don't leave immediately, I'm calling the police."

We hustle to the foyer as Sarah Spenser glides along beside us, buoyed by the swirls of pride-polluted navy blue victory I can see all around her. As Char and I start down the walkway, Sarah Spenser breaks her smug silence, "You were right about one thing, though. Spenser Mining is ready for change. That change is coming. And it is closer than *you* think." She takes a minute to grumble at the rhododendrons, waves goodbye or good riddance, and shoves the door shut.

My arse isn't in the car for more than a minute when my phone starts to sing. It's Peggy, huffing and puffing like she just ran the four-metre dash.

"Get home," she says. "There's trucks and gear goin' up the road. Spenser Mining trucks, taking the Crown access road to out behind your place."

"What the hell are you talking about?"

"Didn't read the paper this morning, did you?"

"I never read the paper."

"What, you think auras or whatever ya call them are gonna tell you everything? Don't be so stunned. Read the friggin' paper."

"Are you gonna tell me or what?"

Newspaper pages rustle as Peggy clears her throat. "Spenser Mining Inc. Partners with Alberta Firm to Explore Coal Bed Methane. Drilling expected to begin this summer," she reads. "What did I tell you? The stench of sulphur and pork fat. Dirty money. The bastards are planning to frack. For a puff of coal gas, of all things."

Turns out there is a shallow coal seam that runs through the woods on the Middle Rear Road, and while there's not enough coal to mine outright, there's enough to frack in order to extract methane gas. The biggest cache starts on the Crown land nestled right beside mine, and runs under my property in the direction the little fracking tunnel would need to go. My little deed of ownership only applies to what's on the surface, not to what's buried in the ground, and it won't be worth the paper it's written on if they find enough of what they are looking for. Because Spenser Mining Inc. has friends in high places. Friends who will be quick to bypass any pesky policies that hinder progress, and drown out any peeps of protest with a rousing chorus of that old, soothing refrain that lulls and lures people into a nervous state of grudging co-operation. We all know the words to that song, here: *jobs, jobs jobs.*

But instead of a mine, this time they'll pound the ground, shoot the earth up with chemicals, and eke out a few wafts of trapped gas from inside an otherwise useless patch of coal. And if our well water becomes undrinkable, they'll say they don't know why. If the trees and the grass and the birds start dying around the tailing ponds, well, that's just nature for you. If people start getting sick, clearly it's because of our poor choices and bad habits. But they'll be quick to remind us how lucky we are, and how grateful we ought to be that this industry came here, out of the goodness of its heart, to build a future for the next generation. Never mind if that future looks like a scene out of a Mad Max movie. And when the gas is gone, they'll leave, taking their money and their magical song about *jobs jobs jobs* with them. But we'll still be here. Sick and starved and broken all over again.

Over my dead body.

9 LOOK AT THAT ONE, MAKING A SCENE

There's more than one way to skin a cat. Char insists that it's the onions planted in the yard whispering that, but she's wrong. I hear it, too. And I know Mama's voice, her words, her loving guidance when I hear it, even if it sounds like onions. There's more than one way to skin a cat. More than one way to stop a pack of rat bastards from wrecking what we hold near and dear.

The poor buddies Sarah Spenser brought in from Alberta to start prepping the site didn't know what hit them. They couldn't figure out why things went missing, week after week. Keys, saws, lunches, toilet paper from the porta-potty. And when they'd see Brenda Baker out for an early morning stroll up the woods road with her hunchback mother Flossie, they'd smile and wave. Just as they'd all nod at Dulcie Cooper when they'd see her down in the ditch at dusk, filling a Sobeys bag with cattails. And of course, they'd humour Shirl Short with polite, protracted conversation every time she showed up, asking if they were up there smoking weed on the job and offering them tea and squares.

The transplanted cowboys couldn't figure out why their truck and dozers wouldn't start either. The odd fella with the tattoos and curled arm at the garage and the Alward boys who clearly know their way around big machines both had the same response when they took a look: they'd scratch their heads and say, "Jeez b'ye, I think your [insert obscure mechanical piece name here] is shot. I can special order that. Gonna take a while." But all the special order parts in the world won't help when there's a half a Sobeys bag worth of sugar being dumped into your gas tank on the regular.

When they finally concluded that the gear was being tampered with, they tried to get the cops involved. But ever since Officer Duke got transferred, the local cops aren't interested in paranoid stories of industrial vandalism out on the Middle Rear Road. So, Spenser Mining Inc. tried to hire a private security guard, not realizing that most of the guys in that business were friends of Cracker Parsons. And God love Cracker, he'd already put the kibosh on anybody working for them Come From Aways out to frack up Crow Fortune's land. In the end, Spenser Mining Inc. paid a sketchy young guy named Weasel Tobin Jr. ten bucks an hour to do the job. Until he started coming to the boss with stories of a half-naked, wild-dreadlocked, snake-dancing woman flitting around in the woods during his shifts. Clearly, the guy was drunk and on drugs just like his old man they heard, so they fired him. Nobody else would take the job.

On the bureaucratic end, things should have gone a bit smoother for Spenser Mining Inc. After all, they have a long history of greasing the paperwork wheels by lining politicians' pockets. But somehow every piece of paperwork got hung up. Or lost. Or both. Exactly how does a stack of such important documents end up behind a radiator, in the ladies' washroom, or in the janitor's closet? In the wrong building. If you ask everybody's favourite little paper-pushing Natural Resources Department bureaucrat, Becky Chickenshit, she'll tell you she's never seen the likes of it in her life. And with that precious baby bump, and her slowly brightening eyes behind her thick-rimmed glasses, who'd have the heart to hassle her about an errant paper pile or two, after all she's been through?

Tsk, tsk, tsk. It's as if the whole dirty Spenser Mining Inc. scheme is cursed, now isn't it?

Constricted rage brings a charming coyote howl tone to Sarah Spenser's voice when she calls me. "What are you people trying to pull? We have every right to extract gas from that land."

I feign a little wisdom-tinged obliviousness. "Sarah, dear, surely you must know by now that you can't force these kinds of things. If the Universe isn't co-operating with you, well maybe it isn't meant to be. Maybe you should find something else to extract. Your head from your arse, perhaps."

"Have your fun," she snipes, "but when you're done throwing your little tantrum, this project will move forward. It's only a matter of time." She pauses. Inhales sharply, begins again with a fresh menace lacing her voice, "And once we find what we're looking for, don't be surprised when that otherwise worthless scrap of land you think you own is appropriated and turned over to us for further development. For the good of the people, you see."

"With all due respect, Saint Sarah, go fuck yourself." I don't even bother to make the loud angry click sound when I hang up on her. I don't have time for that one and her threats and tactics. I've got threats and tactics of my own to plan.

[...]

I stare at my reflection in the trailer door glass. Put an edge
of genuine into my best Viva Rica smile. Smooth the gaudy
green blouse I had to borrow from Peggy over and around
my growing girth. Play with my hair, which is coming back
inexplicably curly and glinting with silver. The hair is finally
long enough to make people forget that there are tumours in
my brain, and the belly is finally big enough to make people
call me "radiant" and touch me without permission. I refrain
from biting them or cursing at them when they do. That
wouldn't be good for sales.

*Hello. My name is Crow Fortune. Imagine spending your eternity
as a vibrant piece of a precious eco-system, with a glorious tree on a
peaceful property overlooking the Great Bras d'Or. With* Crann Na
Beatha, *your final resting place will be clean, green, and serene, as
part of our Sacred Memory Forest.*

Yes. Clean, green, serene. That's good. People like words
that rhyme.

Or how about this:

*Good day. I'm Crow Fortune. Are you uncomfortable with high-
pressure sales tactics from traditional burial providers? Do you
believe that we can be conscious consumers who value people over
profits, even in death? Would you or your loved ones like to know
more about* Crann Na Beatha, *an innovative eco-cemetery that
uses state-of-the-art tree-growing burial pods, hand-crafted by a
Swedish entrepreneur and imported by local Buddhists?*

Swedish, like Ikea! And Buddhist, like the Dalai Lama!
Might as well cut to the chase.

*Look. I'm Crow. Scruffy Effie's daughter. Effie's dead, Smart
Alec's alive, and the Spensers are gearing up to poison the bejezus*

out of our land. We're trying to stop them by turning it into a tree-
hugger cemetery before that pack of greedy bastards gets their fracking
act together. Know any hippies with one foot in the grave and a few
grand to spare?

C'mon almighty Universe. Don't make me go chasing ambulances or hanging around the old folks' home in Town, or staring at people on the street looking for those with a dose of the death aura in order to make this work. We don't have time to diddle around here. She's a race against the clock.

"Wouldn't your mother be proud, God rest her soul. When's the little bundle of joy due, Crow, Dear?" That's what all the old dolls say every time they see me out and about. I pretend I'm not looking to see if any of them are close to kicking the bucket, and I pretend there's not a slew of the new and improved *Crann Na Beatha* business cards and information brochures in my purse. Instead, I smile and say, "Oh, Mama would be in her glory. She's looking down on us from a front row seat in Heaven, waiting for this baby. Due August twelfth. Now when are you gonna give me that recipe for those delicious squares of yours?" Even though I don't believe in Heaven. Or due dates. Or squares. Unless it suits me.

[···]

"You smell different after you've been down The Wharf," Peggy muses, as I make my way into the trailer after an early evening wade in the calm, warm water. She's busy scrubbing down my cupboards with Javex. "You were getting all mouldy bread and canned ham. Now you're mint and sawdust."

"Gotta get outside and blow the stink offa ya," I say, a pitch-perfect imitation of Mama's most sage advice. I try to ignore the heady haze of gold and purple ripples that have been emanating from Peggy with increasing intensity for the last few months. "Why sawdust, I wonder."

"I don't make the smells, I just smell 'em. Sawdust used to make your mother cry."

"You throw it in her eye?"

"No, smartass. When we were small, every time the Old Man cut down a tree, she'd go out and gather up the sawdust in a bag, and she'd bawl because all the little wood chips missed their mother. So she'd go try to glue them back together, and end up with her arse tanned for using up all Ma's bread flour for paste. She was an odd bird, that Effie. Do I ever miss her."

"She never told me that story."

"There was a lot Effie never told anybody."

Peggy busies herself with water boiling and cupboard rummaging, while I mop beads of sweat and the traces of tears from my puffed-up face with my puffed-up hand.

"Peggy, why didn't she tell me the truth?"

"About what?"

"About anything. About my father. About where she went and what she did with her hands? Christ, she missed my graduation because of it," I say, trying not to look and sound like I'm sooking. And failing.

"As far as she was concerned, Alec was the man you deserved to believe was your father. They were best friends, and the messy truth was a technicality." Peggy resumes her scrubbing. "She felt awful about not being there for you that night of your grad, you know. But that woman in the accident. She needed Effie's help. It was damn near a miracle the way she healed."

"Probably best Mama wasn't at the grad. Not my finest moment."

"The hell it wasn't!" Peggy's fists fly to her hips as she spins around to face me. "I was never so proud of you in your whole life as when you marched out of there with your head held high. You showed them. Talk about guts."

"You were there?"

"Of course," she says, a little indignant. "Your mother called and said they needed her hands at the hospital, and I couldn't have you there with nobody in the crowd. Stood near the back though, so as not to embarrass you with the noise."

"That hooting and hollering was you?"

"What did you think?"

"I thought some asshole was making fun of me."

"No dear, some asshole was cheering you on." She thumps over to the table where I'm sitting and plunks a cup of tea and a plate of squares down in front of me. "Here. Eat. You and that baby've got nothing to come and go on. It's that fruit tea you like, and the squares have some ahh-gaahh-vee juice or whatever ya call it in them. If the dog would lick his arse to get the taste out of his mouth, blame Charlotte."

She goes back to her cupboard scrubbing, moving with a surprising ease and grace that pushes her halo of gold and purple ripples out faster and further, until I can almost feel them gently nudging up against me.

"Peggy, did she really drive off that bridge on purpose because she was sick?"

"Everything happens for a reason," Peggy says, the Javex water sloshing on the floor as she scrubs the fridge door with a cloth she forgot to wring out.

"That's bullshit."

"Not bullshit if the reason was she knew she was a goner, she didn't want people to see her suffer and waste away, and she had insurance that would give you the money you'd need to buy the land, now is it?"

As she moves to trudge across the linoleum floor to tackle another cupboard, her foot slides on the careless puddle she made. Peggy would have landed flat on her arse if I hadn't seen it coming, and moved close enough to catch her by the flailing arm, helping to steady her balance.

"Goddamn floors," she grumbles. "Me with a cracked hip, that's the last thing we need."

"Peggy, will you do me a favour?" I say, going back to my tea as she goes back to her cleaning bender.

"No, probably not." Her tone is quick and cold. But the unspoken warmth radiating from her—which I can see and now feel with an almost jarring clarity—says otherwise.

"I'm serious. I need you to promise me something. If I, say, get hit by a garbage truck or choke on Char's shitty agave squares, or if the tumours start up again and—" I can't quite bring myself to finish that thought, as I feel a breathtaking boot to the ribs courtesy the life inside of me. "Promise you'll tell my stories."

Peggy's hands stop scrubbing and come to rest on the kitchen counter. She turns her head to stare down the ancient linoleum floor that just tried to fling her on her arse. For a moment, she is still. Swallowed up by a memory or an idea or the smell of Javex and the hypnotic hum of the bees in the pale-pink clusters of tiny roses outside the kitchen window.

"Nope," she snaps, eyes flashing, aura receding. "Tell your own stories. You're not getting off the hook for that, missy." She flicks a handful of scrub water at me, her ample arms and face twitching to shift to something lighter than talk of death. "Listen, ya lazy brat. Got your hospital bag packed?"

"I'm not due for four weeks." I bite into and promptly spit out a piece of Char's horrendous excuse for a square. "The baby doctor said first-timers almost always go over."

"Is that right, now?" she says. "Well, I don't know what doctors think they know, but Charlotte keeps going on about the rose bush blooming early. Consider yourself warned."

And right on cue, the little critter kicks my lung, pucks me in the bladder, and makes me piss myself just a little. So I go pack a hospital bag, just in case. Then I go outside to smell Mama's roses, and see if maybe they'll start telling me things I don't already know. But all I hear is the industrious hum of bees getting ready to call it a day. And then, the grating whine of chainsaws, followed by a blood-curdling scream.

I expected to be dead by now. I assumed that by summer I'd have long since been Gem-Mortalized, resting in sparkly multi-faceted peace on Mama's end table. I figured I'd have knocked a few easy items off my Fuck It Bucket List. Jotted down a few pages of memories, had some last laughs with my friends, dressed up like my trampy teenage self, and hauled the odd skeleton out of my family's closet, just to waltz it around for everyone to see. But here I am, not dead, very pregnant, and going around in one of Peggy's old floral muumuus. Mama would approve, no doubt. *Only a streel would go around with a pregnant belly hanging halfway out of one of them tight tops, anyway.* And now I'm pulling on a goddamn pair of rubber boots, slathering myself in homemade fly dope, and dragging my muumuu-clad pregnant arse out into the woods to find Char screeching her guts out at Sarah

Spenser's transplanted cowboy minions who've begun cutting down trees at the edge of my land.

Spenser Mining Inc. doesn't care that its exploratory permit has yet to wheedle its way through a series of bureaucratic snags. Spenser Mining Inc. doesn't care that there's a conflicting application in the works, looking to have the back half of my property licensed as the *Crann Na Beatha* Cemetery, which would effectively stop anybody from disturbing the earth and the trees here for a few hundred years. Spenser Mining Inc. doesn't care that Char says she can hear the trees crying, pleading, as their friends, their lovers, their ancestors, their children are ripped to pieces by hired assassins. These boys have orders to clear the land. To make way for the carnage yet to come.

I tromp up over the hill, knowing goddamn well that no one can hear me yelling over the squeal of chainsaws. I yell myself hoarse anyway. Char, with Daktari in tow, suddenly dips out of sight. Moments later, the saws stop and the boys wielding them disappear too, but even from this distance I can see plumes of panic rising. Twisted ribbons, like bruised banana peels, tinged with a sickening orange sherbert colour. An urgent anxiety fills the air. By the time I get to the source of all the fuss and silence, I understand. Char has scurried up into the high branches of a matriarchal maple — a mere spitting distance from where more tall trees on the other side of the property line are expected to fall — to stand on the platform of rickety old boards and road signs that served as my teenage treehouse escape. With Baby Daktari clinging at her hip.

"Bruce the Spruce warned me! Murderers!" Char shrieks, in full banshee mode. She has one arm wrapped tight around the baby, while the other arm takes mad, sweeping accusatory aim at the trio of thoroughly confused, scared shitless guys on the ground. One of them pulls out his phone.

"I'm going to call the boss," he stammers.

"No, man, the police. Before something bad happens," the guy beside him whispers.

"Don't bother with the cops." I try to sound smooth and sure, and not at all like an out of breath muumuu-Mama with serious doubts about the mental stability of the howling tree chick. "But you should definitely give Sarah Spenser a ringy dingy. She's going to want to see what happens next."

When Sarah rolls up in her gleaming white SUV and emerges from behind the tinted windows in an equally gleaming white pantsuit, Char and Daktari are already making themselves very much at home in the treehouse. And the boys from Alberta who were supposed to be cutting down the adjacent trees are sitting around a small fire, having a beer with Willy while Peggy cooks up a pan of baloney and home fries over the open flame.

Sarah marches toward the fire. The poor buddies she hired to cut the trees stash their beer at their feet and try to look like maybe they're hostages. Slightly drunk, relaxed, well-fed hostages who avoid eye contact, but nod and murmur "ma'am" as she sweeps past them.

"What is the meaning of this?" Sarah Spenser looks and sounds much less powerful with the mud nudging up over the edges of her high heels, mosquitoes entangling themselves in her fragrant hair, and a teensy trace of frothy spittle gathering at one corner of her pouty pink mouth. Then there's her aura. A thick yellow swamp of sulk, threaded with strands of corroded orange pride and toothless red fury.

Peggy sniffs over her shoulder, beyond the smell of baloney and potatoes. "Anybody else smell that?" she yells. "Smells like defeat." Which, according to Peggy, literally smells like feet. Sweaty feet.

"We'll see about that, now won't we." Sarah squelches her heels out from the mire, swatting at mosquitoes with one hand and discretely dabbing her rage froth with the thumb of the other. I watch as something new emerges from her aura swamp. Something dark and sharp and thorny. Moving fast. "August thirteenth, we start drilling. And in a few days, all of this, all of you people, will be gone."

"The people will lay our bodies on the line!" Char starts raving from her perch. "To protect our Mother, we will root ourselves to the land. Your metal monsters and the demons of greed and destruction are no match for the immovable forces of nature!"

But Sarah Spenser isn't listening. She's getting back into her SUV and driving away. No doubt she's calling her Alberta business partner to reassure him that all the proper political strings are being pulled. And she's likely transferring a gob of money to a private security firm in Ontario that'll send steely-eyed muscle heads out into the woods of Cape Breton to protect and secure her precious assets and investment from a little band of backwoods ne'er-do-wells.

Char is too loopy, Peggy's too old, Willy's too hemiplegic-ally palsied, and I am too pregnant to be camped out in the woods, getting eaten alive by bugs, kept awake at night by the sweltering late July air, and screamed at by the birds before sunrise. But here we are. Watching. Waiting.

At night, I dream about my great-grandmother, the infamous Black Agnes O'Toole, kissing the dirt floors of the

house on the Halfway Road, praying that her hellish journey—from the laundries in Ireland, to servitude in the sticks
of Newfoundland, to taking the hand of a man they called
Black Bernie—had reached a happy end. I dream about my
nanny and the miners' strike in 1925, how she sat cocked on
her mother's hip when the company goons opened fire on
the crowd of starved and desperate men, women, and children. I dream about Mama, her body and mind buoyed by
a blessedly painless limbo even before her car hit the water.
And of course, my eyes snap open when I hear Mama whisper, *Get your bony arse out of bed before I kick it out.*

My bony arse hurts, Mama. Everything hurts. A couple of
nights of sleeping in the woods, keeping vigil over Char and
her baby in their treehouse, waiting for Sarah's next move,
praying to anything that'll listen for the *Crann Na Beatha*
licence to be approved before some crook in a suit can rubber stamp the drilling. It's enough to make a body ache.
Some days, I feel like dying. But not today. Today, there's shit
to do.

They roll in just before dawn, in quiet black waves. A
dozen of them stood on the edge of the property line by the
time the sun had stretched over the mountain. They didn't
say a word. Just stood there, with their batons and shields
and an air of authoritative arseholery. The hired guns from
Ontario came dressed for a riot. Me? I'm still in a flowery
muumuu and rubber boots.

"Well that's a little much," Peggy says when she and Alec
show up with tea and scones and diapers and more fly dope.
"Should have worn a gas mask and mixed up a couple of
Molotov cocktails to make them fellas feel like they're earn-
ing their keep, at least."

"You wanna fight there, thugs?" a voice cackles from the treetops. "Shove your heads up your arses and fight for air!"

The gentlemen of Phalanx Security Inc. do not respond to Char's invitation. They don't respond to the early morning mosquitoes and blackflies, or to the fact that it must be hotter than the hobs of hell inside those thick, black uniforms. They don't even flinch when Peggy flings a mittful of mud at the captain's shield. To the untrained eye, this wall of man and muscle looks immovable. But to these thoroughly squirrelly eyes of mine, there is a way in. A way out. Hints of it flit all around the captain's head. I just need to push a few buttons to see if what I think I know is actually true, and then see if I have the guts to go out on a limb again with my fledging sense of what makes people tick.

Willy could sleep forever on a tack, so I crawl into the tent and wake him.

"Get up, b'ye."

He flashes a fresh-from-a-dream smile. "Time for some morning nature lovin' is it?"

"No. You got a wedding to go to."

"Whose?"

"Ours."

[···]

If there is indeed a divine Universe that conspires to help the plans of the righteous pan out with a spooky sense of ease and synchronicity, while giving the finger to forces of greed and stupidity, well, it gave us a glimpse of itself today. Within a couple of hours, people had begun to arrive at our little standoff site, armed with casseroles and squares and more booze than you could shake a stick at. Tents and tables sprang up all over the back half of my land. Allie's brothers showed up with a band. Father Delahanty brought a white archway and platform, the leftover manger set from the Christmas pageant. Bonnie from the Hairport even brought a fancy flower crown and a silky white-ish muumuu for the bride to wear. And when the top of it didn't fit quite right, Peggy pulled out that shiny old peacock brooch and used it to cinch the bodice shut.

"A Fortune family heirloom," she whispered, "to keep your boobs tucked in."

By noon, word was out that Crow and Gimp were getting married in the woods out on the back part of the land. By the time we clambered up onto the little platform to officially be united in holy matrimony by Brother Smart Alec Gyaltso, there were forty or fifty people gathered to watch and share in the celebration to follow. But maybe the cosmo-licious Universe of joyful abundance had nothing to do with it. Maybe this is just the kind of magical shit that people around here make happen. When it really counts.

Meanwhile, the black-clad gentlemen of Phalanx Security Inc. just stood there the whole time, sweating balls, hungry enough to chew the leg off the lamb of God, and not sure what to make of the whole spectacle as it unfolded on our side of the line. And after I tossed my bouquet of prickly rambling roses and onion stalks directly at Allie and Wendy, I walked up to the guy who looked like he was in charge. The one whose aura had started off the morning with faint flickers of baby blue and unfinished business but who is now engulfed in a sky-blue longing, even as his face stays locked, stony and stern.

"This here's the best part of a Cape Breton wedding," I

say to him. "Called 'the Time.' Biggest party you ever did see. Times can rage on for days and days, especially when they're outside and the weather co-operates, which it will. You'll be here for the long haul, watching us celebrate love and life, buddy."

I lean in as close as my belly and his barricade stance will allow, and speak with a hushed sweetness. "Look, I know you're in this for the money. I also know that right now, you resent the fuck outta being here. You had something special planned for this weekend."

I blurt out my best guess at what my vision, with its swirls of colourful love and longing and fear, seems to suggest.

"A big family gathering. You were gonna propose to your girlfriend, weren't you? But you got called away to work and she's so pissed. Maybe she'll even break up with you over it. Imagine what kind of hero you'd be if you could get your ass back home and surprise her."

I glance up and can see from the sway and shifts of the colours around him that he's movable. They're all movable in this moment. But before I can test the power of my own persuasion any further, Peggy's hand drops down onto my shoulder. A thick envelope is thrust into my hand.

"Here," she says. "Everybody chipped in for a wedding gift. Betcha there's enough in here to make these fellas wanna head back to where they belong instead of standing around here."

Once the gentlemen of Phalanx Security Inc. decided that what was in that envelope was a far better deal than what Sarah Spenser had nickeled and dimed them into taking, our little post-wedding party was free to spill across the property line and our little tent city bloomed in and around the very spot where Spenser Mining Inc. intended to drill in a few days. And when the other crooked bitch showed up just before the sun went down, to see a big old wedding Time in full swing, she looked like her head was set to explode.

"Welcome to our wedding." I beam.

"You're trespassing on Crown land. Once the Minister of Natural Resources signs exploration rights over, you'll either get out of my way or be arrested."

I'm dazzled by the display of searing anger and frustration rocketing and ricocheting around Sarah Spenser's head. Against the backdrop of sunset, it looks like she's burning and sizzling in her own self-made hell, and I can't help but laugh. Which makes her rage burn even brighter.

"Tommy Murray, isn't it? He's the minister supposed to sign them papers?" Peggy sidles over, half-laughing to herself. "His wife was in that really bad car wreck. Over twenty years ago, now. Night of Crow's graduation, I recall."

"Your point?" There's that frothy spittle in the corner of Sarah's pouty mouth.

"No point," Peggy says. "Just sayin'. His wife made quite a miraculous recovery from that accident." Peggy links her arm to mine, with a wink and a nudge. "Effie met her once. I wonder if they'd remember. I should ask him."

"Now, if you'll excuse us," I say, rubbing my giant belly and grinning at the way strands of pink in Peggy's aura are stoking Sarah's rage into a smoky blue confusion, "we're having a celebration here."

Peggy and I turn away, without even waiting to see her and her storm clouds off. I find my new husband, and my two best friends, all of whom are already three sheets to the wind, and we laugh and cry and dance and eat squares and casseroles beneath the stars, held snug in the warm embrace of family and friends and the place that needs us.

Oh, but it's all fun and games until the chick in the off-white silky muumuu and flower crown goes into the porta-potty to take a long-overdue piss, and comes out set to have a baby.

"Labour? Are you shitting me?" Willy slurs as he takes my face in his hands, his eyes filling with tears, mirroring back the bonfire's glow.

"Shut up before I tear your lips off," I growl, as I slap his hands away and brace for more bone-shifting agony. I put my hands on his shoulders and lean hard on him, trying to sway with and through the pain as it builds, spreads, peaks, and retreats over the span of a few minutes. I look up to see a wall of my drunk friends form behind Willy, feet planted firmly to brace and keep him upright as my weight and my wails push against his soused and unsteady frame. Willy's arms—the good one and the bad one—are wrapped around me tenderly as Char, Allie, and Wendy hold us all in place.

"This is totally your fault," I say through teeth clamped tighter than a vice, which makes him weep and smile even more.

A guttural cry surges from my throat as my legs tremble and I buckle forward. Heads turn and stare, but the faces are blurred by shades of soft pastel concern. A bigger crowd of faintly shimmering shadows forms around me in the moonlit clearing, until a booming voice bosses them back to tending the fire, singing some songs, and having another drink. Peggy comes hustling over.

"Smell woke me. You three get down to the trailer, lay a bunch of towels out on the bed, then put the tea on and start sobering up." Peggy shoves Willy, Char, and Allie out of the way and in the direction of the trailer. "Missy Death Doula, you look like the straightest of the pack here," she says, taking Wendy by the arm. "Help me get her to the trailer."

"I'll call an ambulance," Allie says.

"Doubt they'll make it in time. There's only two, and they're both on calls. And the hospital called a code census." Leave it to Peggy, who went home for some quality time with her scanner, to know what's what. "Besides, my mother had all eleven of us at home. It's not rocket science."

All of a sudden I'm kicking myself for not taking one of those damn breathing classes. For not slathering coconut oil on my perineum three times a day to make it more stretchy and supple. For not doing this when Mama was alive, so she could be here to say *Quit sooking and get 'er done, child.*

"Here," Peggy says, placing my hands around her forearms. "Squeeze the bejesus outta me. This is what I been growin' a goodly layer of fat for all these years. Just don't push yet. I'll not have your baby born in the woods like a g.d. wolf cub."

By the time we make it to the trailer, my contractions are coming with barely a breather between them. The tea is made. Willy is pacing, Char is dancing, and Allie has already boiled a pot of water and torn up a bedsheet because that's what they do on TV.

"All right, I better check your micker-twicker," Peggy says as she and Wendy ease me onto the bed.

"Jesus, it's a vagina!" I shriek. "And it is ripping in two right now!"

"Char, Allie, come grab a leg," Peggy says, low and calm, as if there aren't hundreds of frantic, panicked, lime-green light shards slashing and piercing the expansive ash-coloured cloud that looms above us.

"She's not havin' it right here? Right now?" Willy props himself up against the wall in the hallway, a soup of fire-engine red and delicate cream swirling around him.

"This child's not waiting." Peggy has flecks of a carefully guided gold now tingeing her neon panic. "Bossy and impatient already. Wonder where that comes from?"

My spine instinctively curls around my screaming centre. Sensations I never dreamed of now come to nightmarish life in places I didn't know existed. There is moaning. There is screaming. There is farting. The real miracle of childbirth is how nobody ever breathes a word about how revolting and surreal and hellish it all is, until it's too late.

Wendy coaxes breath into and out of my body. Peggy tells me when to push, when to back off, when to bear down. I obey.

"Willy, get over here," Peggy barks. "Your child is about to come into the world. A baby deserves to be greeted by its father."

Tears stream down Allie's face. Char starts singing "Stairway to Heaven," and for once, she gets all the words right.

This must be what some kinds of dying feel like. A mind-numbing, time-freezing, soul-cleaving agony that crushes you into a ragged ball of hurt. Then — in a rush of release that defies all prediction, all expectation, all logic — it is over. The pain. The fear. Every single misgiving you've ever had about anyone or anything. Gone. The messy horror of what you've just endured, wiped clean from your soul. Until something different starts, as if all the elements that broke apart and dissolved in the dying have come back together in a form that you couldn't have fathomed until you woke from the tyranny of pain. And you find yourself surrounded by ungodly beauty. This must be what some kinds of reincarnation feel like.

July twenty-third, right at the stroke of midnight, my baby girl is born. And maybe I am reborn then, too.

Before I even hear her take her first screamy breath, I see what my daughter brings with her into this world. A slew of iridescent orbs cascade from between my trembling thighs, filling the room like I just gave birth to a cosmic bubble blowing machine instead of a tiny human miracle. Seconds later, a waxy infant is laid across my chest, still tethered to my insides by a stubborn placental slab. Her eyes are puffed shut. Her skin is thin, there's crust in the crevices of her arms, her legs, her neck. Her head is lumpy and hairless. She promptly poops all over me. I kiss her slimy, crusty, bald head and tell her she is the most beautiful thing I've ever seen.

"She smells like a pine tree," Peggy says, wiping gobs of snot and tears with the back of her bloated hand. "As blessings do."

Somewhere farther down the Middle Rear Road, an ambulance rips along, sirens wailing. Out in the woods behind my trailer, the Time rips along too, and as word of my baby's birth spreads, people plan the food they'll bring and the hours they'll spend planted on my land until it's safe from Spenser Mining Inc.'s harm. And from the kitchen, I can hear Peggy muttering about the smell that came quick on the heels of pine tree. The lingering scent of baby powder, of the chaos yet to come. But me? All I can see are the rainbow bubbles around my daughter's head. And then I hear Mama's voice singing softly, sweetly,

There was liquor on the barroom floor,
And the bar was closed for the night.
When out of his hole came a little black mouse,
and he sat in the pale moonlight...

EPILOGUE

The Swan Song

It is with heavy hearts that we announce the sudden but peaceful passing of Stacey Theresa "Crow" Fortune, age 39, on August 8. Crow passed away at home, in her sleep. She is survived by her precious baby daughter, Raven Jewel Fortune, her husband Willy "Mr. Crow Fortune" Matthews, best friends Allie Walker and Char MacIsaac, a number of aunts and uncles, and her father, Brother Gyaltso Smart Alec Spenser. She was predeceased by several relations, including her much adored maternal grandmother, Lucy, and her dearly missed mother, Effie, who loved Crow more than life itself.

A wake and funeral are to be held at Crow's home, under the direction of Wendy MacDermid, and burial will take place on the family land, up the Middle Rear Road. A tart cherry tree is to be planted on the edge of the property to mark the place where her body will be laid to rest, and visitors are welcome to come sit, sing, laugh, caw, and cry in the shade of Crow's tree any time. In lieu of flowers, donations can be made to the Crann Na Beatha *Memory Forest Trust Fund. As per Crow's wishes, we share the following piece she wrote shortly before her death. Because that one always needed to have the last word, now didn't she. This is Crow Fortune's Swan Song:*

If you are reading this, it is because I did exactly what I came here to do. *Ladies and gentlemen, a round of applause, please, for the one and only Crow Fortune! She did it! She died! Just like she said she would do.*

I don't know if there's such a thing as a good death, but if there is, I hope I had one. Hope I didn't make too much of a mess, or cause too much of a scene, or wreck anybody's good time, and if I did, I'm sorry. Because even though I apparently succeeded in doing exactly what I came here to do, and even though it's no secret that none of us will be getting out of this life alive, there's still a tinge of failure that comes with the whole dying deal. There was no divine intervention from the benevolent Universe, no last-minute miracle of a happy ending, no grand triumph of righteous fate over snivelling misfortune. Just me, my quick blip of a weird, sad story, the end. The biggest failure of my whole life, this dying thing. And just look at what I've left behind: my old friends, my new family. A people and a place I didn't realize I needed until far too late. But better late than never, I suppose.

As I sit here drinking my too strong, too sweet cup of Mama's Stovetop Sludge, my eyes flitting back and forth between the small, lumpy, bald head of my newborn baby and the massive, smooth arc of orange in the sky that heralds the failing of daylight, I can't help but think about what will happen when I'm gone. Is Willy gonna be able to properly manage this kid's mop if she's cursed with the cruel genetics of my bird's nest hair? Will Papa Gyaltso go turning the "Itsy Bitsy Spider" into some sort of preachy Buddhist lesson, and will Nanny Peggy teach little Raven Jewel how to curse right? Dear God, what if my daughter gets all her fashion tips and dance moves from Char, and her coping mechanisms from Allie? These are the details I instinctively fret about whenever I find myself shrouded in a cloud of dark, quiet inevitability. Watching. Waiting. *Oh death, you sneaky bastard, you.*

And then there's the bigger, more grandiose questions about what will happen when I'm gone. Where am I going? Anywhere? Nowhere? Somewhere? Somewhere good? Will there be tea and squares and laughing and crying and swearing there, because if there isn't, well then I don't want to go. Not that I'll have a choice. When my body is tucked into the earth inside a cozy burial pod, with a tenacious little tree being fuelled by the leftovers of my existence, will the flickers of energy that steered my flesh and bones through the world simply evaporate? Will they too be absorbed by the earth and the tree and the land I loved? Or will my gaudy spirit hitch a ride on the saltwater wind, and swirl away to a place where there's nothing but golden light and good memories, and the sound of Mama gently whispering, *Get your bony arse out of bed, before I kick it out.*

When I showed up here, with all my assorted sins and shames neatly packed in a classy bag of big-city smug, the people of this place had every right to drag me by the scruff of my neck down to the fire hall, with an angry mob awaiting to pelt me with lobster shells and fiddle bows and beer caps and various tartans. They could have revoked my Caper Papers on the spot for talking like such a filthy traitor. For making like I was somehow better than everyone and everything here just because I ran away to bury my accent, my fuck-ups, my roots. But they didn't. Every piece of this place conspired to hold me together, even as I fell apart. To remind me who I am, and why.

Unfortunately, knowing damn well that I was going to die didn't turn me into some peace-pissing, bliss-barfing, gratitude-grabbing beacon of spiritual guru greatness. Pity. I could have done some good with that. Whipped up some wicked brochures and built one hell of an empire. Maybe turned the whole goddamn island into a world-class New Age spiritual tourist attraction. Oh well. Maybe next life, if believing in such a thing suits me. Which, in the hard moments, it does.

If nothing else, maybe all this brought me to peaceful grips with my life. It made me think and say and do all the stupid, shitty things I thought and said and did, because that's what people do when they're living. Even when they're dying. It made me notice that there are shades of beauty in the strangest places. In the strangest people, too. It made me stop looking for truth, and start seeing meaning.

Lately, that dream I had right before and after I came here—the one with the cackling birds, the hellish land, and the lone tree that would stalk, grab, and trap me—has come back. But it's different now. I don't wake up in the middle of it, sick and terrified. That dream doesn't wake me up at all. And rather than squeeze me to death, the tree just picks me up from the dirt, and holds me tight in the mythic madness of its branches. From so high up, I can see every shimmer and shadow that plays between the water and the sky, and I swear I can hear all the people I've ever loved gathering, their voices calling and cawing in riotous tones like a pack of black, beady-eyed birds who've stumbled upon some sort of treasure.

I know now that I'm not in a nightmare. I'm home. Cradled in the strong, snarled arms of this glorious mess of a family tree. Smack dab in the middle of a story about a long line of lunatics and criminals. Right where I belong.

ACKNOWLEDGEMENTS

In its early days, this work was supported by the Toronto Arts Council, with funding from the City of Toronto. For that, I am deeply grateful.

This book owes its very existence, in part, to a complete stranger. An anonymous woman on a Parents of Multiple Births listserv many years ago responded to my overwhelmed new-twin-mom post with a story about a young woman who died suddenly, just after giving birth. It was intended to give me a glimpse of how fortunate I was, how much worse it could be. Instead, it gave me an existential crisis, a case of hypochondria, and ultimately, the story of Crow. So, random internet lady, wherever you are— thank you. Your message had an impact.

That existential crisis eventually led me to explore Buddhism, as a way to view life and death. I am deeply grateful for the teachings and writings of Pema Chödrön, and the practice of Tonglen, upon which Brother Gyaltso's "Tree Meditation" in chapter eight is based.

I'd also like to acknowledge that my writing process for *Crow* had an eclectically kick-ass soundtrack, some of which is evident in the brief lyrical references throughout this book. Such songs include: "Stairway to Heaven" by Led Zepplin; "Me and Bobby McGee" by Kris Kristofferson; "Luckenbach, Texas" by Waylon Jennings; "Mamas, Don't Let Your Babies Grow Up to Be Cowboys" by Waylon Jennings and Willie Nelson; "The Red-Headed Stranger" and "Blue Eyes Cryin' in the Rain" by Willie

Nelson; "Take Me Home, Country Roads," "Grandma's Feather Bed," and "Matthew" by John Denver; and those songs and artists not quoted but identified by name and song title in the text.

And now, for the people to whom I owe the biggest thanks my heart can muster:

To the team at Goose Lane Editions, especially publisher Susanne Alexander and editor Bethany Gibson, for their steadfast commitment to helping Crow's voice and story take flight.

To Marjorie Simmins, for her guidance, and for seeing the "embarrassment of riches."

To Cassandra Yonder, for sharing her insight with me as part of my research, and for her work at www.deathcaring.ca.

To Alex Pearson, for chasing the "Golden Hour" light for my photo.

To Lindsay, for the tea and the intellectual commiseration.

To Lila, for the love, the laughs, and the adventures.

To Jody, for the love, the laughs, the adventures, the body guarding, and the ass-kicking whenever I needed it.

To my brother, Neil, for keeping me grounded... or getting me grounded? Probably both.

To my dad, Fraser, for instilling in me a love of outlaw country music and songs that tell stories, for his sense of humour, and for seeing the potential for spontaneous combustion.

To my mother, Valerie, for being both my toughest critic and my biggest fan. For a life and a lineage filled with strength, stories, and weird sayings. For giving me a genuine love of words. Especially the curse-y ones.

To Nanny, whose fierce love still lives in my bones.

To my daughters, Coco, Neela, and Macie, for making my world bigger, brighter, and more beautiful than I ever could have imagined.

And finally, to my husband, Matthew, for making my tea every morning. For being in this life with me. For making me laugh when I need it most. For his patience, his intelligence, his perspective. For the boundless love and relentless faith that make all things possible.

If the only prayer you ever say in your entire life is thank you, it will be enough.
　—*Meister Eckhart*

Amy Spurway was born and raised on Cape Breton, where she landed her first writing and performing gigs with CBC Radio at age eleven. She holds a BA in English from the University of New Brunswick and a degree in Radio and TV Arts from Ryerson University. Her writing has appeared in *Babble, Elephant Journal, Today's Parent,* and the *Toronto Star.* She lives in Dartmouth.